# THE ART OF APOLOGY

LUCY MARIN

Quills & Quartos
PUBLISHING

Copyright © 2024 by Lucy Marin

All rights reserved.

This is a work of fiction. Names, characters, businesses, places, events, locales, and incidents are either the products of the author's imagination or used in a fictitious manner. Any resemblance to actual persons, living or dead, or actual events is purely coincidental.

No part of this book may be reproduced in any form or by any electronic or mechanical means, including information storage and retrieval systems, without written permission from the author, except for the use of brief quotations in a book review.

No AI training. Without in any way limiting the author's [and publisher's] exclusive rights under copyright, any use of this publication to "train" generative artificial intelligence (AI) technologies to generate text is expressly prohibited. The author reserves all rights to license uses of this work for generative AI training and development of machine learning language models.

Ebooks are for the personal use of the purchaser. You may not share or distribute this ebook in any way, to any other person. To do so is infringing on the copyright of the author, which is against the law.

Edited by Jo Abbott and Jan Ashton

Cover by Pemberley Darcy

ISBN 978-1-963213-64-5 (ebook) and 978-1-963213-65-2 (paperback)

*To the memory of dear Buddy. You will be missed.*

# CHAPTER ONE

Elizabeth Bennet briefly caught the eye of Mr Fitzwilliam Darcy as she took a seat on the edge of the assembly room. She did not have a partner for the set, and this was the only empty chair. As the dance began, she glanced at him several times and was certain he looked her way too. As soon as he had entered the room, Elizabeth had been drawn to his tall, elegantly clad figure; she had hardly noticed his companions: Mr Bingley, the Bennets' new neighbour, and his family. But whatever attraction she had felt had quickly vanished in light of his comportment. All night, he had impressed her with his disdain for everything and everyone he saw.

Her dislike became fixed when Mr Bingley came to encourage his friend to ask a lady to dance, proposing Elizabeth. Turning towards the gentlemen, she saw Mr Darcy studying her as he said, "She is tolerable, but not handsome enough to tempt *me*."

Elizabeth felt her eyes widen, and, as he went on to claim she had been slighted by other gentlemen, she swallowed a laugh. Mr Bingley returned to the lines of dancers where Elizabeth's sister Jane awaited him. Feeling as though someone was watching her, she looked about, only to realise it was Mr Darcy. Yet again, their eyes briefly met before he turned away, his haughty expression unwavering. That he had insulted her, and evidently did not care that she had heard him, almost made her feel as though she were living in a farce, and he was the chief actor. Why had he come if all he intended to do was show how little he thought of everyone present apart from his friends? Did he take pleasure in sneering at people he considered his inferiors?

*It is a pity. There is no denying he is handsome, and I would not have objected to speaking to him, perhaps even dancing with him. Now all I wish is to avoid him forever.*

Catching sight of her dearest friend, Charlotte Lucas, across the room, Elizabeth went to her.

"Are you enjoying yourself, despite your lack of partners, Eliza?" Charlotte asked. "It is a pity that Mr Bingley did not bring more gentlemen with him and that the two he did bring are not inclined to dance."

"Mr Darcy might be—if only there was a lady worthy of his attention." Elizabeth fluttered her eyelashes in imitation of a coquette.

In a whisper, she told Charlotte what she had overheard. They laughed about it, but soon, Elizabeth's good mood diminished. It began when Mrs Long sought her out to say, "Do not mind what that man said of you. You are a very pretty girl, and no matter how rich he is supposed to be, he is ill-mannered. Why, he sat beside me for half an hour and said not a word!" She patted Elizabeth's cheek and walked on.

In the period that followed, multiple people spoke to her about Mr Darcy's slight, some with humour, some with pity, and one or two people with thinly disguised delight. Amongst the latter was one lady who had a daughter she was desperate to see married, and she was only too happy to ensure everyone she met thought highly of her girl and poorly of all others. When Elizabeth saw her whispering to various people, occasionally glancing or pointing in her direction, she was sure the hateful woman was discussing the incident and exaggerating what Mr Darcy had said, even though she had not witnessed it herself. Likely, she was also comparing Elizabeth to her daughter—who, naturally, was prettier, more accomplished, and in every way better than she.

With each passing minute, her embarrassment and anger became more acute, causing clashing sensations of icy cold and burning heat throughout her body. She spied Mr Darcy—the hateful man—still calmly walking about the room, his lips curled in dislike as he regarded the people and activities. Immediately, the blood vessels in her head began to throb.

When she and her family were at last preparing to leave, she whispered to Jane, "You cannot imagine how glad I am to be going. What a wretched night!"

All she wanted was the solitude of her bedchamber and the promise of not having to see any of her neighbours for as long as she could manage it. And she fervently hoped Mr Darcy would return to London and she would never have to see him again.

"Mr Bingley is charming and everything a young man ought to be!" Mrs Bennet clutched her hands to her chest and grinned. But then her expression darkened, and she huffed. "But his friend! You would not believe what he said of our Lizzy. How I wish you had been there, my dear, to give him one of your set-downs."

Elizabeth wanted to sigh and sink further into the soft chair; she had attempted to escape the drawing room and go to her chamber, but she had yet to find a reason that would not draw unwanted attention. If she did not find a way to leave soon, she would have to endure listening to her mother recount every moment of the assembly to Mr Bennet, which she suspected would take above an hour.

As her mother mentioned that the detestable Mr Darcy had insulted Elizabeth, she felt heat spread up her neck and into her cheeks. The way her father examined her, his brow arched high, suggested he had noticed.

"What was his complaint?" Mr Bennet asked. "Lizzy does not look excessively upset. A bit hot perhaps, unless her colour comes from embarrassment. Surely this Mr Darcy could not have said anything *that* bad in a public setting."

Hoping to end the conversation quickly, Elizabeth said, "He behaved abominably, and not only towards me, so I care nothing for his opinion. Charlotte and I laughed at how ridiculous the whole thing was and—"

"He refused to stand up with her," Lydia, her youngest and most impatient sister, interjected. "Mr Bingley wanted him to ask her, but he *refused*! He said she was not handsome and deserved to be slighted."

## THE ART OF APOLOGY

"He did not say I *deserved* to be slighted," Elizabeth said, giving in to the desire to roll her eyes as a sign of her frustration. She also made a noise of dismissal that was louder than she had intended and almost worthy of the farce she had felt she was in earlier that evening.

"Lydia, I am sure he said no such thing and that there is more to the story than what we know. Mr Bingley speaks very highly of Mr Darcy," Jane said.

Elizabeth scoffed, but before she could respond, Mrs Bennet said, "No doubt Mr Bingley believes the best of his friend, and it does him credit to have such a generous view. In this instance, he is mistaken. Mr Darcy is a horrible, rude—"

"Mama," Elizabeth said, hoping to change the subject. She failed, however, and her mother continued.

"*Everyone* was speaking of it. I do not know who first overheard him, but they were quick to spread it to the whole room. Mrs Howe is jealous because that daughter of hers is not nearly as pretty as any of my girls, and you can be sure she repeated it again and again. The entire town will be talking of nothing else for weeks!"

Disregarding his wife, Mr Bennet looked at Elizabeth and asked, "What exactly did Mr Darcy say? No, Lydia." Without turning his head towards his youngest child, he held up an admonishing finger. "Your sister will tell me."

Elizabeth wiggled her toes, which were sore after so long in dancing slippers, and told her father what had happened, being as concise as possible.

Mr Bennet's face hardened, and he kept a steady, firm gaze on her. Around them, her sisters and mother resumed their chatter about the assembly. Fortunately,

Lydia and Kitty were more interested in discussing what other ladies had worn—especially the elegant and heretofore unknown Mrs Hurst and Miss Bingley—than Mr Darcy, and Mrs Bennet was never one to forgo the opportunity to speak of fashion.

Unfortunately, when the other ladies began to leave the drawing room, her father requested that Elizabeth stay behind. Once they were alone, he asked that she again describe exactly what had happened with Mr Darcy and what other people had said to her afterwards.

She did her best to satisfy him, then concluded, "Truly it was nothing. Why should I be discomposed by the ill opinion of such a man? I advise you to forget it. That is exactly what I shall do!" She laughed to show the entire affair was amusing rather than distressing, although, admittedly, it had stung—both Mr Darcy's insult and the way people had spoken of it afterwards.

There were some thoughts she would keep to herself, such as the initial attraction she had felt for Mr Darcy. She had not much liked Mr Bingley's family; his sisters evidently thought they were superior to those they had met, and Mr Hurst had looked as if he smelt something foul. Elizabeth had heard Mrs Hurst boasting of Mr Darcy's grand estate in Derbyshire, and it had left her with the impression that there was an understanding between the gentleman and Miss Bingley. On the one hand, she thought two such disagreeable people deserved each other, yet on the other, it disappointed her, for reasons she did not comprehend.

Her father soon dismissed her, having hardly spoken

himself. Elizabeth gratefully kissed his cheek and fled to her chamber.

Rupert Bennet watched as Elizabeth left the room. How could Mr Darcy look at her, the most admirable of his girls, and dismiss her? As much as he often called his daughters silly, especially the three youngest, and thought girls should be left to their mother's care, he truly believed that Jane and Elizabeth were estimable and that Mary, Catherine, and Lydia would naturally become more like them as they matured. It might be another few years, but one day, he would be able to contemplate what fine, sensible, well-behaved young women all his daughters were.

If Mr Darcy could insult Elizabeth, what did that mean for her sisters? Might other gentlemen have a low opinion of them? It seemed impossible, yet…

Bennet sighed and ran a hand over his face. He was tired and should have sought his bed long ago. He found it amusing to hear his wife and daughters speak of their evening entertainments, if only so he could tease them, but he had never liked keeping late hours. The best thing he could do for himself was to forget the entire business of Mr Darcy and his ill-conceived words. After all, what could *he* do about it; he had not even been present when the sorry episode happened. Accordingly, he pushed himself out of the armchair and made his way to his chamber.

At breakfast the next morning, Bennet found he could not rid himself of the irritation of knowing a man he had never met—which for some reason made his vexation worse—had spoken so harshly about his dearest girl. He observed his daughters as they chatted and steadily ate their meal. Unconsciously, he was looking for fault, some reason Mr Darcy had felt it reasonable to act as he had. There could be none, of course; even if Elizabeth and her sisters were the most tiresome creatures in the kingdom, it would not justify him or any other person speaking poorly of them, especially in public.

In as much as he could be glad about anything to do with this disgusting business, he was relieved Mr Darcy had not taken it into his head to insult Jane. She was too tender-hearted to laugh it off as Elizabeth had. None of the younger three would have cried over it, but there was a little something—almost like an itch at the back of his consciousness—telling him that overhearing such a dismissive statement would have injured Mary and Kitty. As for Lydia, he could not say why, but instinct suggested it would have been terrible for her too.

*Instead, that wretched man chose my Lizzy!* How could he have seen her—Bennet's most worthy girl—and refused to dance with her? How could he call her not handsome? It was preposterous! Any man would be fortunate to earn her regard. Slighted by other gentlemen? Was this Mr Darcy blind or merely stupid? There were hardly ever enough partners for all the women at the assemblies. It was a frequent topic of conversation in drawing rooms across the area. If Mr Darcy was any sort of gentleman, he would have participated more, ensuring the single young ladies went home with fond memories of the evening.

*What kind of father would let an insult to one of his daughters stand unchallenged?* The thought surprised him, but in an instant, he knew it was true. He was far from being a young and foolish man and had no intention of calling out Mr Darcy, but the man *must* be told that what he had done was unacceptable.

Elizabeth might laugh about what happened and soon forget it, but Bennet would not.

## CHAPTER TWO

Darcy was in his apartment reading when he was informed that he had a caller. He considered refusing to see whoever it was. The name he was told—Mr Bennet of Longbourn—meant nothing to him. There must be some mistake; surely the man wanted Bingley, not him.

Or he had heard of Darcy's wealth, and that was his motivation in coming. *What will it be today? An excellent investment opportunity, perhaps property in the neighbourhood I should want for some nonsensical reason? No, I suspect it is the usual—a daughter, a sister, a niece...some girl I am sure to fall madly in love with. How does my income and knowledge of my estate always end up circulating so quickly? I do not speak of it.* He was sick of how jealous people became of his wealth, how *that* was what they valued in him.

Sighing, Darcy closed his book and set it aside. It was not particularly engaging, and he might as well see this Mr Bennet. It would be better to make it known at once that he was only in the neighbourhood for a short while, and he had no intention of making friends or buying anything beyond a few small items—if the Meryton shops had anything to tempt him—and he certainly would *not* be falling in love with some country miss of no importance. Afterwards, he would take a long ride. The exercise would be welcome, and although he had intended to go out with Bingley later, his friend's meeting with the estate's steward was lasting far longer than he had anticipated. Darcy needed to do something active; he was not accustomed to sitting around all day like an old man. Or as Hurst did; he apparently had no interests beyond napping, eating, playing cards, and participating in sport. What an awful life that would be! Then again, he mused, was it so different from how many ladies spent their time, if one substituted sewing or some other feminine art for sport?

Moments later, Darcy entered the drawing room to find an older gentleman awaiting him; from the quality of his attire, he was neither poor nor especially wealthy. The man paced in a straight line in front of the windows, his head bent and hands clasped behind his back. Darcy assumed he was Mr Bennet; he certainly hoped a second man had not come to importune him. He cleared his throat to signal he was present, causing the other man to cease walking and face him.

"Mr Darcy, I presume?"

Darcy nodded. "If it is Mr Bingley you wished to see, you will have to return tomorrow. I might convey a message, if you like."

"Rupert Bennet of Longbourn," he said, a sharp edge

to his tone that Darcy did not care to be curious about. "My business is with you, sir."

Darcy inwardly sighed and again reviewed the possible explanations for Mr Bennet's call. Because he expected it to be one of the usual reasons, despite the man's abrupt manner, Darcy was shocked by what Mr Bennet said next.

"How came you to insult a lady in a public place? Were you not bothered that you might be overheard by her and our neighbours, which, by the bye, you *were*?"

Interesting, Darcy thought, only just recognising Mr Bennet's anger. His deep scowl alone must be an indication that he had a connexion to the lady Darcy had apparently dismissed. He never said what he did not believe, and if he had disparaged someone, they had deserved it. Mr Bennet must be referring to the assembly, as Darcy had only arrived yesterday, but he had no recollection of doing such a thing. There had been no one present worth knowing apart from Bingley and his family—and Darcy was not entirely sure he would include Hurst.

"I am afraid you have puzzled me. What is it you believe I have done?" Darcy said, doing his best to make his disinterest unmistakable. He would not apologise for speaking the truth—if he had indeed shared his opinion aloud—and he wanted the neighbourhood to understand he had no intention of knowing them on more than a superficial level. He was in Hertfordshire for a few weeks or a month to assist Bingley; as soon as he could, he would return to his family and the handful of people beyond them whom he trusted.

Mr Bennet shook his head as though in disbelief. "You insulted my daughter, Miss Elizabeth Bennet. Within her hearing, and that of many others, you told Mr Bingley she was not pretty and refused to be introduced to her."

Darcy's eyes flickered about the room as he tried to grasp the edges of a memory. Then he could picture it. A young lady wearing a gown with violet flowers. Shiny, rich brown hair and fair, smooth skin. She was tall for a lady, perhaps a little taller than his sister, and slender. When Bingley had come to coax him into dancing, Darcy had caught her glancing at them. He had spoken deliberately, wanting to issue a set-down to ensure she understood he found her entirely insipid. Bingley was free to flirt with whomever he liked, but Darcy would do *nothing* that a lady or her relations might believe indicated a romantic interest or obligation from him. That meant not seeking introductions or asking ladies to dance—not in such a place. It was different in London, when he was amongst the *ton* and there were other wealthy gentlemen about. Few, if any, gentlemen of his quality would ever visit this small, unfashionable town. To these feelings was added the fact that he detested dancing. He had only asked Mrs Hurst and Miss Bingley because they expected it of him.

Darcy also remembered the way Miss Elizabeth had met his eye after he had spoken, her expression shocked and then amused. He had watched her walk across the room to a woman whom he recalled being introduced to, Miss Lucas, and had continued to study her as the two ladies spoke.

Mr Bennet's voice recalled him to the present. "You insulted my daughter in a crowded room. You *were* overheard. It is bad enough that she had to listen to you dismiss her. You had no cause to think ill of her. You had not even been introduced! To make the situation worse, causing her yet greater distress, others heard you as well. My dear girl, who is but twenty years old, had to tolerate—a word you are quick to throw about—our neighbours wanting to discuss your vile statements with her all night. No doubt they are speaking of it amongst themselves today and will continue to do so for some time. Do you make it a practice to damage the reputations of young ladies you do not know for no reason other than— Actually, I fail to see why you would, unless it is for your own amusement."

Darcy's cheeks warmed slightly. If pressed, he *might* concede that yes, he knew it was poor manners to attend an assembly and not dance. Further, he might have confined his remarks to telling Bingley to return to his partner, leaving him to disregard everyone other than his friends. There was nothing wrong with his sentiments—he was allowed to think what he liked—or his desire not to feign friendship or even curiosity about any of the local people, but holding his tongue might have been more prudent.

Hoping to end the discussion and send Mr Bennet on his way immediately, he said, "I regret she overheard what was a private exchange between me and Mr Bingley." He refrained from adding that Miss Elizabeth ought not to have eavesdropped and had not seemed disturbed by it while she and Miss Lucas had discussed the brief, forgettable moment. Darcy had presumed that he was the cause of their glee as they glanced at him and smiled at each other. Something in the sound of Miss Elizabeth's laugh had drawn his attention, making it difficult to look away.

Mr Bennet gave a bark of incredulity as though he found *Darcy* amusing. "I am not owed an apology, sir. My daughter is. And I hope for your sake you take the time to consider your words carefully before you approach her to give it."

With that, the man spun about and marched out of the room. After spending a minute reflecting on Mr Bennet's rudeness—both in coming to him like this and leaving as he had—Darcy made his way into the gardens. He would still like to go for a ride, but he had an immediate need for fresh air. He strode along a path, his pace quick and mind racing. What had Mr Bennet meant by his final statement? First, he evidently had supposed that Darcy would issue an apology to Miss Elizabeth directly, and second, he had suggested she would…what exactly? Although Darcy had seen no sign of discomfort in her, perhaps she was one of those ladies who wept at the slightest mishap. If he did speak to her—and he was by no means resolved that he would—and she cried, he would… Well, he did not know what he would do, but he would not take it kindly, and it would sink his opinion of her even lower. What would be resolved under those circumstances? Not that there was anything *to* resolve.

He exhaled sharply and, seeing a wooden bench beneath a nearby oak tree, he sat and contemplated the estate. Bingley was pleased with Netherfield Park, and Darcy hoped he would be happy here. Months earlier, his friend had asked for his help in finding a property in Hertfordshire. Naturally, Darcy had obliged him, and of the few that were available for lease, this had been the most promising. It would be better if the neighbourhood boasted more noteworthy families, but Bingley likely would not remain for more than a few months. If he decided to reside at Netherfield for longer than a year, Darcy would offer him the benefit of his own experience. It was necessary to have some connexions with one's neighbours—especially other gentlemen—but that did not require spending large amounts of time with them. Being *too* friendly, which Bingley often was, could lead to speculation that you meant to marry a young lady from the area and—when you did not—injured feelings were sure to follow.

For the next few minutes, Darcy did nothing more than take in the view. Slowly, his earlier question of whether he had made the wrong choice in how he had responded to Bingley's coaxing the previous night turned into certainty that he had.

"I should have remained silent. Nothing good could come from speaking my thoughts aloud. Surely there were other ways to ensure people understood I am *not* interested in knowing them, and I ought to have simply refused to dance with any young lady," he murmured, then rubbed his forehead and sighed. "I suppose I should acknowledge my unwise decision to Miss Elizabeth."

He sighed once again. Why had Bingley been so set

on Hertfordshire? Darcy knew that it had to do with his late parents; it seemed excessively sentimental to him, but possibly—probably—only because *he* found his present situation disagreeable. Yet, Bingley had promised his father…

Darcy stood and began to walk towards the house. He did not want to contemplate promises made to dead fathers because it reminded him of his childhood friend George Wickham and the many ways he had been betrayed by the cur. It raised his ire just when the peacefulness of the countryside had begun to calm the discontent that had been simmering within him since the summer.

Preferring not to dwell on the subject, he turned his thoughts back to the morning's events. While Mr Bennet's purpose in calling had been unexpected, Darcy still would not be surprised if another man—or woman—attempted to gain access to his fortune, either through marriage or a business arrangement. He began to wish he had not promised Bingley that his visit would last a month. Perhaps he could make up an excuse and return to London or his own country estate before that period elapsed. Tomorrow would not be soon enough.

# CHAPTER THREE

Elizabeth was chatting about the assembly with her mother, sisters, and Charlotte Lucas when her father returned. He had not told them where he was going, but that was not unusual. What was uncommon was the thunderous set of his features as he strode past the drawing room door to the stairs, his footsteps heavy as he ascended. Alarmed and curious, she excused herself and followed him to his book-room.

"What is it?" he said when he noticed her. He stood by a small table, pouring a glass of wine from a decanter.

"I was going to ask *you* that. Is anything amiss?"

She watched with a mixture of wariness, anxiety, and a touch of amusement as he grumbled—his words too low to make out—paced in front of the window briefly, and finally took a seat behind the broad expanse of the antique walnut desk. He nodded to indicate the chair across from him, and she dutifully lowered herself into it.

"I was at Netherfield Park," he announced.

## THE ART OF APOLOGY

"Netherfield? Why?" Had he gone to see Mr Bingley? After all, that gentleman had danced two sets with Jane, and her father might wish to discourage such a mark of favouritism. *Though that would be even more surprising than knowing where he has been this morning.* Elizabeth loved her father dearly, but he was not the most diligent of men. He was intelligent and, when he chose to be, affable, but he was also lazy and claimed that fathers had few responsibilities to daughters apart from giving permission to any man foolish enough to want to marry them.

"To see Mr Darcy." Mr Bennet took a large mouthful of wine.

"Mr Darcy? What business do you have with *him?*" No sooner was the question past her lips than she understood. "Oh, Papa—" How she wished he had stayed at home, as was his custom! His interference would surely only make the situation worse.

As she spoke, he said, "To demand he explain why he dared to insult you, of course."

Before he could go on, she interjected. "I told you last night it was best forgotten. Who cares what he thinks of me?"

"I do!" Quickly draining the wine remaining in his glass, her father stood and went to look out of the window. They were silent for a long moment until he turned to face her. "His behaviour was ungentlemanly, and someone had to tell him. As your father, *I* am the only logical person for the job. It is enough that you had to hear such disparaging remarks. To know that others did too—that they dared to speak to you of it—"

"Papa—"

"No, Lizzy." He gave her a stern look. "It had to be done, and so I did it. Believe me, I took little pleasure from it. To think I believed Mr Bingley seemed respectable when I called on him earlier this month. Young and a little stupid, perhaps, but harmless."

Elizabeth's brow furrowed. "Mr Bingley said nothing unkind of me. Did you see him this morning too?"

"I did not, but what manner of man must he be to have such a person for a friend? We cannot help who our relations are—and Lord knows, we seldom manage to influence how silly they behave. I am less inclined to judge a man by his family than by those he *chooses* to associate with."

She stood and, keeping her voice calm and persuasive, said, "Mr Bingley struck me as a charming, delightful, and not at all stupid gentleman. I liked him. Dislike Mr Darcy as much as you will. I assure you, there is nothing he can do to make me forget or alter my first—decidedly poor—opinion of him. But give Mr Bingley a chance to prove himself. Do not judge him by his friend." Elizabeth's plea was both what she felt was right and because she had seen how flattered Jane had been by his attention. Her elder sister tended to think too well of people, but there was something about Mr Bingley that inspired Elizabeth to trust him. She spoke of how friendly he had been and how he had impressed everyone with his good manners.

Soon, Mr Bennet's countenance eased. He returned to his chair and, after chuckling, said, "You should have seen Mr Darcy's expression! He was clearly shocked by my reprimand. I shall be interested to see whether he apologises to you. He said something about his regrets to me, but I told him *you* were the one he needed to address."

"I do not care whether he does."

Her father waggled a finger at her. "But you should, my dear, you should. If he does, we might laugh at how difficult it was for him—because I assure you, it will take a Herculean effort for such a man to lower himself to apologise to a young lady he sees as beneath his notice. If he does not, then we might laugh at all the ways he avoids doing what is right. I have known many men like him. He will find some way to excuse himself, to blame you or me or who-knows-what to give himself permission to avoid humbling himself."

Elizabeth giggled. "I still hope he goes away soon. However, I very much anticipate Mr Darcy providing me with endless reasons to laugh at him while he is in the neighbourhood!"

BINGLEY REPORTED WITH AN ODD AMOUNT OF enthusiasm that they would attend the same church as the Bennets did. He made the announcement after dinner on Saturday.

"Everything Miss Bennet said of it tells me it is exactly the sort of church I prefer," Bingley said.

"You prefer a church?" Miss Bingley sniggered, as did her sister. "I seem to recall how difficult it is to get you out of bed on time to attend services whenever we are in Scarborough and our relations insist we go."

"You are speaking nonsense," Bingley retorted. "I

happen to like going to church, especially when it is a charming country parish, such as this. It is different in London or even a larger town when one has been up half the night at some ball or party. Miss Bennet says that the parson is excellent. What was his name? Jones or Cole or something like that. It does not matter. We shall meet him soon enough. He is middle-aged, I believe, and has been here for…"

Darcy ceased listening as Bingley continued to sing the praises of a gentleman and church he had never encountered. It did not much matter to Darcy where he attended services while in Hertfordshire. He imagined Bingley's true pleasure was the prospect of seeing Miss Bennet again; he had often mentioned her since the assembly. Darcy conceded that she was very pretty, and Bingley said she was also guileless and interesting to talk to. If Bingley wanted to know her better, Darcy had no objection—presently he did not, at least. Bingley was young and enjoyed the company of young ladies.

*Not that I consider myself old,* he reflected. He was only four years Bingley's senior, but at times, he felt much older. He had always thought that had more to do with his circumstances—the early deaths of both his mother and father, a large estate to manage, and the care of his sister. To add to that, his family placed many expectations on his shoulders, notably about choosing a proper bride.

"You need look no further than your cousin Anne," his uncle, the Earl of Romsley, had said to him the previous winter. "My sisters both hoped you would marry. You would gain Rosings and an excellent property

THE ART OF APOLOGY

to leave your second son, and she does have excellent connexions." He had laughed, no doubt thinking he had made a joke, given *he* was the most impressive connexion of the family.

The countess had repeated the suggestion not two months ago. "You ought to take a wife. It would do you good to have more company when you are at Pemberley, and now that Georgiana is no longer at school, she will spend more time in Derbyshire too. She needs a lady with her."

His aunt, Lady Catherine de Bourgh, was more insistent, often speaking as though the matter was already settled. As for Darcy's paternal relations, they believed he should follow in his father's footsteps and marry a lady of high rank and great fortune. For his part, he was in no rush to settle down, and he had told his family so repeatedly. In another few years, he would select a suitable lady, and they would have a perfectly ordinary marriage.

It occurred to him that Bingley had also been orphaned at an early age and was responsible for one of his sisters; Mrs Hurst had already married by the time their father had died. The difference must be in their circumstances. Miss Bingley was five or so years older than Georgiana, and Bingley did not suffer under the same weight of family and societal expectations as he did. For all their wealth, Darcy did not know that anyone pursued Miss Bingley for her dowry as Wickham had his sister, and several of Darcy's acquaintances had spoken to him of Georgiana's impending entry into society. They had done so casually, to be sure, but he had understood that they were already contemplating the size of her fortune and excellent breeding and how an allegiance with her would benefit them. Was it any wonder he despised and distrusted people unknown to him and whose situation in life was so decidedly beneath his own? The danger he faced in apologising to Elizabeth Bennet was that she and her family would immediately seek to form a connexion with him.

*Indeed, I would not be surprised if Mr Bennet's visit was part of a scheme.* First, convince Darcy he must apologise, then trade on his guilt for having insulted the girl—not that he had any, but they would assume he did—and before he knew it, they would have tricked him into proposing to her. *That* would never happen!

The next morning, the Netherfield party took the pew across the aisle from the Bennets. They had arrived at the church with only time to nod a greeting to them and others before the service began because the ladies had been slow to prepare. Darcy usually thought Mrs Hurst and Miss Bingley dressed fashionably and elegantly, and he did today as well, but here, in this modest country parish, on a Sunday morning of no special import, they had taken it too far. Knowing it was mean-spirited of him, he wondered whether they intended to advertise their sense of superiority, to ensure everyone looked at them instead of attending to the parson. With effort, he banished the thought. They were his friends; mostly he considered them his friend's sisters, but still, they were more than mere acquaintances.

*I shall not look*, he silently vowed. In the minutes he

had been in the church, he had repeated the statement several times. What, or rather whom, he would not look at were the Bennets. He sensed their eyes on him, but he was determined to be wise and not give them a single thought. It was not so easy, however, and Darcy's explanation for why he was so conscious of the family's presence was Mr Bennet's reprimand, which still left him feeling both indignant at the affront and wishing he had remained silent at the assembly.

When he was no longer able to resist, he glanced towards the Bennets, taking care not to make it obvious lest he be seen. His mouth went dry, and when he swallowed, his throat hurt due to the lack of moisture. All he had managed to see was *her*. Miss Elizabeth sat at the end of the pew, her gaze steady on the parson and her chin tilted upwards. Her spencer and bonnet were both a rich blue, which only enhanced the colour of her hair and skin.

That did not explain why his heart raced. *It is only because I suppose I ought to apologise to her, regardless of why they want me to.* He would be careful of the consequences —ensure Miss Elizabeth Bennet knew there would be no friendship between them. It was simply a task, an unpleasant chore, and one he would do to satisfy Mr Bennet and prevent him from complaining to his friends. This entire stupid affair only served to remind Darcy why he disliked these confined societies where nothing of note ever happened and everyone was far too familiar and comfortable with each other. *A tempest in a teacup indeed.*

When the service ended and they stood to depart,

Bingley slapped Darcy on the shoulder and said, "That was excellent, was it not? Truly one of the best sermons I recall hearing in a very long while."

"Yes. Certainly," Darcy muttered, trusting his friend would not notice how distracted he was. He was attempting to determine what he would say to Miss Elizabeth. The business of apologising would take no more than a minute, and then he could return to Netherfield —as long as Bingley did not insist on spending the entire morning chatting to people.

Darcy took his time leaving the pew and walking down the aisle. He spotted Miss Elizabeth immediately as he left the church, pausing a moment near the door to watch her as she stood, talking to one of her sisters whose name he did not know. He walked towards her with his characteristic long stride, his approach commanding enough to send the other Miss Bennet scurrying off. Miss Elizabeth turned towards him and made a shallow curtsey, but she did not speak.

"Miss Elizabeth. I hope you are well," he said, giving her a nod that was curter than he had intended.

"I am, thank you."

Her cold demeanour almost made him turn and walk away. Maybe he had been mistaken about her, and rather than having been waiting for an apology, she had as much interest in hearing one as he had in giving it. The thought gave him a momentary pleasure because it meant he could simply say some other innocuous statement, about the weather perhaps, and leave her be. But his hope was soon extinguished when he considered the more likely explanation for her manner. She was one of those ladies who would act offended or distressed until a gentleman said whatever he thought might please her, after which, they would be all smiles and giggles and fluttering eyelashes. Good Lord, he despised girls like that! *One, two minutes and the task will be done. I shall never have to speak to her again!*

"I regret that you overheard the manner in which I referred to you the other evening. At the assembly. When I was speaking to Bingley. Please accept my apology." He had added the part about his friend to remind her it had been a private conversation. Albeit one had in a crowded public place.

She regarded him for a moment, still acting aloof, before saying, "Thank you."

He felt his brow furrow and forced his features to ease; he might be puzzled by her response, but he did not want her to know it. "Is that all the reply I am to expect?"

She averted her gaze long enough to adjust her bonnet, then met his eyes again. "An apology given under duress is not an apology, Mr Darcy. A true apology must be felt here." She tapped her chest above her heart. "You do not regret what you said. The lack of sincerity in your tone told me as much. I do not believe you even regret that I heard you. The only reason you have spoken to me today is because my father dared to tell you that you behaved inappropriately. Am I mistaken?"

Heat rose up the back of his neck. She was correct. He did not regret that she had heard him; he had *meant* for her to hear him, to discourage any pretensions before they were begun. When he did not immediately answer, she continued.

"You do understand that your behaviour deserves censure, do you not? I must believe you are not so lost to good manners that you are unaware how wrong it is to share your ill opinion of any lady with so many other people about. Particularly one to whom you have not even been introduced and who has done you no harm! Do you have any notion how hurtful it can be to hear yourself spoken of in that way and to know others knew of it?"

What would he have said if she gave him the opportunity to speak? He did not feel capable of uttering a single word because the only ones that came to mind would be spoken in anger in light of her reprimand and embarrassment that she understood him so well. The latter feeling would only increase the former. But if he were capable of being reasonable, he might ask whether she would mind less if they *had* been introduced—why that made a difference, he did not know, but both she and her father had mentioned it—or he might tell her that he *did* know what it was like to have people speculating about you in your presence. How often had he felt as though a thick black mass had formed in his stomach when he heard people gossiping about his wealth or sharing some nonsensical and false story about his supposed liaisons and habits.

"I do not care what your opinion of me is," Miss Elizabeth said, and the disinterest in her tone convinced him she spoke the truth. "I *do* care that I have had to endure far too many people commenting on what you said of me. You must realise that everyone is speaking of it. Well, *everyone* is a slight exaggeration." She chuckled, but her show of good humour was not for him. "But ladies and gentlemen I like, and even some I do not, have all wanted to discuss it with me, some to offer consolation, some to laugh at me, a few even to laugh with me. I do not blame you for your low opinion of me."

"But I do not—" Darcy interjected. The tips of his ears burnt, and he hoped they were hidden by his hat.

"Oh, but Mr Darcy, you *must* think poorly of me. After all, I am only *tolerable* to look at, and what value is there in a lady if she is not pretty? And let us not forget that I was *slighted* by other men and not good enough even to be introduced to you."

Aghast at having his words so saucily thrown back at him—and hating how they sounded coming from her—Darcy opened his mouth to assure her she was wrong. Then he saw a sparkle in her eyes that stopped him. The heat in his ears had spread over his entire face as she spoke, but currently, he felt as if a bucket of icy water had been poured over him. She was laughing at him, teasing him. Not only was it in her eyes, but the corners of her mouth were twitching as though she was struggling not to smile. He ought to be insulted, and he was, but part of him was also…intrigued, he supposed, or ever so slightly amused.

"What would you have me say?" he asked.

"Nothing you do not truly feel or believe," she said. "At present, you do not regret what you said. Perhaps you never will. That is your right. I shall never ask you to apologise for your feelings."

"Would you believe me if I said I knew I was mistaken?"

She shrugged. "If you only wish to express regret for speaking of me aloud where others overheard you, then I shall accept it."

"That is all I am to expect of you?"

"At present, it is all I can offer you. You said such... disagreeable things of me without us ever exchanging a word. My looks you could see, and I cannot fault you for finding them wanting, but believing I was overlooked by other men implies my character is somehow lacking and my company to be avoided, even for the length of a set."

He attempted to interrupt her and assure her that he did not think she was unattractive; truly, she was rather pretty. Had he failed to notice it at the assembly? She continued at once, however.

"I promise that if the day ever comes when you can genuinely say you regret speaking of me as you did, I shall humbly accept your apology. Good morning, Mr Darcy." She gave him a cool, polite smile and went to join her father.

# CHAPTER FOUR

"What did he say to you?" Mr Bennet demanded. Elizabeth gave a soft chuckle and smiled, which she hoped would ease her father's agitation. He was far too bothered by Mr Darcy's behaviour at the assembly. To be sure, she had felt a momentary pang at being dismissed so easily—not because she had hoped to attract him but because no young lady wants to have their charms dismissed. She remained resolved to forget all about Mr Darcy, as she had told her father, and wished he would do the same.

After explaining the essence of her conversation with the gentleman, she added, "A simpleton would have seen that his apology was not serious, so I did not accept it."

"You did not?" Her father appeared taken aback.

She shook her head gleefully. "I told him that he ought to learn to apologise properly, and if he ever does, I shall graciously forgive the past. Since I expect he will never lower himself enough to admit he was wrong to insult me in a crowded room, I need never worry about having to speak to him again!"

She grinned and waited for her father to laugh or smile. She knew how to respond to both; what she did not know was what to do when he scowled. He was looking around the churchyard, she assumed for Mr Darcy.

"Papa—"

"Let us find your mother and sisters. I would like to go home. We shall discuss Mr Darcy anon." He lightly touched her elbow, leading her first to her mother and younger sisters, then to where Jane stood with Mr Bingley. Both times, he only said, "It is time for us to go."

Bennet was not fond of Sundays. He grudgingly accepted the necessity of going to church, but what transpired at Longbourn vexed him. Years ago, his wife had decreed that it was a day for family, and thus, he sat in the drawing room with her and their daughters and prayed tedium and frustration would not be the end of him. In the past, Mrs Bennet had complained about his habit of hiding behind a book, but it had been a decade or so since she had given up her attempts to make him speak to them more than occasionally. As far as he was concerned, she managed to say enough for three people, and the girls were probably grateful not to have to listen to him as well.

Mary was in a corner, reading a religious text, which she claimed was the only suitable material for the Sabbath. Jane's and Elizabeth's heads were bent over their sewing, Elizabeth's left eyebrow occasionally arching as her mother or one of her sisters said something particularly nonsensical. His two youngest daughters sat with his wife, their animated conversation leaping haphazardly between fashion, gossip, their desire for greater entertainment, and hopes that there would be an endless parade of parties for them to attend in the coming months.

Today, his gaze was drawn to the ladies more than it commonly was; he found himself studying his daughters. It was Mr Darcy's fault, of course, and he again struggled to comprehend how he had spoken so harshly of Elizabeth. Mostly, he observed the youngest three, becoming lost in his reflections.

Mrs Hill and a maid brought in tea and cake, and glancing at the clock on the mantel, Bennet calculated he had been contemplating his family for above half an hour. As though thick clouds parted before his eyes, he understood that his girls needed him to…teach them. Guide them. Mr Darcy had been wrong to insult Elizabeth and, more to the point, in what he had said of her. But if he—or some other man—had refused to dance with Mary, Kitty, or Lydia, could Bennet have entirely blamed them? More likely, he would have said he had made a sensible choice and that spending the length of a set in company with one of the girls was sure to give even the stoutest of men a headache.

*I ought to encourage them to…be better.* He was shocked by the notion that his girls were not as admirable as they ought to be, but he knew at once that it was true.

Elizabeth served him a cup of tea and thick wedge of spice cake. "Are you well, Papa?"

He struggled to erase whatever signs of confusion she must have seen in his expression and shook his head. "It is nothing. I simply remembered a letter I meant to write yesterday but forgot. I must attend to it tomorrow." He tapped his temple.

She smiled and went back to her seat, leaving Bennet to his reveries. He supposed Kitty and Lydia would be the easiest to correct. *I shall demand they...do something useful every day. Read a book or cultivate a talent.* First, he would have to know them better because, shamefully, he could not name any of their preferred pastimes, other than giggling and gossiping.

He slowly sipped his tea, wishing there was someone he might consult with. His wife would be useless and say that the girls were perfect as they were, immediately followed by complaints that they did not always follow her advice on how to dress or speak to gentlemen, and, the chief cause of her frail nerves, none of them were yet married. No, he was on his own, and he was resolved. He said another prayer, this time that he would not falter.

At length, he decided that the best service he could do Mary would be to build up her confidence. For his darling Elizabeth, he reluctantly admitted that it might be good if she tempered her sarcasm and tendency to cling to first impressions, refusing to accept that they might be mistaken. While it was true that *he* shared those habits, he drew on years of experience to form his portraits of people, thus making them more accurate than hers could be.

*And what of Jane?* His eldest girl was almost too good, and Bennet worried about her suffering disappointment. Several times, he had heard how much Jane liked Mr Bingley—and that the young man appeared enchanted with her—but what if his interest faded or he was like the arrogant Mr Darcy and they simply had not yet seen that aspect of his character?

Bennet sighed. What Jane most wanted, and what she deserved, was a family of her own—a husband and children she could bestow all her affection on. But what could *he* do about it?

Mrs Bennet laughed loudly, drawing his eye. *I might do as she asked when we learnt a young gentleman was moving into Netherfield. I can be welcoming, speak to him, get to know him. In that way, I may decide for myself whether he is worthy of Jane, and if he is, I can encourage their connexion by providing opportunities for them to talk without my wife intruding and scaring him away with her fussing and nonsense.*

No doubt, it would be disagreeable work, but what manner of gentleman would he be if he did not do all he could to ensure the happiness and well-being of his ladies? What manner of gentleman was he that he had neglected to do so for years?

ELIZABETH HAD NOTICED THAT HER FATHER WAS behaving oddly all day. Usually, he hid behind a book while the family sat together on Sundays. Instead, whenever she looked his way, he appeared to be watching them, sometimes scowling, other times with his head tilted to one side as though contemplating a difficult puzzle. At dinner, he said little, even when she spoke directly to him, and continued to observe them; she did not even see him look at the food on his plate before scooping it up with his fork and bringing it to his mouth. Should she be concerned?

*Perhaps I shall discuss it with Jane, though I am sure she will tell me I am being fanciful or grow anxious for him unnecessarily.*

"I shall prepare the invitations at once!" Mrs Bennet said.

Her mother's voice was loud, and it was either that or what she said that appeared to shake Mr Bennet out of his distraction. Elizabeth noticed his head jerk up and his eyes fix on her mother; she turned to regard her as well.

Mrs Bennet's expression was gleeful, and she patted Jane's hand as she said, "You will wear your—"

"Do pardon the interruption, my dear," Mr Bennet said. "I know it is none of my concern, I am only here to pay the bills and smile prettily to our guests when you insist upon it, but invitations to whom and for what purpose?"

It seemed incredible that he had missed everything that had been discussed throughout the meal—on a subject that had first arisen earlier in the drawing room—and it only proved to Elizabeth that he had been contemplating very serious matters.

Colour bloomed in her mother's cheeks, and she

took a large sip of her wine before responding. "If you had paid any attention to me earlier, Mr Bennet, you would already know what we are speaking of. The dinner party!"

He waited a brief moment as though expecting further explanation, but when none was forthcoming, he asked, "*What* dinner party?"

Mrs Bennet exhaled forcefully before replying. These signs of exasperation between her parents were a game to them, Elizabeth supposed. At times she found it amusing, but at others, it was fatiguing, and she wished her mother and father liked each other more.

"We must have Mr Bingley to dinner to welcome him and his family to the neighbourhood. He was so taken with Jane, and it will give him an opportunity to know her better. You *will* be kind to him."

The last sounded more like an order than a request, and Elizabeth expected her father to say something sarcastic or laugh. Instead, his response shocked her. "I should like to spend time with him. But let me be clear. While I accept the wisdom in having Mr Bingley to Longbourn, I shall not stand for that friend of his entering this house."

"Papa," Elizabeth said before her mother could speak; she was wary of an argument resulting if her parents began debating the matter, as they surely would. "We cannot *not* invite him. He is Mr Bingley's guest, and it would be very rude to ask everyone but him."

"No, Lizzy, I do not agre—"

"I would not dare insult Mr Bingley by excluding his

friend!" Mrs Bennet cried. "For Jane's sake, it is *vitally* important that Mr Bingley thinks well of us."

Mr Bennet regarded Jane; she was blushing, and her eyes were lowered. After a brief silence, he asked, "Do you particularly want Mr Bingley to think well of you, Jane?"

After glancing at him, she nodded.

Elizabeth rested a hand on his arm and, speaking more for his ear than the others, said, "He is unobjectionable, and Jane *does* like him. And consider this. Being here, amongst a smaller party, will force Mr Darcy to practise good manners. He must have been taught them, and he will know that everyone is watching him, waiting for him to make a fool of himself yet again. I need not talk to him. Indeed, I have no desire to. For Jane." She fixed him with a look that was meant to hint that he was at risk of being curmudgeonly. Of all her sisters, she was the only one who would dare to suggest he was not behaving reasonably.

He sighed. "Very well. But you are to have nothing to do with the man, Lizzy. Other than greeting him politely, none of you girls are to speak to him, and if I hear so much as a hint that he has said anything even slightly disagreeable to or about you or your sisters—"

"He will not dare to because he knows you will not tolerate it." She smiled, imbuing her expression with warm affection.

Her father patted her hand. "You are a good girl. One day, you will meet a man worthy of you, and I shall endeavour not to hate him for taking you away from me."

She chuckled, and they both resumed eating, while Mrs Bennet spoke in detail about her arrangements for the party.

# CHAPTER FIVE

"Thank God we are away from those people and shall not have to see any of them again today!" Miss Bingley exclaimed as she entered the drawing room at Netherfield. She sat on one of the silk-covered sofas, Mrs Hurst taking a place beside her and nodding in agreement.

"Why did you make us go to that church?" Mrs Hurst asked. "Surely there was no need to go at all, or we might have found a more...acceptable one in a nearby town. What is the largest town hereabouts?"

"As I have told you," Bingley said, "we are in the country, and it is expected that we attend on Sundays. Besides, it is an excellent way to become part of the community. I met ever so many people in the short time we spent in the churchyard. I liked being there, and I shall be glad to go again."

Darcy just caught sight of Miss Bingley's eyes flickering upwards as he passed by her to go to the window. Hurst was sitting in a chair by the fire, a newspaper

## THE ART OF APOLOGY

hiding his face, and Bingley had taken a place across from his sisters. Darcy found the conversation pointless, and it would surely only lead to the Bingleys and Mrs Hurst squabbling. They had already done so several times in his hearing, all because the ladies did not like the county in which their brother had taken a house.

*If anyone should feel fatigued, it is me.* Darcy's tendency to be unsociable had worsened since Ramsgate. He knew it, yet there was nothing he could do about it—nor did he want to, truth be told. He had every right to be in a foul mood, given the way his once-friend George Wickham had attempted to ruin his and his sister's happiness forever. Georgiana remained much affected, and Darcy prayed she would improve under the care of their aunt Lady Romsley and her new companion, Mrs Annesley.

*I shall return to my former self in time. There is no need to force myself to more cheerfulness than I feel. Anyone who is a true friend will not care.* When they were lately in town, Bingley had enquired whether he and his family were well, afterwards expanding this to include other matters that might be concerning Darcy. His questions were posed in a manner that suggested he recognised something more than his usual responsibilities was weighing on him. Naturally, Darcy had denied all suggestion that there was anything amiss.

"Darcy," Bingley called, "do you not agree that the parson was excellent and the church is charming?"

He turned from the window where he had been mindlessly watching the wind rustle through the trees and shrubs, and said, "It is a perfectly acceptable country church. I have been in worse."

"That is not a ringing endorsement, sir," Miss Bingley said, then chuckled. "I believe you agree with Louisa and me that the entire neighbourhood is…I hate to say terrible, but there is nothing to like about it. You are simply too kind to admit it, knowing how it would disappoint my brother."

Darcy acknowledged her with a quick nod but remained silent. In actuality, his views on the neighbourhood did not entirely align with hers. True, the people he had met were not the sort he preferred to spend time with, but—just as with the church—he knew there were other places that would be more trying to live in, even temporarily.

Presently, it was important to Bingley to be in Hertfordshire. Whether he remained here for months or for years, Darcy would not speculate, but his friend wanted to familiarise himself with the county because his mother had passed her childhood in it, only leaving upon her marriage. Mrs Bingley had died when Bingley was still a young child, and he had few memories of her. Darcy knew what it was like to want a connexion to a dead parent and the need to seek it. That was why he had immediately agreed to help his friend find an estate he might lease in Hertfordshire.

"I do wish you had taken an estate somewhere more fashionable," Mrs Hurst said. Darcy had heard the same exact words from her at least half a dozen times. "Mama would not expect or want you to suffer for her by actually residing in the county. A sensible man would have

## THE ART OF APOLOGY

simply found a decent inn and stayed a night." She and Miss Bingley regarded each other and nodded, the latter adding her agreement in a loud and hearty voice.

Bingley's cheeks turned red. Darcy went to sit near him, quietly offering his support. There was nothing he could or would say; it was a family dispute.

"I disagree, and *I* am the one who spoke to Papa about the matter—not you. He regretted not spending more time here. I wish we had so that we might have known her family before they all died or moved away."

Miss Bingley's eyebrows rose and fell, a silent sign she did not share his sentiments, but Mrs Hurst's countenance indicated a degree of understanding.

"It would have been...pleasant," she said. "But Papa was occupied with his business and family in Yorkshire, and now, there is no one here for us to know. I do wish you had made it a visit of a few days rather than lease an estate."

In Darcy's opinion, there was no need to repeat herself; she was becoming reprimanding, and he was annoyed on his friend's behalf.

"At least he did not purchase it," Miss Bingley mumbled.

"Be as superior as you like," Bingley said to his sisters. "But I also expect you to be gracious. If that is too difficult, you may return to London. I shall do well enough without you here. I do not need you to run my household, Caroline. Darcy has managed Pemberley very well without the benefit of a lady while Miss Darcy is so young. You and Hurst have a home of your own, Louisa, if you are so anxious to be amongst people more to your liking." He stood and, to Darcy, continued, "I need fresh air. Would you care to take a walk?"

Darcy also stood, nodded politely to the ladies, disregarded Hurst, who was still hiding behind the paper, and followed Bingley from the room.

BY MONDAY MORNING, MRS BENNET WAS READY to deliver her invitations to the forthcoming dinner party. Elizabeth admired her mother's ability to move so quickly from conceiving the idea of holding such an event to being prepared to tell those lucky people who would be asked to partake in it.

"John will deliver these," Mrs Bennet said, tapping a short pile of notes and naming their manservant, "and these we shall deliver ourselves." She held a much smaller group of invitations aloft.

The ladies were in the parlour after breakfast. Mr Bennet had already gone away. Elizabeth did not know where; her father seldom spent much time with them when he could avoid it. In truth, she was already anticipating taking a long, solitary walk and thus removing herself from her mother and younger sisters' company. She loved them dearly, but that did not mean she wished to be with them all the time. The day was long, and she would dutifully and gladly give them all the attention they desired later on.

Her mother shuffled through the cards she meant to hand out herself and moved one into the other pile. "We shall go to Lucas Lodge first, then Netherfield, and afterwards, I wish to call on my sister."

Lady Lucas for gossip and to show off that *she will be the first to host Mr Bingley, Netherfield so that she might throw Jane at that gentleman, and finally Aunt Philips for more gossip, ideally how Mr Bingley is surely already madly in love with Jane and will soon propose.* Elizabeth bit her lips together to avoid laughing at her joke.

Aloud, she said, "It sounds like you have arranged a delightful morning, Mama, but I should not go. You know my father insists I avoid Mr Darcy as much as possible."

Her mother scoffed. "I do not care what that man has said."

"Mr Darcy or Papa?" Kitty said, sounding baffled, but Mrs Bennet continued as though she had not heard her.

"Mr Bingley must see us at our best, and that includes being forgiving of his odious friend. I would be glad to never see him again, and if he so much as looks at one of you girls askance, I shall kick him! But"—her mother took a deep breath, evidently meant to calm herself—"Mr Bingley will look upon us more kindly if we overlook his friend's rudeness. Lizzy, I hope that you and Mr Darcy will soon come to an understanding."

Lydia guffawed, and Mrs Bennet shot her a disapproving look and said, "Oh, not that sort!" Then she continued giving her instructions to Elizabeth. "You need not say anything to him. Be polite, allow Mr Bingley to see how happy we are to know him, and I shall be satisfied. Your father and his odd notions are unimportant."

Since Mr Bennet's decree would permit Elizabeth to act as she most desired—both in avoiding Mr Darcy's company and this morning's proposed calls—she preferred not to overlook them. However, her mother insisted, and there was no getting out of it.

A short while later, having completed her preparations, she sat with Jane in her chamber as her sister finished her own.

"I wish Mama did not insist I go," Elizabeth grumbled.

"I am glad you are coming with us," Jane said, her voice soft and soothing. "It means so much to my mother, and I hope that once you spend more time with Miss Bingley, you will see what I did at the assembly—that she is really very agreeable. I dare say Mr Darcy will improve upon acquaintance too."

"You are encouraging me to disregard—*disobey*—what Papa said. I am proud of you." It was unlike her older sister, and Elizabeth was not sure whether or not she approved of this show of defiance. "But it does not make me any more inclined to make calls today."

"Of course I am not saying you should disobey my father! I just think it is important that you provide Mr Darcy with the opportunity to apologise, and—"

Elizabeth laughed. "He already has apologised. After church yesterday, as I told you, and he did a very poor job of it. It was obvious how reluctant he was to speak to me, and *that* is because he believes it to be unnecessary. Admit it, you *are* telling me to disregard Papa's orders. I would expect it of Kitty or Lydia, but not you or Mary."

Jane blushed. She sat at a small table covered in pieces of jewellery and other accoutrements and began to arrange them, no doubt as a way to avoid looking at her sister. "I cannot believe Mr Darcy is truly so disagreeable. Mr Bingley thinks well of him, and he is such an amiable, kind gentleman, he would not be friends with someone who was not likewise respectable and good."

"Then how do you account for his behaviour at the assembly?"

There was a slight pause before Jane responded. "I do not know why he acted as he did, but he must have had a very good reason—something that has nothing to do with you. You were merely the unfortunate target of his unhappiness. Everyone has those moments when they are quick to anger."

Her voice full of the genuine affection she felt for her sister, Elizabeth said, "You just want everyone to be friends, or at least amiable acquaintances. Very well. I shall go and astonish you—and Mr Darcy—with my politeness."

## CHAPTER SIX

Darcy sat through the Bennets' call—which fortunately was not prolonged—without saying more than murmured greetings. He ought to have retreated to another room as soon as he heard they were there, but something had kept him in the drawing room with Bingley and his family having a rather repetitive conversation about travel. The Bennet ladies had come to deliver an invitation. Mrs Bennet had barely looked at him when she assured him they would be happy to see him at Longbourn; her chin had been pointed in the right direction but not her eyes. Her voice, like her manner, had lacked the warmth she displayed when speaking to Bingley and his relations.

For the remainder of the visit, Darcy had remained silent and observant. While he had not been able to avoid seeing—or hearing—the younger Miss Bennets and their mother, what chiefly captivated him was Miss Elizabeth. What a conundrum she was! He did not know what to think of their exchange the previous day or what

## THE ART OF APOLOGY

he ought to do next. Other than curtseying upon arrival, she had done nothing to acknowledge his presence, which only added to his confusion.

*Disregard the matter and do my utmost to forget about her and her family. How I wish I could quit Netherfield immediately!* Once Bingley demonstrated that he was becoming accustomed to his new duties, Darcy would leave.

For a minute or two after the Bennets' departure, Darcy stayed sitting in the same chair, not truly listening to the conversation taking place around him, until the evident frustration in Bingley's tone drew his attention.

"Well, I think it was very kind of her," Bingley said. Catching Darcy's eye, he continued, "Do you not agree that it is kind of Mrs Bennet to arrange a dinner to welcome us to the neighbourhood?"

Darcy shrugged. "Kind, yes, but also a rather dreary prospect."

Mrs Hurst and Miss Bingley tittered.

"I think it sounds like a jolly good time!" Bingley exclaimed, his face beginning to resemble a ripe plum. "It will be an excellent opportunity to know my new neighbours. I want them to have a good impression of us all, which means I expect you to be on your best behaviour, Caroline."

Miss Bingley rolled her eyes. "I shall endeavour not to show the discomfort I feel amongst these people. Will that do?"

"Very nicely," Bingley said through clenched teeth. He spoke no further, but his eyes flickered towards Darcy, who suspected his friend was recalling that *he* had done nothing to hide his disgust at the assembly.

*That cursed evening! How I wish I had suffered a headache or had found another excuse not to attend.*

"The woman is unlikely to serve even one decent ragout," Hurst said. "But it is important to establish connexions with what gentry exists near one's estate, or so my parents always say."

"There you have it!" Bingley said, clapping his hands together. "In three days' time, we shall go to Longbourn. I am already anticipating seeing the Bennets again."

*And I am looking forward to seeing Miss Elizabeth again.* Initially taken aback by the realisation, Darcy soon recognised its value. He would again apologise, this time being sure not to sound as dismissive and unwilling as he had the day before. The task would be done properly, he would better mask his disdain for the people of Meryton in the future, and Bingley could happily anticipate however many months he chose to pass in the county that had been beloved by his late mother.

ELIZABETH CONTINUED TO BE CONFUSED BY her father's behaviour. He was his usual self with her and, as far as she knew, Jane, but she happened to witness him speaking to her younger sisters, which was unusual; he seldom sought any of them out. The first occasion was when she and Mary were reading in the parlour shortly before dinner on Monday. They sat in different corners of the room, and when her father entered it, he glanced at her and then went to sit with Mary. Curious, Elizabeth kept her book open in her lap but ceased reading. Instead, she strained her ears to listen to their conversation. It might be wrong, but she reasoned that if he wanted to keep the subject secret, he would not have spoken to Mary with her nearby.

"What are you reading?" he asked.

To no great surprise, it was a book of sermons. In Elizabeth's opinion, its only value was as a sleep aid.

"Ah. I do not believe I have read it myself," Mr Bennet said. "What advice do you find in it?"

Mary spoke for several minutes, reciting the dubious lessons she had discovered in the tome. Upon occasion, Mr Bennet's eyebrows would rise slightly until he abruptly lowered them, giving Elizabeth the impression he was struggling to appear interested and not disgusted.

After several minutes, he said, "So, this...gentleman argues that proper young ladies should always be silent when in company with young men, apart from brief comments on the most uncontroversial subjects?"

It was almost enough to make Elizabeth laugh out loud. As if *she* would ever behave in such a manner.

"He does," Mary confirmed. "Whatever education we might have, it can never rival that of a man, and neither can our understanding of the world. Our innocence might lead us to say or do something that gives the impression we are flirting or might be open to...inappropriate behaviour. It will make us seem lacking in proper seriousness and deference, and no man wants to marry a silly woman, to have such a person as his wife and mother to his children."

Instantly, Elizabeth understood Mary better than she thought she ever had. Their father had married an ignorant woman—much to the detriment of all their daughters—and their two youngest sisters were on the path to becoming excessively silly, unduly coquettish, and utterly empty-headed and ridiculous. She fairly burned to know how he would respond; he kept her and Mary waiting for a long moment, so long that Mary spoke before he did.

"It is a woman's job to ensure the gentleman in her life knows that she views him as superior, that she will always do as he directs and put her own opinions and needs second to his."

Elizabeth could see why many gentlemen would find it an appealing thought, but she would be miserable to be shackled to a man who expected blind obedience, who never gave a care to what she wanted and felt. It was how Mr Darcy would act, which was why she would never like him or even tolerate his company. A true, honourable gentleman would think first of ensuring his wife and daughters were comfortable and happy.

Her cheeks heated when she realised that her father might favour such an unequal arrangement. It was true that men were accorded more rights to decide for themselves and the ladies under their protection, but what the law said and how people acted did not always align. There was no denying that her father did not provide a particularly good example of how a gentleman ought to treat his wife, and, with regret, Elizabeth admitted he did his daughters no favours by refusing to be involved in their education.

Her observation of Mary and him was no longer surreptitious; she *needed* to know how he would respond.

If he did nothing to counter Mary's view, *she* would have to for her sister's well-being.

Mr Bennet cleared his throat and said, "I believe there is an in-between that would serve both ladies and gentlemen better. A lady should always strive to behave respectably, but one who is too reserved, or excessively sombre, is unlikely to find many people who want to talk to her—especially at an occasion where they expect gaiety. And consider that if a young lady never speaks, if she is reluctant to share what interests her, how might gentlemen or other ladies discover whether they would enjoy being her friend or husband? There is nothing wrong with sharing your opinion—as long as you are willing to listen to and accept other people's opinions in return."

Mary furrowed her brow, and he continued. "Consider how Jane and Lizzy act in company. No one can fault Jane's manners, though I suspect she keeps a little too much of herself hidden from the world. Some would say that Lizzy shares her opinions too freely. That sort of boldness will appeal to some but be disapproved of by others. I happen to like it, but your mother fears it will mean Lizzy remains unwed. I suspect the right man will come along, one who appreciates her quick wit and liveliness."

Elizabeth blushed to hear herself spoken of in such a fashion. She was aware of her mother's sentiments, but was there some message her father wished to impart to her? He must know she could hear him.

"My recommendation to you and your younger sisters is to choose which of them would best suit you as a model to follow—not to replicate or attempt to emulate but as a guide for how to behave in society," Mr Bennet said before pausing and checking his pocket watch. "We must prepare for dinner. Perhaps we shall return to our conversation later?"

He patted Mary's hands, stood, and left the room. Elizabeth stared after him, wondering whether an impostor had replaced her father. Turning to Mary, she suspected that her sister felt the same.

# CHAPTER SEVEN

Bennet was used to feeling disappointed whenever he looked at his wife, often wishing he could return to his younger self and make a different choice of marriage partner. He would never admit it aloud, to be sure, but he had been infatuated by her beauty and coquettishness and had acted in haste by proposing to her.

But he could not wish away his wife, and to lessen the chances of any other gentlemen finding fault with his daughters, he would see whether there was anything he might do to bring about some improvement in Mrs Bennet. She would never be a wit, but he might ease the anxieties that he suspected caused her many complaints. Deciding it would help to show an interest in her activities, at dinner on Monday, he asked how she had spent the day and listened attentively, made a similar enquiry Tuesday morning regarding her plans for the day, and that evening took a seat next to her when they went into the parlour after dinner.

"My dear," he said, "I want your opinion."

"*My* opinion?" She peered at him through narrowed eyes.

Bennet nodded. "I had an unexpected letter from my cousin and heir, Mr Collins."

"Odious man! What does he want? Hoping to discover you are on your deathbed, I suppose."

She was still a lovely woman, and he recalled that he had once found her caring and amusing. Perhaps these aspects of her character remained hidden beneath layers of nerves and shrewishness brought on by disappointment in him, their marriage, and their failure to have a son. He spoke softly, not wanting to be overheard by their daughters.

"I shall show you what he wrote, if you like, but I must warn you, it was a struggle to read the thing. I am afraid he is not at all sensible. As to what he wanted, he claims a desire for us to be reconciled, now that his father is dead. He will inherit Longbourn, and there is nothing we can do about it." He shrugged. "I do not believe any of us, including the girls, would enjoy his visit, but he wishes to come. I can see the benefit of establishing a connexion, but is now the time for it? Would it be better to put it off?" Hosting Mr Collins may be diverting, but his attention should be spent on his wife and daughters. *And improving myself.*

His wife sniffed loudly and pressed a handkerchief to her cheeks as though the conversation was upsetting her. "I do not see why I would ever want to know him."

He nodded understandingly. "As unpleasant as the subject is, his letter has made me think about what will happen to you and the girls once I have died, should any of them remain unwed." The words were unexpected, but they felt right. "But that is a conversation for another day. I do not believe now is a good time to meet him. Mr Bingley has just entered the neighbourhood, and the militia will soon be here. It is enough for us to keep an eye on all of those men, to say nothing of Mr Darcy, to be sure our daughters are being properly respected. Do you not agree?"

Again, she regarded him as though wondering whether he was playing a joke on her. It shamed him that she had ever had reason for her suspicion.

Slowly, she said, "Mr Bingley?"

Lowering his voice further and leaning towards her, he said, "It is far too early to know whether he and Jane will learn to love each other, but they must have time to know each other without unnecessary distractions. I believe we should…go about this softly. For now, we should merely observe. Let us not speak of what the future might hold until *they* have decided themselves. Do you agree, my dear?"

"Mama, Lydia says she will wear my pink dress to the dinner party, but *I* want to wear it!" Kitty complained, effectively ending Bennet's conversation with his wife for the moment.

CONTINUING TO STUDY HER FATHER, Elizabeth noted how he attempted to engage her mother in conversation at meals. He did not laugh at her but appeared to gently coax her towards topics other than fashion or Mrs Philips's troubles with her servants. Remarkably, even after one dinner, Elizabeth was convinced she saw a difference in her mother; Mrs Bennet seemed less fidgety and had not complained once of her nerves or aching head on Monday evening. After dinner on Tuesday, her parents had a serious-looking discussion, albeit one that might have ended too soon when Kitty and Lydia interrupted them. While giving part of her attention to Jane, with whom she sat, Elizabeth tried to determine how she might discover *what* they had spoken of.

Soon, Kitty and Lydia left the room, announcing an intention to go to their chambers to sort out something related to their costumes for the dinner party. Mr Bennet departed as well, and—assuming he was going to his book-room—Elizabeth decided to follow. She wanted to talk to him about his recent behaviour. Approaching the room a couple of minutes later, she was near to astonished to find that her youngest two sisters were within with their father. The door was slightly ajar, allowing her to see them, and she crept as close as she dared and listened. It was wrong of her, but she could not fight the impulse.

"I have been remiss in discussing your comportment with you both," Mr Bennet said. "I am afraid you are both out too soon—especially you, Lydia—but we cannot undo it. I should have taken a greater role in your education, but again, we cannot undo the past. I shall be considering the matter seriously and determining what we might do going forwards."

"But that is not what I wished to speak to you of

tonight. What I want to say is that, when you are in company, you *will* behave with decorum and prove to me that you are mature enough to be in society. If you cannot, there will be consequences—possibly even a return to the nursery. Am I understood?"

Elizabeth leant against the wall, her legs feeling too weak to bear her. Was she dreaming? It could not be, because even in her most elaborate imaginings, she had never dared to believe her father would take such a firm stance with Lydia and Kitty. Undoubtedly, they needed it, and the sooner the better, in her opinion, lest they shame the entire family. She and Jane had attempted to correct them, but the girls had never been willing to listen to them. Why would they, when their parents permitted them to run wild?

For several minutes, Mr Bennet explained how he expected them to behave in company, ending by saying, "I shall observe you henceforth and, no doubt, shall have more to say on this subject."

Elizabeth heard the sounds of crying and assumed it was Kitty, who was by far the most sensitive of all the Bennet sisters.

Speaking more gently than he had before, her father said, "There is no need for that, dear girl. My wish is that you and your sisters are all admired as respectable women."

"This is because Mr Darcy—" Lydia cried.

"The reason is not important," he interjected. "I am your father, and I am telling you what I expect. You will obey me. To your chambers and to bed with you. No chatting or looking through your ribbons or whatever you intended to do. Think carefully about what I said. Good night."

Kitty almost ran from the room, not stopping to acknowledge Elizabeth—if she even saw her. Lydia huffed loudly and stamped past, her lips curled in anger.

Not knowing what she would say to her father, Elizabeth slowly turned and went to her bedchamber to compose herself before returning to the parlour.

# CHAPTER EIGHT

The dinner party at Longbourn had been much like any other Darcy had attended. *What am I thinking? It was much worse than many of them.*

Watching the Bennets interact with each other had been distasteful—absurd, really. As he sat in the carriage with the Bingleys and Hursts to return to Netherfield afterwards, scenes from the evening came back to him despite his desire to erase them from his memory. The chief example was possibly Mrs Bennet fawning over Bingley, with the willing and enthusiastic assistance of her sister, Mrs Philips. Darcy expected the women to beg, even bribe, Bingley to propose to Miss Bennet within the month. Then there were the younger Miss Bennets. He had paid them no attention at the assembly, but observing them was unavoidable at the party, given how few people were present. Miss Mary looked like she wished she was anywhere else, and the behaviour of the other two was nothing short of perplexing; having to bear witness to it made his head ache. One minute they had been laughing and chatting animatedly with the few unattached men present, and the next, they had been whispering urgently to each other, Miss Catherine apparently battling tears and Miss Lydia a desire to scream. Darcy believed the cause was Mr Bennet, who had spent the time they were in the drawing room flitting between his daughters and wife in what appeared to be an attempt to make them behave with decorum. At the table, he had occasionally said one of their names, sending them severe looks and once or twice pointing a reproving gaze at Miss Lydia.

Darcy wished him luck; it would take a great deal of effort to make the Bennets a family worth knowing.

*Apart from the eldest two Miss Bennets. You can say nothing against them.*

He looked about the dark carriage, wondering where the thought had come from. But no one had spoken, and with reluctance, he had to admit it was true. Miss Bennet seemed like the usual sort of pretty but bland lady one commonly met, and as for Miss Elizabeth… Darcy still did not know what to think of her. He had felt a desire—very slight, he assured himself—to speak to her, but when he had twice attempted to act on it by joining in her conversation with others, it had been impossible. She had avoided him all evening, walking away if he was near and not even doing him the courtesy of looking at him when she greeted him. Mr Bennet had glared at him repeatedly, and in the end, Darcy had only spoken briefly to a few gentlemen and otherwise to the Bingleys and Hursts.

# THE ART OF APOLOGY

When they reached Netherfield, Bingley said, "Darcy, would you give me a few minutes before you retire?"

Darcy nodded and followed his friend to the library. Surveying its sparsely filled shelves, he said, "If you decide to remain here longer than a few months or even a year, you really should begin to build a collection."

Bingley sighed heavily. He stood by a table holding several decanters and glasses and, without asking whether Darcy would like a drink, poured wine for both of them. As he gave Darcy his, he said, "Should I bother enquiring whether you found the dinner party agreeable?"

The only reason Darcy did not scoff was because he was taking a sip of wine. "The meal itself was very good. I applaud Mrs Bennet for employing a much better cook than I had expected. I have little to say of the company."

"And I am sure everyone present was well aware of that."

Shocked at the harshness of the words from his usually mild-mannered friend, Darcy flinched. "I-I do not—"

"You know exactly what I mean," Bingley interjected. He regarded Darcy for a moment, then sighed yet again and fell into an armchair; Darcy took a place across from him.

"You know how important being here is to me," Bingley said. "My father charged me with securing an estate, improving my family's social position, and he very much wanted me to establish a connexion to Hertfordshire."

"Because your mother was born and raised near St Albans."

"Exactly. I want to be accepted here." He spoke each word distinctly, and Darcy regarded him, seeing signs of anger and frustration that surprised him.

"I am sure you will be. You cannot be worried—"

"I *am* worried how people will view me."

Darcy furrowed his brow. "Why?"

"Because of *you!*" While Darcy stared at him in astonishment, Bingley took several breaths and shook his head before continuing. "I suppose I ought to be relieved you did not insult anyone this evening—not in words at least—but, Darcy, do you not understand what people think of you? How little they—"

"What do I care about such people?" He quickly swallowed the last of his wine; it tasted sour. He stood, and Bingley did likewise.

"My point exactly! When did you become so intolerant? They are not the most fashionable people, perhaps, but they are good and honest folk and have welcomed us into their society. Already you have given the Bennets—my nearest neighbours—reasons to dislike you, and you have been little better with anyone else. Do you not understand that they will wonder at *me* because of *your* behaviour? I introduced you as one of my dearest friends! Even Hurst was more polite than you were tonight!"

"I shall depart in the morning." Darcy walked towards the door, but his steps faltered at Bingley's next question.

"What has happened? You have never been particu-

## THE ART OF APOLOGY

larly comfortable in company, but since the summer, your mood has blackened."

"It is nothing," Darcy managed to say despite how tight his jaw had become. If he were to confide the truth about Ramsgate to anyone, it would be Bingley, but he could not. He and his family had vowed not to divulge it. Even more to the point, to speak the words, to see Bingley's horror and sympathy and listen to his condolences, would be impossible.

"You are not obligated to tell me, and I do not know that it matters to the situation. Leave if you wish, but if you do, Darcy, I do not believe our friendship will survive."

It felt like an anvil had settled in his stomach; he turned to face Bingley, who ran his hands over his face before speaking further.

"I heard many people talk of you—tonight, on Sunday, at the assembly. They did not say anything to me directly, but I heard their whispers and saw their discomfort when I drew near. From what I understand, it was you insulting Miss Elizabeth that truly turned everyone against you, although your manner before that infamous moment had already made them question what sort of man you were. You have done nothing to improve their initial impression."

"What do you expect me to do about it? What is it that you want me to do or say?" *Have you already decided you agree with them, that I am no longer worthy of being your friend?* There were not many gentlemen Darcy considered genuine friends. He had many acquaintances, but with the exception of his cousins Bramwell and

Fitzwilliam, he was not close to any of them—apart from Bingley.

"I want you to show them the Fitzwilliam Darcy I know—or perhaps I ought to say *knew*. The gentleman who is a loving brother, trustworthy nephew and cousin, kind and generous to his servants, and who can be the most excellent friend, albeit one few would call lively. I want them to see that I am a good judge of character and that they can like and trust me because my friend and my family are pleasant, decent people. I want to stop having to be the only one who is making an effort to be accepted."

Few people ever dared speak to Darcy in such a manner. His father had, of course; what parent did not have occasion to reprimand their children? Currently, only his uncle the earl believed he had the right to, along with his aunt Lady Catherine, who corrected everyone she met if they did not do as she demanded. That *Bingley* of all people was so upset by his behaviour shamed Darcy. He wanted to argue that he *had* been a good friend; it had been *he* who had assisted in finding Netherfield and securing a favourable lease, he who had agreed to spend a month—at least—here to offer whatever guidance Bingley needed.

But did any of that excuse disappointing his friend as he evidently had? Twice in a week, two different gentlemen had told him his behaviour was not what it should be. Darcy did not particularly care about Mr Bennet's opinion, but Bingley was another matter entirely. And what would his beloved mother or father think, were either still living? If he was honest with himself, he would have to acknowledge that he had allowed his sour mood—which had nothing to do with the people of Hertfordshire—to make him feel a deep disdain for them. To be sure, there were some people he genuinely would never like, but did they not deserve his civility, regardless?

*Miss Elizabeth does. I could have simply reminded Bingley how little I like to dance, or said I had a large, painful blister on my heel.* In reality, the metaphorical blister that affected him was on his heart. *Good Lord, how I wish I had made an excuse not to go to that damn assembly, or even told Bingley that I was not fit for company!* He had thought it before, but at present, and perhaps for the first time, he fully admitted the truth. He had let his unhappiness cause him to act rashly and to wound a young lady for no reason apart from the unlikely possibility that she would take his request for a set to indicate he was attracted to her. It was badly done, but he was not prepared to admit it aloud.

Bingley's voice pulled him from his reflections. "If you are gone in the morning, then you are gone, and I suppose we might speak eventually. We are sure to end up at the club or some party at the same time. If you are still here…"

Darcy waited patiently while Bingley looked towards the window, the view hidden by thick brocade curtains. "We go to Lane Park on Friday. Mrs Best was kind enough to invite us to her soirée, and I…hope you will treat those people as they deserve. I do not expect you to befriend them, but they are now my neighbours, the families I shall spend my time with while I am here, and I would like to be on good terms with them."

"I under—"

"I am going to my apartment. Good night."

Bingley left the room without even glancing in his direction again. Darcy returned to his seat and remained there for some time, considering everything that had happened and what he would do next.

## CHAPTER NINE

From Elizabeth's perspective, the dinner party at Longbourn had gone as well as possible. She had been pleased to see her friends, and while her mother had made too much of Mr Bingley, none of her flattering comments, not even her over-enthusiasm, had stopped him from admiring Jane. The couple had spent most of the evening together, and before retiring that night, Jane had shyly admitted to Elizabeth that she liked him more than any other gentleman she had ever met.

Before breakfast the following morning, Elizabeth sat and drank a cup of tea with her father. He asked whether she had enjoyed the event, to which she replied in the affirmative.

"I was glad to see you avoided Mr Darcy," he said.

Elizabeth laughed. "He made it easy by avoiding everyone apart from his friends. My mother will be satisfied with the evening. I expect she will want to talk about it extensively at breakfast with much to say about the many, many looks Mr Bingley gave Jane and how they made her blush. She will be very happy that her daughter is winning the contest to secure Mr Bingley's attention."

To her surprise, his expression was not amused as it usually would be; rather, he seemed displeased, perhaps even admonishing. "Your mother works hard to ensure our guests are comfortable, and she wishes only the best for you girls. Granted, she could show a little more discretion—she hardly knows Mr Bingley—but I appreciate the impulse behind her actions. You should not be so quick to laugh at her, Lizzy."

She attempted to hide the colour that must surely be covering her cheeks by bending over her cup and taking a long, slow sip.

"Do not mind me," he said after a brief pause. "I did not sleep well."

"I am sorry to hear that, Papa." Looking at him more closely than she previously had, she saw that his eyes were heavy and partly closed. "What are your impressions of the evening? I thought dinner was excellent, particularly the chicken."

Mr Bennet gave her a small smile. "Yes, the meal was excellent. I spoke to Mr Bingley and thought he was amiable, as you told me, but I am not yet convinced. Tell me, what would you do to…encourage Mary to embrace society more? I worry she is too sombre and will become more withdrawn if something is not done soon."

Despite her efforts to conceal her astonishment at the question, she could not entirely keep it from her voice as she said, "I do not know." Seeing him watching her, waiting impatiently for more, she finally added, "I would try to convince her not to compare herself to her sisters, especially not to Jane and Lydia. My mother considers Mary the least pretty of us, and she knows it. I cannot say with certainty, but I have wondered whether she uses her studies as a way to distinguish herself from us. She *is* the serious one, prepared to dedicate her days to sober reflection and music, whereas the rest of us prefer less demanding pastimes and livelier tunes. And-and..."

She exhaled noisily. "I believe she wants to ensure no one views her as they do Kitty and Lydia, silly girls who spend too little time thinking of matters beyond their appearance and how many men favour their company."

"And reading so seldom, it makes people wonder whether they know how," he interjected. "I doubt either of them has voluntarily opened a book this year."

She nodded and observed him closely, not quite optimistic that he intended to act on her information. "Jane and I both feel Mary has become worse since Lydia entered society."

Her father averted his eyes and began to nod. As though speaking to himself, he said, "Yes, there might be some truth in that. I must attack both fronts at once."

"Pardon me?"

"Nothing, nothing." He still did not look at her and shortly waved a hand towards the door. "Were you not going for a walk, my dear?"

Taking that to mean he wished to be alone, Elizabeth stood, placed her empty cup on the tray, and left the book-room.

THE NEXT OCCASION Elizabeth would have to see Mr Darcy was on Friday when she and her family were spending the evening at the home of Mr and Mrs Best. She was not certain he would be there, although she knew the Netherfield party had been asked. Mrs Best told them so when she called on Tuesday. She spent the entire twenty minutes she was at Longbourn telling them how much her son, Edward—who had not been at the assembly due to ill health—was looking forward to meeting Mr Bingley and Mr Darcy but most especially to seeing Elizabeth again. It was almost enough to make her wish for her own bout of ill health.

There was nothing wrong with Mr Edward Best, other than his conversation was lacking, he had little sense of humour, and he was not particularly handsome. However, that spring, he had decided he liked her above all other young ladies, and his mother seemed to believe Elizabeth ought to be flattered by his infatuation with her. She was not. Mr Bennet had already informed the Bests that they should have no expectations that a match between her and the young man would be met with approval, but it had not made any difference to his or his mother's deportment towards her. No doubt, her father had treated the matter partly as a joke, thus making it easy to overlook his warning.

As for Mr Darcy, Elizabeth admitted to being curious whether he would attend the party. Given how disdainful he was whenever she saw him, she rather expected to hear that he had returned to town or wherever his estate was. If he was at Lane Park, would he continue to act as poorly as he had every other time she had seen him? Was it possible he might decide to embrace his present situation and attempt to make friends? The thought made her snigger. It was exceedingly unlikely that Mr Darcy knew how to undertake such a task. *And it would be difficult for him, given he has offended everyone in the neighbourhood. I doubt he would be willing to make the effort! The thought of all the apologies involved would surely make him faint.*

She also wondered how her father would behave. It was surprising enough that he insisted he would go with them—he usually preferred to stay at home to 'revel in the quietness when Longbourn is free from all you women', as he often said—but then a brief conversation with Mary early that morning added to her shock. Mary came to her chamber while she was preparing for a walk.

"I cannot believe I am saying this, but my father has encouraged me to dress my hair differently tonight," Mary said, her eyes wide and slowly shaking her head. Gesturing to the sides of her face, she continued. "He mentioned the way you always have curls. I told him I thought it would not suit me, but he thinks it will. Has he ever spoken to you of such a thing?"

"No," Elizabeth replied, drawing out the word as she recalled their discussion the previous day and the conversations she had overheard him having with her younger sisters. It was difficult to believe he truly intended to take a hand in, well, *improving* them was the only way she could explain it. Yet, it seemed that he did.

"Why would he begin now?" Mary sounded alarmed. "Does he expect me to adopt such a coiffure? You agree that it would look horrible on me, do you not?"

"For questions one and two, I cannot say." *Though I would like to know, especially regarding the first!* "As for it suiting you…" She ran her fingers through a strand of Mary's hair. "I fear it is too fine to hold a curl, but together with our maid, we might arrange it in a way that both he and you would approve of."

"But—"

"Think how it will please Papa," Elizabeth said gently. "You are very pretty, Mary, and I would very much like everyone to see it—you especially. Now, you sit here and let me play with your hair for a few minutes. Do you remember when you, Jane, and I used to do that, when we were all still in the nursery?"

Her walk forgotten, Elizabeth spent the next while with Mary, ultimately settling on more than just how she would arrange her hair for the party; they also adjusted her costume to add more colour. The changes were subtle but enough for their mother to remark that Mary looked very well when the family gathered for dinner. What Elizabeth would remember most was her father's satisfied expression.

Arriving at Lane Park, Elizabeth saw at once that Mr Bingley, his family, and even Mr Darcy were there. All three Bests greeted them, after which, the Bennets went in various directions. Mr Bingley was at Jane's side almost before she was rising from her curtsey, and Mr Edward Best insisted Elizabeth take his arm so that he might escort her farther into the room, where he promised to show her the refreshments laid out along one wall.

"My mother has arranged for us to be entertained by

# THE ART OF APOLOGY

musicians from Hertford. I do not know exactly how many there are—two or three. Oh, and a singer. You play and sing so well and will find it diverting, will you not? I told Mama you would. We shall have a hot supper later on too," he assured her. "Listening to music always makes me so hungry. Is that not odd? It is the same when I see any sort of performance. Mama has arranged a feast. Would you like anything now? A drink perhaps? Wine? Punch?"

"No, thank you," she said before he could go on. She managed to extricate her arm gently from his and looked about the room, hoping to spot one of her friends. It would provide her with an excuse to separate herself from him; she did not want to encourage his belief that she might develop a *tendre* for him. It was saying something that even her mother, who longed to see all her daughters married as soon as possible, did nothing to promote the match. "Oh, there is Charlotte. Please excuse me, Mr Best. I must ask her something."

Before he could respond, she left, trusting that the growing crowd of guests would prevent him from following her.

Soon, they sat down to watch the small musical ensemble. It had clearly been Mrs Best's intention that Elizabeth and her son might sit together, but Elizabeth carefully avoided both and slipped into a chair where she was partly hidden from view. There was a draught, and she was glad for her wrap, which she pulled tightly across her shoulders. Soon, she was engrossed in the performance and any discomfort was forgotten.

Until she noticed Mr Darcy watching her.

He was sitting across the room, his position perfect for seeing her with few obstructions. What did he want? No doubt he was finding fault with everything about her—her looks, where she was sitting, the expressions on her face as she listened to the various pieces. *He is the most vexing man I have ever had the misfortune to meet!* She did her best to pretend he was not there, even leaning this way or that so it was more difficult to see him, telling herself it was part of the promise she had made her father to avoid him.

Mr Darcy's examination did not end after the musicians had finished. There was an interval before supper, and as she spoke to different people—Mary, followed by some acquaintances—she spied him turned towards her. Twice it seemed that he intended to approach, but she moved elsewhere, knowing it would make it difficult for him to find her, given the size of the room and the number of people.

*Why will he not admit that I do not wish to talk to him?* It occurred to her that she was mistaken, that he had no desire to be in her company, and any time she had seen him looking at her it had only been to ensure he did not accidentally find himself close enough that he was obligated to exchange a few words with her. *Not that he feels it is necessary to abide by the social niceties!*

If she had been of a more liberal mindset, she would remark that he might be making an effort to be pleasant this evening. When he had dined at Longbourn, just two days ago, he had largely stood apart from the other guests when they were in the drawing room, and she doubted he had said much to his companions at the table. Tonight, he was speaking to her neighbours—not just his friends—and while he did not smile or laugh or even look particularly engaged by the exchanges, it was possible he was attempting to be polite. Regardless, one person with whom he would *not* converse was her!

Her good fortune ended about twenty minutes later. Mr Edward Best had found her and was sharing his impressions of the music while she listened with growing impatience when Mr Darcy joined them.

"Miss Elizabeth," he said, offering her a slight bow.

"Mr Darcy, how did you like the performance?" Mr Best asked, saving her from having to address the gentleman. "I was just telling Miss Elizabeth that I thought it one of the finest I have ever seen."

"Did you? How...interesting. And you, Miss Elizabeth, what is your opinion?"

She shrugged and opened her mouth to make an excuse to leave them, but before she could, Mr Best again spoke. His lack of manners made her wonder whether perhaps he had imbibed a little too much wine or whether his recent illness, and thus absence from company, had left him over-eager for people other than his parents to speak to.

"Miss Eliza is an excellent singer. Have you ever heard her? And she plays the pianoforte better than anyone I know. Any lady, I mean, not someone who earns money for it."

"I have not had that pleasure," Mr Darcy said.

"If you do, you are sure to agree with me!" He smiled broadly at her, and Elizabeth straightened her spine so she would not squirm—especially when she noticed Mr

Darcy's arched brow as his gaze flickered between her and Mr Best.

"I am glad Mama arranged this party," he continued. "It is so good to see all my friends again. It may have only been a fortnight since I last did, but it feels like half a year has passed."

"You were not at the assembly," Mr Darcy remarked.

"Unfortunately, I was ill. I am very sorry I missed the dancing, especially the opportunity to escort you." He nodded at Elizabeth. "I understand you lacked partners, but had *I* been there—"

"If you would excuse me, I see my father," she interjected. "I believe he is looking for me." Her cheeks burned as she walked away.

# CHAPTER TEN

Darcy went from watching Miss Elizabeth walk away to staring at the man next to him. He had been introduced to Mr Edward Best earlier that evening and had thought him the usual sort of young man who spent his life in a small rural community—simple but inoffensive. Not long after the Bennets had arrived, it had been evident that he was infatuated with Miss Elizabeth, which Darcy found oddly irritating. Or perhaps what he meant was baffling. To be sure, Edward Best was not a bad looking fellow, but he was a bit soft. As soon as Darcy had the thought, he stopped himself. It was not especially kind, and if Bingley knew of it, he would be disappointed. *What would he say? Likely that we do not know young Mr Best's circumstances. He might be recovering from a broken limb that has kept him from his usual exercise.*

Currently, Darcy decided he preferred his explanation for the man's full cheeks and the slight roundness of his belly, which were sure to get worse with age; he spent more time at the table than at sport. He must also be stupid to have said what he had regarding Miss Elizabeth's dance partners. Darcy recognised that it was hypocritical of *him* to question another person's ill-chosen words, but he had not known Miss Elizabeth when he insulted her; Mr Best liked her, might even think he was in love with her!

"It appears she does not wish to speak of that evening, so I expect you will not mention it again. I hope —for Miss Elizabeth's sake—everyone ceases to remind her of it," Darcy said, satisfied with the other man's chagrined expression. Because he believed it was the right thing to do, Darcy then engaged him in conversation for several minutes, asking him the sorts of questions one is supposed to ask of people they have just met. Thus, he discovered Mr Best was indeed not fond of sport or walking for pleasure, but he enjoyed cards and other parlour games. He also was not much of a reader, and once Darcy discovered that, he could think of nothing else to say to the man.

All evening, Darcy had noticed Bingley glancing his way as though seeking reassurance that his friend's behaviour was what he wanted it to be. It was another source of vexation for Darcy, and it was almost enough to make him vow to arrange his hasty departure from the neighbourhood. But he did not want to lose Bingley's friendship, and while he believed Bingley's concerns about his reputation being damaged amongst the local population were unfounded, he was not prepared to risk it. Not yet, at least.

And, funnily enough, he was beginning to *want* to

apologise to Miss Elizabeth. Was it seeing how annoyed she was at Mr Best's comment about the assembly? It would be too much to say she was distressed by it, and if she had laughed about it—as he was sure she had done that night—he would forget about it, but she had not. Instead, she looked like she wanted to upbraid him or maybe even deliver a swift kick to his shin. The flash of *something* in her eyes before she had walked away was almost captivating.

Not *almost,* Darcy was forced to admit, just as he was certain that Miss Elizabeth had the most beautiful eyes he had ever seen; they radiated her emotions.

Leaving Mr Best, Darcy joined Bingley, who was standing with Miss Bennet and several other people whose names he could not recall but felt he should. Bingley pulled him aside so they could speak privately.

"Why were you scowling at Mr Best?" Bingley asked. Bingley looked more concerned than reproving, which was just as well. As much as Darcy wanted to maintain their friendship, there was only so much scolding he would accept—and he had tolerated more than enough the other night.

"Was I? I did not mean to."

"I saw you and Miss Elizabeth speaking to him, and she did not look pleased when she walked away. I asked her whether she was well, and she said she was."

Darcy told him what had happened. "I hoped for an opportunity to show her I can be polite. She is with Miss Lucas now and appears to have suffered no harm from my company—or that of Mr Best."

"Darcy…" Bingley said, his tone conciliatory.

He waved away whatever his friend meant to say next. "Think nothing of it. Come, let us return to Miss Bennet and her friends."

For the rest of the party, Darcy remained with Bingley, and after an elaborate if not toothsome supper, they returned to Netherfield. He did not speak to Miss Elizabeth again, but he was keenly aware of where she was—and that she was avoiding him.

As she did whenever possible, Elizabeth went for a walk early on the morning after the Bests' soirée. In her opinion, the day was perfect for such an excursion, the autumn weather being neither too hot nor too cold, the sun appearing between the clouds often enough to provide a lovely warmth to her skin and added brightness to the countryside, and the breeze light. She reflected on the previous evening and determined she must ask her father to tell Mr Best—senior or junior, as he liked—that she was not interested in more than a friendship, really an acquaintanceship, with Mr Edward Best, and this time, he needed to be more direct about it.

*Perhaps then he will cease to hover whenever we are together!*

In thinking of the party, she could not help remembering Mr Darcy. "Yet another irritating gentleman," she muttered. "Really, no decent person should be expected to keep company with more than one at a time!"

She was satisfied that she had managed to avoid his company for the most part, but he had *looked* at her so often! It seemed that whenever she happened to catch a glimpse of him, his gaze was on her. She made a noise of frustration and shook her hands in an effort to dispel her simmering frustration; it was much more agreeable to appreciate the quietude of the country and remember what made her happy.

Some while after setting out from Longbourn, she heard the unmistakeable sounds of a horse approaching. Elizabeth wondered who was riding the creature and hoped she would not be obliged to do more than say good morning—if even that—before they parted and she took advantage of her remaining solitude; she would have to return home for breakfast soon.

She was already smiling politely in anticipation of the expected greeting, but when she saw who it was, she fought not to scowl instead. Mr Darcy. Why did it have to be him? Swallowing the unpleasant emotions that had reappeared as soon as she recognised him, Elizabeth nodded and turned to follow the path back to Longbourn.

"Miss Bennet, please, a moment of your time," he said.

Elizabeth's steps halted, but she did not face him. By way of dismissal, she said, "Good morning, sir," and resumed walking.

"Will you not speak to me for a few minutes?" His voice was too firm to make her believe he actually *wanted* to talk to her. "I had hoped we might yesterday, but obviously, we did not have the opportunity. I consider it fortunate that we met."

She stopped again and kept her back to him.

"Whereas I do not. My father has insisted that I not talk to you. You can hardly wonder why."

"I am only asking for a few minutes—"

She spun round to look at him. "Which I *cannot* give you. My father has forbidden it. Even my sisters have been told to spend as little time with you as possible. You know why and cannot blame him!"

Mr Darcy's cheeks were flushed, and his jaw appeared clenched. She was surprised he did not simply decide to forget about apologising to her again—assuming that was his purpose—and depart. Instead, he cleared his throat and spoke, his posture rigid and voice just as stiff.

"I am willing to admit I made a mistake. A few moments of your time are all I require."

If he had looked at all contrite—even if he had *sounded* contrite—she might have listened to him. Instead, she said, "I have told you, my father has forbidden—"

"He is not here."

"I commend you on your powers of observation. You must also have noticed that we are on a public path. Anyone might come by. Have you not learnt that people here talk to each other? I doubt there is a single man, woman, or child in the vicinity who has not heard of your insult to me and dismissive deportment to everyone at the assembly. If we are seen speaking, it *will* be gossiped about. My family—*my father*—will know. Are you asking me to disobey him? To risk his disappointment and anxiety?"

"Anxiety?" he interjected, his brow furrowed as though puzzled or taken aback by the implication.

"That you might injure my feelings and make me doubt myself, my worth as a person. I assure you, I would never allow you or anyone else to make me believe I am less important than they are, especially not for something so trivial as my looks or because I was unable to dance a set at a public assembly where there were not enough gentlemen present and some of those that were are too arrogant to even permit themselves to be introduced to the other participants. Frankly, Mr Darcy, regardless of what my father has told me, I have no wish to see you, let alone speak to you. You told me everything I need to know about you that night. Good morning, sir."

With that, she pointed her toes in the direction of Longbourn and stamped away. It took her almost the entire walk home to resume her previous good mood. How that man vexed her!

DARCY WATCHED ELIZABETH BENNET'S RETREAT —which was becoming a habit—and only returned to his horse once he could no longer see her. Never—*never*—had he met such an obstinate girl. And he had met scores of young ladies, many of them giving every sign that they were prepared to do whatever necessary to distinguish themselves from others, even if their behaviour would only earn them censure. He could well imagine what his aunts—either Lady Romsley or Lady Catherine—would have to say about Miss Elizabeth's conduct. Speaking to a gentleman of his quality in such a fashion? It was not to be borne.

"The entire Bennet family is unreasonable!" he grumbled, belatedly looking about him. The last thing he wanted was for such words to reach Bingley's ears; it would make his friend even more displeased with him.

But really, what was he thinking? Was he truly going to allow Bingley—friend or not—to force him to humble himself to such people as the Bennets or anyone else in this insignificant neighbourhood? No, he was not. Especially not *her*.

Avoiding the direction she had gone, Darcy encouraged his horse to take the path as quickly as it would go for as long as possible, using the rush of wind across his skin to cool his temper. Only then was he able to recall the interview with Miss Elizabeth with anything like rational thought. As unwilling as he was to admit it, he came to several important conclusions. First, he ought not to have attempted to convince the lady to hear him when she was reluctant to, especially once she informed him that her father had forbidden her to speak to him. Second, it was possible that Mr Edward Best had hurt her with his ill-advised comment suggesting people were gossiping about her, which had added to her reluctance to do anything that might result in yet more talk. On the whole, Darcy thought it unlikely; rather, he imagined she had found it irritating. There was something about her that suggested strength—possibly that she did not shy away from telling him how disagreeable she found him. Third, while he would seek to apologise and improve his standing with the Bennets and wider local society, it would not be for Bingley's sake alone. It was an important reason, but it was that combined with knowing it was the right thing to do that would make the effort worth the while. He *should* have behaved with greater decorum at the assembly and when he went to Longbourn for dinner, whatever his feelings and discomfort. He would have to try again to apologise to Miss Elizabeth and do so in a manner she found acceptable.

The thought occurred to Darcy that the even greater reason was to have an excuse to speak to her again. It was not that he liked her all of a sudden, but having her attention on him meant he would have the opportunity to closely observe her fine eyes and delicate features, to insist she give all of her conversation to him alone, and that, he decided, would not be so terribly unpleasant as he had imagined at the assembly.

## CHAPTER ELEVEN

Returning to Longbourn, Elizabeth found that—try as she might—she could not put the unexpected encounter with Mr Darcy from her thoughts. It was unbearable that her reflections were lasting so much longer than the meeting itself had! Why could she not set it—him—aside once and for all?

"I shall say this for him," she muttered to herself, "he is one of the more interesting characters I have met. Unfortunately, for both of us, it is not in a good way. What in his life led him to become so arrogant and aggravating that I want to shake him?" Maybe if his brain was rattled sufficiently, it would give him some sense.

Elizabeth had always had a dislike for perfunctory apologies as she believed Mr Darcy's had been. As she had told him in the churchyard, an apology ought to be heartfelt, or it was as worthless as asking someone how they were and walking away without waiting for their response.

## THE ART OF APOLOGY

"Do I *want* him to know me well enough to genuinely regret what he said at the assembly?" For Mr Darcy to give her an expression of regret that would truly satisfy her, they would have to become far more familiar with each other, which meant spending time together, and *that* she had no interest in—and she was certain he did not either.

And yet...she could not deny she thought of him often, and the snippets of conversation she had overheard him having with various people at Lane Park had suggested he could be interesting—when he extended himself.

With great effort, Elizabeth was able to put him from her thoughts. It was a very good thing he appeared to be trying to be civil, but they had better avoid each other for however long he remained at Netherfield. It meant he would never sincerely apologise, but she did not care.

Later that day, she was in the parlour with her parents and sisters. They were again discussing the recent news that a regiment of the militia would soon settle in the neighbourhood.

"I shall not have you girls chasing after the soldiers," Mr Bennet said after her mother's enthusiastic assertions that Elizabeth and her sisters would find having the regiment there extremely diverting.

"Oh, but Mr Bennet, there can be no harm in it," Mrs Bennet said.

"By 'it' I suppose you mean flirting and throwing themselves at men?" he interjected.

"They will like us above all the other girls in the

neighbourhood. What fun we shall have!" Lydia exclaimed before joining Kitty in giggling gleefully.

Mary, sitting beside Elizabeth, sighed and regarded the pair with her lips pursed in disapproval.

"And bring shame to us all? I think not," her father said. "Mr Darcy has opened my eyes. If he could look at Lizzy and say such disparaging things, I can—"

"You cannot still be going on about that disagreeable man!" her mother exclaimed. "And I would have you stop speaking as though Lizzy is better than her sisters."

"Lizzy's comportment is undeniably more admirable, and that is what concerns me at the moment." Mr Bennet briefly regarded Jane. "I cannot fault your manners either, my dear."

Jane offered him a smile; she otherwise looked upon her sisters and mother with sympathy.

"No soldier will enter this house," Mr Bennet stated firmly.

This, naturally, resulted in more complaints from her mother. He listened for a moment, shaking his head as she spoke, eventually saying, "It is enough that I allowed you to invite our esteemed"—this was said in a mocking tone—"new neighbours. I am resolved. We cannot avoid meeting the officers, I suppose, but we shall not befriend them—not until I am assured our daughters can behave appropriately in their company."

He pushed himself out of his chair and left the room, seemingly having had enough of Mrs Bennet, Kitty, and Lydia's whining. Elizabeth followed him to his book-room.

"Ah, Lizzy, did you have a particular reason to accompany me, or was it just an understandable desire to escape the company in the parlour?" her father said as he made himself comfortable in his customary place behind the desk.

Elizabeth sat across from him. "Both, I suppose. I *did* want to talk to you about something. I agree that Lydia and Kitty must be more closely watched, and for that, I was glad for what you said, but can you not trust Jane and me, Mary too? What have we done that you feel we would run after gentlemen just because they are handsome or are wearing uniforms?"

"Have you forgotten what happened at the assembly?" He arched a bushy eyebrow.

"I can hardly do that when everyone is intent on reminding me. Besides, *I* did nothing wrong that night."

He shrugged. "Mr Darcy has proved useful as a reminder that we cannot be too careful when admitting new people into our circle." His voice lowered, he continued; Elizabeth was not sure she was meant to hear his next words. "Frankly, I wish Mr Bingley had not taken the estate. An elderly couple with no young gentlemen as relations would have been preferable."

"Papa..."

Meeting her eyes, he said, "How am I supposed to know which gentlemen I can trust with you girls, especially when they are so wholly unknown to us? Mr Bingley appears amiable enough, but I might be mistaken. Perhaps it is all a disguise and he is as much a reprobate as any other young man about London."

Elizabeth laughed. "Be reasonable. Would you have my sisters and I remain unwed? Mr Bingley *is* amiable, even if his taste in friends is dreadful. I cannot say much good about his family either. If he chooses his wife carefully, she will help him learn more discernment."

"We need not depend on the Mr Bingleys of the world to provide husbands for your sisters or you. There are other men. Young Best, for example. He likes you, and I have known him all his life, and his father since we were boys."

Elizabeth gaped at him; a wave of nausea passed through her. "You are not serious! I appreciate that you are concerned about the sorts of gentlemen we might meet, and I agree it is wise to be cautious, but there is no need for extreme measures. You have laughed at his infatuation yourself and claimed you would never give your consent to a match between us—not that I would ask it of you. Just because Mr Darcy does not like my looks or, I dare say, anything else about me, there is no reason to change all your previous views on Mr Best. Do you recall why you object to him? He did not go to university, he is far from the most intelligent man, and he is immature."

Her father ran his hands roughly over his face, only speaking after a pause. "I have lately been rather painfully forced to acknowledge that I have not been the father you girls deserve. I have left too much to your mother, and as much as I respect her, I do not believe she is as…capable as she needs to be."

This was an astonishing statement, though upon reflection—and given her father's recent behaviour—she should not be surprised. "That is why you have begun attending social engagements with us and spending more time in the parlour?"

He nodded, but before he could speak, she continued, not wanting to miss her opportunity to give her opinion on Mr Best. She mentioned his name, saying, "I wish you would talk to him and his parents and discourage any hopes where I am concerned. I know you have hinted as much to his father before, but it is time to ensure they understand and accept my decision."

Mr Bennet made a noise of surprise. "Why now? What has brought this on?"

"I have grown fatigued of him following me around, acting as though we...*like* each other or, worse, might be on the point of an understanding." She felt the heat building in her cheeks and ears and hoped it was not visible.

"Very well. Despite what I said a moment ago, I would not want you to marry him." He sounded begrudging, but she was satisfied he would do as she had requested. "It is unlikely you would be happy with him. Well, Lizzy, that is two gentlemen you wish to avoid—or should wish to." He regarded her over the rim of his spectacles and said, "Mr Darcy."

She rolled her eyes; she had not needed him to specify whom he referred to. Telling him of Mr Best's allusion to the events at the assembly, she said, "It is reminders such as that which mean I shall never forget what sort of man Mr Darcy is. Why would I want anything to do with him? Why would any of us? Jane will be kind to him because he is Mr Bingley's friend, I suppose."

"You have not talked to him again? He has not approached you?"

Elizabeth shook her head and, briefly, averted her eyes. Why was she unable to say that she had seen the man just that morning? Was it because she knew it would upset her father? Or perhaps because he would repeat his demand that she never speak to him. *I wonder what Mr Darcy would have said had I been willing to listen.* She reminded herself to be careful; curiosity could be dangerous when not employed wisely.

"Good. While you are avoiding him, you can spend more time with your younger sisters. I shall talk to Jane about it too. I would appreciate you imparting some of your..." He gestured vaguely with his hands, unable or unwilling to say what would likely sound disparaging. "Did you know that neither Kitty nor Lydia speaks more than a few words of French? You are better at the language than Jane is, so you might work with them on it. I suspect if I tried, it would only end in tears—my own as much as theirs." He tapped his chin, and more to himself than for her ears, he added, "And I must make sure they are reading those books I gave them."

Unfortunately, she expected his resolution to do better by his children would not last longer than a week or two, but until then, she would attempt to do what he requested and hope she was mistaken. "Is there something in particular you would like me to do with Mary?"

"It might be too much to expect you to cure her of her fondness for ponderous tomes—that is a job for me—but you are the only other girl who plays the pianoforte. Teach her livelier pieces or ones she can play without sounding so...deliberate. You should not be able to hear the strain the musician is expending. It robs a performance of any enjoyment it might have held."

They sat in silence for a moment, him wearing an expression of deep contemplation. Soon, she slipped out of the room, leaving him to his thoughts.

## CHAPTER TWELVE

Two days after seeing Miss Elizabeth, Darcy attended a town meeting of local gentlemen with Bingley. He could not help but notice the many hearty greetings Bingley received, whereas people were noticeably more formal, and even cool, towards him.

The men were discussing necessary improvements, beginning with the roads, which always seemed to be an issue no matter where one went, and Mr Bennet raised concerns regarding ongoing flooding in the village nearest to his estate. Darcy had said little throughout the morning, preferring to simply listen and later talk over the event with Bingley, all in a quest to help his friend become familiar with life in the country and the responsibilities of a landowner. Presently, he stood slightly apart from the others but close enough to listen as Bingley spoke to several gentlemen.

"I asked Darcy whether he would like to come, and I was glad when he agreed," Bingley said, Darcy presumed in response to some comment or other one of his companions had made.

*And it is yet another occasion to improve how these people view me,* he thought more sourly than he liked. He really ought to give serious consideration to leaving Hertfordshire. Surely, if he made an appropriate excuse, Bingley would not object. Given how often the thought had occurred to him and that he had done nothing about it, he wondered why he was so reluctant to go; was it simply his promise to Bingley to remain a month? It was not as though his friend truly required his advice; he was more than capable of sorting out what he needed to know, and there were many men in this room alone who would be pleased to assist him, should the need arise.

Bingley continued speaking within his group. "Darcy has been managing his estate for five years now, while I am new to the endeavour. His knowledge, which he freely shares with me, has been very helpful, and I am grateful for it."

*Laying it on a bit thick,* Darcy thought, doubting that people would like him just because Bingley praised him.

"Five years?" Mr Goulding said. He turned his pale blue eyes to Darcy speculatively, remarking, "You were young when you inherited, sir."

It seemed a prying question, but Darcy swallowed his annoyance and offered a tight nod; he did not appreciate the reminder of *why* he had been barely three-and-twenty at the time. "Regrettably, yes."

Another man whose name he could not remember asked, "You are from the midland counties, are you not?"

Darcy inclined his head.

"I heard Derbyshire," yet another man said, and over the next while, several people made comments about Pemberley all without Darcy having to open his mouth. How people had learnt so much about him and his estate, he did not know, especially not in a small, out-of-the-way neighbourhood such as this. He felt the coldness of vexation creeping over him and, glimpsing Bingley out of the corner of his eye, saw that he was regarding him with disappointment. It was only then that he understood that his discomfort was causing him to stiffen his spine and scowl. He forcibly relaxed the muscles in his face and shoulders. Despite how it might appear to Bingley, Miss Elizabeth, or anyone else, he did not *want* to be disliked. The notion was somewhat of a surprise to him, perhaps born of feeling excluded from the present gathering. At the very least, he would prefer to be respected. His position in life should be enough reason for people to view him favourably—and it might have been, had he not spoken so thoughtlessly at the assembly. Everything led back to that one brief yet fateful moment.

Accordingly, Darcy did his best to sit and chat with the other men. He found they were interested in hearing of his experiences at Pemberley and how he and his neighbours had confronted various issues, including those they were presently struggling with in Meryton. He presumed they were seeking novel approaches to try, which was admirable. When he went to the table to refresh his cup of coffee, he was surprised that Mr Bennet joined him.

The older gentleman cleared his throat and gave every appearance of being reluctant to ask anything of him. "I would appreciate learning more about the drainage works you mentioned."

Darcy nodded once. "I shall ask my steward to send you the information. He keeps excellent records, including about what did and did not work as well as what we intend to try in the future."

"Thank you."

They remained where they were, Darcy because Mr Bennet did not move away, leaving Darcy with the impression there was more he wished to say. Had his daughter told him of their unexpected meeting? If Mr Bennet chose to again reprimand him, Darcy would walk out of the room and immediately set out for London; nothing would stop him.

At length, Mr Bennet said, "I was at school and later Oxford with a chap named Frederick Darcy. He and I were good friends, but we later lost touch. Life takes over, leaves us with little time for correspondence, let alone visiting friends. It did not occur to me until lately that you share a name. His grandfather had an estate in, goodness, was it Staffordshire? Or perhaps Shropshire. He would not happen to be a relation of yours?"

Darcy felt stupid for how shocked he was—and that it made him inadvertently gape and stammer as he replied. "I believe you must mean my cousin—my father's cousin. His maternal grandfather lived in Shropshire, near Shrewsbury. He inherited the estate about fifteen years ago. The Darcys usually attend Cambridge, but I recall that my cousin went to Oxford to please his mother and grandfather."

Mr Bennet explained that he and Frederick Darcy had first met when they were about ten or eleven years old. He asked after his old friend in what went beyond a polite enquiry, if Darcy had the right of it. It encouraged him to answer more freely than he otherwise might have; if he hoped it would improve the older gentleman's opinion of him, he did not acknowledge it.

"My cousin is very well. My sister and I often refer to him as our uncle, given he is of a similar age to our late father. I only mention it so that, if I do, you understand why." He paused and silently told himself not to ramble like an idiot; it was unlike him. "He and his family visited my sister and me at Pemberley in June. We meet in London frequently too. He has a house there, as do I. He has two children, a son who is at Cambridge and a daughter who is about Miss Elizabeth's age." Darcy stopped suddenly and watched to see how Mr Bennet would take his casual mention of his second daughter.

Mr Bennet cleared his throat. "Well. It is an interesting coincidence. I suppose there is some resemblance between you and him. In person, I mean. I thought very highly of your cousin. Everyone who knew him did. He is a gentleman in every sense of the word."

"He is an excellent man," Darcy said, his tone quiet and chastened. He believed Mr Bennet was comparing Frederick Darcy to him, and it was evident he considered only one of them worthy of praise.

"If you are so inclined, please do send him my regards. As I said, I regret that our connexion was lost. I would be pleased to rectify it, if he agrees." He gave Darcy a stiff nod and walked away as Darcy was saying that he would.

"You are distracted. Is there a particular reason?" Bingley asked.

Admittedly, Darcy was lost in thought as he and Bingley rode back to Netherfield a little later. He shook himself and said, "I apologise. Did you say something?"

"I thanked you for going with me. I was worried I would be asked something I had no notion how to answer." Bingley grimaced, then laughed. "And I was. Am I really expected to know what arrangements have been made for the spring? It is months away. I have hardly thought of Christmas, let alone next year!"

Darcy appreciated his friend's ability to find the humour in almost every situation and gave him a brief smile. "My steward and I are always thinking of these things—what we have done in the past and how successful it was, what repairs and other work should be attended to after the harvest and then after the winter snows have gone, what new agricultural techniques are being developed, and so on. It is never ending, I am sorry to tell you."

Bingley's eyes were wide, and he slowly shook his head. "I am beginning to understand why you are always reading all those treatises. That last one you gave me was—"

"Dry and dull," Darcy suggested, to which Bingley nodded enthusiastically. "My situation is different from yours. I know I shall be master of Pemberley next year and the year after that until the day I die. You might not be at Netherfield beyond this winter."

"That is true." Bingley glanced at him before turning his eyes back to the path. "I saw Mr Bennet speaking to you. Did he say something…upsetting?"

Darcy assumed he wanted to know whether there had been another disagreement between them. Later, he would have to give consideration to how to draw the line between wanting to make up for the poor impression he had given the neighbourhood when he first arrived and tolerating this ongoing suspicion and feeling like he was constantly being observed and judged. "He told me he went to school and attended university with one of my cousins." He considered his conversation with Mr Bennet and the other gentlemen—and his recent meeting with Miss Elizabeth—and asked, "Am I truly so…unpleasant, Bingley?"

His friend took a long moment to respond, then shrugged. "No, but also yes, upon occasion. Especially lately, as I told you the other day. I am sorry, Darcy, but you seem to want to hate everyone and everything at present."

This time, it was Darcy who needed a period to contemplate before speaking. "You owe me no apology. Rather the opposite. I did not realise it—*I*—had become so disagreeable. There is a reason, a…situation this summer affecting a member of my family. I would tell you, but my uncle has decreed we are to be silent about it. I understand why, and indeed, I hope to keep knowledge of it to as few people as possible." He was struck by how that might sound, and added, "It is not that I do not trust you—"

"No, no," Bingley interjected, waving a hand dismissively. "Other people's secrets are not ours to share. If one of my sisters were involved in some sort of scrape, I might not be inclined or feel able to tell you. Not that I am suggesting Miss Darcy—"

Darcy had felt the blood drain out of his cheeks as soon as Bingley mentioned sisters, and at that inopportune moment, Bingley looked his way. His demeanour must have shown the dread he felt recalling the events at Ramsgate.

"Oh," Bingley all but whispered. "I-I pray everyone is well."

Darcy hastened to nod and swallowed, hoping to clear the lump in his throat. "We are all healthy, and there is no reason we shall not forget about it in time."

"I am very glad to hear that. If there is anything I can do, any way I might be of assistance…"

Darcy nodded again. "You are a good friend, Bingley." *Perhaps better than I deserve.*

## CHAPTER THIRTEEN

At the end of the month, the Bennets went to an evening party at Lucas Lodge. True to his recent behaviour, Mr Bennet went with them; he did not even grumble that it meant leaving his comfortable armchair in the parlour, so snugly placed near the fire, which was sure proof of his desire to ensure his daughters were properly chaperoned and protected from gentlemen who would not hesitate to treat them poorly.

Mr Darcy was one of the guests, as were the other residents of Netherfield Park, but Elizabeth easily disregarded him. She noticed him looking in her direction several times—once it seemed his gaze went from her to her father and back again—but he did not try to approach her; thus she was not required to put any effort into rebuffing him. Fortunately, the Bests had taken whatever her father had said to them to heart, as Mr Edward Best and his mother avoided her company. Some members of the militia were there—the colonel of the regiment and about half a dozen of his officers.

At one point, Lydia loudly whined that she wanted to dance, Kitty joining her chorus, and they demanded that Mary, who stood next to the pianoforte chatting with Maria Lucas, play appropriate music. Elizabeth, too, was nearby, and to her delight, her father was with them in an instant.

"Lower your voices and cease your complaints," he ordered. "If Lady Lucas intended for her guests to dance—"

"But she will not care, Papa," Lydia interjected.

"And the officers said they would like it," Kitty added.

Mr Bennet fixed his hard gaze on first one and then the other of his young daughters. "There will be no dancing tonight, but even if there were, you are *not* to stand up with any officer unless I give my express permission. Both of you will remember that you are gently-bred young ladies and act accordingly, or we shall return to Longbourn where you will go to your rooms at once and remain there until I no longer feel the need to severely reprimand you. Am I understood?"

Lydia opened her mouth—no doubt to argue—but Kitty stopped her by shaking her arm and telling her to be quiet, "...lest Papa drag us to the carriage. It would be so humiliating!"

Elizabeth was surprised by Kitty's actions, and her father evidently was as well. He regarded her, his brow arched, and she shrugged in a silent agreement that it was unlike Kitty, who was prone to follow Lydia's lead in all things.

Not long after, Elizabeth sat at the instrument at

Lady Lucas's request and played several songs. Mary was also asked to perform, albeit with less enthusiasm. Elizabeth had done as her father had asked and had attempted to discuss music with her sister. They had had a mild row when Elizabeth had tried to explain to Mary that there were some pieces only the most talented and trained person should perform; that would never include either of them, given they had only sporadically had access to masters. Eventually, and after Mr Bennet had also spoken to her—apparently kindly and encouragingly, from what Elizabeth had been told by her sister—Mary had agreed to learn several simpler songs.

Elizabeth was beginning to wonder whether there was something amiss with her father—an illness that could account for the alteration she saw in him. Surely Mr Darcy's silly insult was not enough to bring about this much change! But she should be glad not suspicious; if he kept it up, it might make a material difference to the comfort of their family and the well-being of her sisters. He had ceased teasing her mother as often, which meant Mrs Bennet complained of his cruelty less, and Elizabeth found she rather liked the result. It had been years since her parents had seemed to do more than merely tolerate each other, and she had forgotten how pleasant it was to live in a relatively peaceful home.

Late in the evening, she was standing with Charlotte when the strident, nasal voice of Mrs Best caught their attention. Elizabeth had not realised she and her son stood not half a dozen feet away, although she was aware that Mr Darcy was even closer. She did not believe he knew she was there, however; his back was to her and had remained thus since she had spied Charlotte and come to speak to her.

"You must stop acting as though someone has died, Edward," Mrs Best insisted. "What does it matter if Mr Bennet has said you must forget that daughter of his? I dare say he has done us a favour. You will find a more appropriate, agreeable girl upon whom to bestow your affections. One who is more *tolerable.*" She sniggered, and Elizabeth felt her back stiffen. "Miss King, for instance. You ought to make the effort to know her better."

"She is not pretty," Mr Best said in a manner that reminded Elizabeth of her four-year-old cousin when he was told to do something he did not want to. "Miss Elizabeth is exceedingly pretty."

"Yes, well, Miss King has a rich uncle who is a bachelor and is old and ill. He will certainly leave her a nice bit of money. A decent dowry will make up for her lack of other attractions. And unlike Miss Elizabeth, she does not think herself better than everyone else. The whole family thinks they are superior, though I have never understood why."

Charlotte grasped Elizabeth's hand; she tilted her head, silently asking whether they should step aside to avoid hearing more. Elizabeth indicated a wish to remain where she was; if the woman was going to disparage her family, she wanted to know exactly what she said. Out of the corner of her eye, she saw Mr Darcy beginning to move away; evidently Mrs Best noticed as well, as demonstrated by her next words.

"Mr Darcy, how are you this evening? I was telling

my son and husband earlier how glad I am that you and Mr Bingley have come to the neighbourhood. Was I not saying just that, Edward?" In what was presumably supposed to be a whisper but was too loud, she added, "Tell Mr Darcy how happy you are to make his acquaintance."

"I am pleased to make your acquaintance," Mr Best said dutifully but not eagerly.

"This is a pleasant evening, I suppose," Mrs Best said. "Lady Lucas does like to entertain us. A few too many invitations, in my opinion, which I have always felt indicates a rather unbecoming arrogance. Why should we always be coming to Lucas Lodge?"

*You need not accept,* Elizabeth thought, exchanging an incredulous look with Charlotte.

"But I cannot fault them for trying. You know Sir William had a shop before he was given his honours for making some trifling speech. I am afraid the man makes far too much of it, but he is a good sort, I suppose, and this has been a...*pleasant* party. We cannot all provide quite the same level of amusement to our guests, can we?"

She giggled, clearly implying she was a better hostess than Lady Lucas, which—in Elizabeth's opinion—she was not. Her parties were not as diverting as she seemed to believe, and Elizabeth had long considered Mrs Best mean-spirited. She must now add vindictive. Lady Lucas and Elizabeth's own mother also loved to gossip, but neither of them was deliberately cruel.

"I find myself well amused," Mr Darcy said with a level of civility she had not expected. Charlotte arched her brow as though asking Elizabeth what she thought of his remark.

"I am sure I am happy to hear it, but I flatter myself that you enjoyed yourself a little bit more when you were at Lane Park. Unfortunately, my husband is not here this evening. I know he would like to speak to you more. He told me how much he valued the conversation you had the other evening, and at that meeting you gentlemen had to talk about roads and what have you. I know that you will now say you found his company agreeable, for he is a fine man, if I am permitted to say as much about my husband. I congratulate myself for choosing my spouse wisely. To be sure, few who were being honest would say that my husband is less agreeable company than Sir William. And Mr Bennet prefers his witticisms to actual conversation. Both men could use a little more...refinement, shall we say? Mr Bennet is a gentleman and can have no excuse, but I blame a lack of education for Sir William's deficiencies."

Elizabeth's ire was near to boiling point, and the bright pink spots on Charlotte's cheeks suggested she felt the same. Yet, neither of them was willing to make their presence known. To her other inducements to remain where she was, Elizabeth added yet another: she wanted to know what Mr Darcy would say to such uncharitable statements, if anything.

"The Lucases and Bennets are good friends, as you might have noticed," Mrs Best went on, apparently certain that he would approve of her sentiments. "Knowing both families as I do, I am hardly surprised. Edward and I were speaking of the Bennets when you joined us. How clever of you to recognise their falseness as soon as you met them! They are always putting on airs, especially Miss Eliz—"

"Actually," Mr Darcy interjected, causing Elizabeth to lean slightly towards him in order not to miss a single one of his words, "I believe the Bennets are a most respectable family. Have you happened to hear that Mr Bennet went to school and university with my father's cousin and dearest friend? I regret that my foul mood the night of the assembly has made anyone believe I do not think well of them."

The lightest touch of a feather would have knocked Elizabeth to the ground, such was her shock. She longed to applaud, for he had managed to silence Mrs Best. The sliver of profile she had of Edward Best showed that his complexion was ashen, indicating that even he understood Mr Darcy's set-down.

The gentleman gave the Bests a shallow bow that was nearly impolite in its execution and began to move away. His and Elizabeth's eyes met, and he looked startled—his steps faltered, and his lips parted as though he was going to say something. But then his gaze flickered to Charlotte, and he closed his mouth, inclined his head, murmured, "Ladies," and walked on.

Elizabeth watched as he went to join Jane and Mr and Miss Bingley. It was only when Charlotte spoke, causing Elizabeth to turn back towards her, that she realised the Bests were no longer nearby.

"That was quite a shocking scene, was it not?" Charlotte said. "I mean both what that odious woman said and what Mr Darcy did. Have you noticed how differently he is behaving tonight? He is conversing with people, even seeking them out, and what he said about your family was complimentary. What could have brought about such a change?"

"I have no idea," Elizabeth said as her gaze drifted back to the gentleman. "No idea at all."

## CHAPTER FOURTEEN

The incident involving Mrs Best and Mr Darcy was much talked of by the Bennets when they sat together in the parlour after returning from Lucas Lodge. Kitty and Lydia's agitation at what might easily turn into a scandal—by local standards—had the benefit of preventing them from complaining about everything they had not been able to do, chiefly dancing and monopolising the attention of the young soldiers in attendance. Elizabeth sat in a chair next to her father close to the fire. He said nothing while listening to the pair go on and on about the exchange between Mrs Best and Mr Darcy, despite not having witnessed it since they were at the other end of the room when it took place. What Mrs Best had said and then what Mr Darcy had, his tone of voice, his looks, the manner in which he had walked away from the lady and Mr Best all deserved comment. Somehow, Mr Best had become almost a villain to her sisters; Elizabeth had no notion how their minds had made such a leap. Mrs Bennet also had many complaints about Mrs Best—how dare she say such things about *her* girls and husband! And she had not stopped there, certainly not, she had also besmirched Mrs Bennet herself and their dear friends the Lucases; the affront, the ignorance, she had never liked her, and as for her son, there never was a stupider, more oafish boy known to man, she had said it was how he would turn out the day she first met him when he was an infant, and time had proved her correct...

"It was exceedingly kind of Mr Darcy to speak of us so generously," Jane said. "Mr Bingley was right to praise his friend, even if his goodness was not as evident as it might have been before now."

"Papa, is it true that you know one of his cousins?" Mary asked.

He nodded and said, "If I recall correctly, my old friend was his late father's cousin. It must be twenty or more years since we exchanged letters. I believe I last wrote to inform him of Jane's birth, and he told me that he had lately married."

There was more chatter amongst them, mostly about subjects other than Mrs Best and Mr Darcy. Soon Lydia and Kitty announced they were going to their chambers.

"Only five minutes of giggling together, if you please, then to your separate bedrooms and to sleep," Mr Bennet said. "Good night, my darling girls."

Kitty kissed him on the cheek, but Lydia was less willing to accept his current propensity to limit her activities and only granted her mother such a favour.

"I shall ensure they do as you requested," Jane said before she too left the room. Mary went with her.

"Well, Mr Bennet, I hope you intend to have a serious discussion with Mr Best tomorrow," her mother said when only the three of them remained. "I do not know how I shall ever be able to say a civil word to Mrs Best again!" She sniffed loudly.

"I shall indeed call on him," he assured her. "I could hardly do less, given how I acted when Mr Darcy insulted our Lizzy."

"But you were wrong about Mr Darcy. I always said we did not know the entire story, and Mrs Long told my sister that she heard Mr Darcy say he was in a foul mood at the assembly, which must be his excuse. I am sure something particular happened to cause it. I could tell just by looking at him that he is as fine a gentleman as I have ever met. So handsome and rich. And he is Mr Bingley's particular friend. Why, they are as good as brothers, I expect, which means when Mr Bingley and Jane—"

"*If* Mr Bingley and Jane are ever anything more than acquaintances, then we shall concern ourselves with his connexion to Mr Darcy. Remember what we spoke of, my dear," he said gently. "We must allow Jane to know this young man—and him to know her, though I am less worried about his impression of her. Only a fool would fail to recognise her exceptional quality."

"Oh yes, yes. Very well," her mother said, waving her hand in a gesture meant to suggest he did not need to go on. Elizabeth presumed they had discussed the matter, though she had not known it previously. "But I am telling you, he is half in love with her already, and I know my girl. The more he shows that he likes her, the more she will be unable to stop herself from liking him. They will be married before we know it. I am going to my apartment. I suppose you and Lizzy have been waiting for me to leave so that you can finally talk without the rest of us here to intrude."

To Elizabeth's surprise, her father only laughed. "Not at all. I do have something I wish to say to our daughter, but then I shall seek my chamber. Shall I say good night to you then, my dear?"

Her mother adjusted her shawl and shrugged. "I suppose. If you like. Sleep well, Lizzy."

Elizabeth stood to kiss her cheek, only returning to her chair once her mother had left the parlour.

"It was certainly an eventful evening," her father said. "How early do you suppose Lady Lucas will be here to talk it over with your mother? Shall we have to wait until after breakfast?"

Elizabeth laughed. "That will depend on how late she keeps Charlotte awake to discuss it tonight!"

He chuckled and patted her hand. "I own I was surprised to hear of Mr Darcy's actions. If anyone other than you had reported it to me, I doubt I would have believed it. What is your opinion? Have we been too severe on him?"

Elizabeth shook her head. "I do not trust him. The next time we meet, he might once again be his arrogant, disagreeable self. I shall continue to believe my first impression of him was right."

"You seem to delight in hating him," her father observed.

Once again, she laughed. "What if I do? Besides, I do

not agree. You know how I like to study characters. I am confident I have a good understanding of his."

"On so little acquaintance?"

"Papa, you are in a strange mood, and I am too tired to puzzle it out. I shall retire." She began to stand, but he stopped her with a light touch on her arm.

"I shall not keep you, but before you do, I wish to leave you with a piece of wisdom I have acquired over the years. Do not rush to decide people's goodness or lack of it, and avoid stubbornly clinging to opinions that might bear to be re-examined."

Her brow furrowed and she stared at him. "Are you suggesting I am mistaken about Mr Darcy?"

He pursed his lips, and there was a short silence before he said, "I do not know him well enough to say for certain. Upon further acquaintance, I might decide we should forgive him—or that he will never deserve it due to some fundamental character defect. My observation was more general than that. You never know when your first impressions might lead you astray—either approving of someone you should not or disapproving of someone you should. I recommend both you and Jane practise a little more care in that regard."

"She is too prone to like everyone, and I am too prone to hate them?"

In answer, he kissed her hand and wished her a restful sleep.

Darcy was pleased the party at Lucas Lodge had provided him with an opportunity to speak in

## THE ART OF APOLOGY

praise of the Bennets and to attempt to demonstrate his desire to be on better terms with Bingley's new neighbours. Having given more thought to his recent conversations with Bingley and everything that had happened since he had come to Netherfield, he had been forced to admit that his behaviour towards others was worsening, and if he was not careful, it would soon deserve even more severe censure than he had recently received from his friend and Mr Bennet. He had never been particularly comfortable amongst strangers, and this tendency had become worse after his father's death, when he had increasingly been the subject of gossip and speculation, chiefly regarding when and whom he should marry. With his breeding, connexions, and wealth, he was viewed as an extremely eligible match. On the one hand, it was an enviable position to be in; few ladies would refuse an offer from him, and when he found the woman he wanted to marry, he was confident he would succeed in securing her. On the other hand, it was natural that he wanted to be valued for the man he was, not for the size of his fortune or who his parents had been.

In that light, should he not ensure people saw in him a character who deserved praise for his affability and goodness? He *was* a good person; he was confident that his servants, tenants, and friends would agree—even Bingley, despite his recent unhappiness with him. But he was also judged on how he treated others, and by those not dependent on him or who liked him based on their history or because they were his relations. He recollected an important lesson his father had imparted to him: if you find you have made a mistake, the gentlemanly response is to set about correcting it as soon as possible. It might be too late for him to significantly improve Miss Elizabeth's view of him, to say nothing of Mr Bennet and his other recent acquaintances, but he should make the effort nevertheless, if only because it would please Bingley. And, admittedly, Darcy was bound to feel a sense of pride in himself for undertaking the task, which would be agreeable, given how low he had been since the summer.

The morning after the Lucases' party, Darcy had accompanied the Bingleys and Hursts to St Albans, which they had wanted to visit, given the tie to the late Mrs Bingley. They had remained several days, and Bingley had managed to discover a handful of residents who recalled his mother's family. At times, Darcy had felt like an intruder and wished he had remained at Netherfield Park or returned to London. Bingley and his sisters had spoken of their parents a great deal, and Darcy believed it had affected the ladies such that they had gained an appreciation for why Bingley was determined to fulfil his father's wish for them to have a connexion to the county. Privately, his friend had told him that he hoped it meant his sisters would make more of an effort to establish friendships in Meryton.

"You might say the neighbourhood is not fashionable enough, but I like it," Bingley had said to him. "I might like to settle there. For good, I mean."

"Choosing an estate based on fashion would be a dangerous proposition," Darcy had replied, wondering whether he had ever disparaged Meryton in such a manner. "If you would be happy living there, there is no reason you should not."

The morning after returning to Netherfield, Darcy decided to take a ride. It had been a few days since he had last seen Miss Elizabeth. She was much in his thoughts, which was natural since he would not accomplish his goal of reconciling himself with Bingley, the people he had lately met, and especially his conscience, until he had succeeded in apologising to her.

"Which will surely be such an easy matter," he muttered sarcastically.

Riding was a favourite pastime, and, possibly, he would meet the lady, as he had previously. If he did, he would attempt to speak to her again. As far as he knew, Mr Bennet had not rescinded his ban on her talking to him, but she might be willing to overlook it, especially after his behaviour at Lucas Lodge. He did not know how else to go about his task; it would be impossible if she kept avoiding him. If only he could convince her to listen to him for a minute or two, he might persuade her to agree that he was attempting to do as she and her father had requested and apologise.

Today, he had managed to coax his lazy oaf of a dog to accompany him. Glancing down at the creature, Darcy wondered whether perhaps he ought to hope he did *not* meet Miss Elizabeth. She might despise him for his unfashionable choice of canine companion. Was she that sort of lady? He did not believe so, but he hardly knew her—which was why she had said he could not truly regret his remarks at the assembly.

"Come on," he grumbled. "Can you not go any faster?" His horse—as fine a specimen as any in the country—whinnied, almost as if he had taken Darcy's words as an insult. He patted the long, brown neck, and said, "I was not speaking of you but rather of—"

Suddenly, off ran the dog, showing more energy than he ever had in his life, leaving Darcy to chase after him.

"Budge, where are you going?" he cried, alarmed when he ran through undergrowth that was impossible for Darcy to cross. "Bud, you maddening thing! If you get lost, I-I…" There was no way to end the threat; the truth was, he would continue to search until there was no reason to keep doing so. His sister would be heartbroken if anything happened to Budge, and there was nothing Darcy would not do to keep his sister from sorrow, especially after her ill-fated sojourn to Ramsgate the summer past.

A few minutes later, a single bark provided Darcy with the clue he needed to find his dog. "Stay exactly where you are, Budge, or you will be sent to your bed without dinner for a week!"

Rounding a tall stand of vegetation as he spoke, Darcy almost fell from his horse at the combined sensation of surprise and deep embarrassment.

# CHAPTER FIFTEEN

Miss Elizabeth Bennet was crouching, patting a clearly enthralled Budge. She looked up at Darcy, a wide smile on her face, and laughed. Her eyes danced, and it was impossible to deny that it made her especially lovely. For a second, he forgot to breathe.

"Did you call your dog Budge?"

He dismounted, using the moment he had his back to her in a largely vain attempt to regain his composure. "I did." He spoke the words slowly, then rolled his eyes and continued, "He began his life with a much more dignified name, but he was—still is—lazy and would fall to the ground acting exhausted wherever he was. My sister, who was only ten or eleven at the time, would always urge him to budge. She said she liked the way the word sounded, which was her excuse for saying it so maddeningly often. The silly thing—the dog, not Georgiana—would not move no matter how much we prodded him. Eventually, he would only respond to Budge or Bud."

Her lips twitched, telling him she was finding it difficult not to laugh; he could not blame her. "What sort of dog is he? I do not have a perfect understanding of breeds, but I do not believe I have ever seen a similar one."

Budge was neither large nor small, and he was almost entirely white, with fur that always appeared in need of grooming. But he had his own appeal, with big dark eyes and a mouth that made him look like he was smiling no matter the circumstances.

If Miss Elizabeth wanted to speak of his dog for the next hour, Darcy would oblige her. That she was willingly asking him questions, looking at him with friendliness, was a victory he had longed for—more than he had realised until this instant. "His parentage…is uncertain. One of the groundskeepers at my estate found him when he was a young pup. Georgiana loved him at once, and so we kept him."

"But he is *your* dog, not your sister's? I assume as much given he is here and she is not."

He sent a silent prayer to the universe that he had not become as red as a ripe strawberry. "He appears to prefer me." He quickly went on, not wanting to admit that Budge showed signs of illness whenever Darcy went away without him. "You have an affinity for animals, I see."

She turned her gaze to Budge, who was lying down, his eyes half closed, and continued to stroke him. "I have always quite liked them."

"Do you have any pets of your own?"

"Not any longer. We used to have a cat, properly my

mother's, but she was free with her affection and often demanded attention from my sisters and me. Not unlike how this fine fellow is." Budge gave a soft bark. "She died last winter. I suppose my mother will get another cat eventually, but it is too soon."

"I am sorry," he said with genuine feeling. "I know how much sorrow the loss of a beloved pet can cause."

She said nothing at first and kept her eyes on Budge. Darcy watched her, a sense of peace gathering around him, whether it was from the beautiful place or the beautiful lady with him, he could not say. *Or perhaps it is just because she is kind to my dog and has not yet fled my company.* She had even sounded amiable when she addressed *him*.

Standing, she said, "I ought to continue my walk." Budge rolled over until he was half on her feet, causing her to chuckle and Darcy to silently promise him a treat for finding a way to delay her departure.

"I would like to apologise to you."

Miss Elizabeth regarded him, her brow arching gently. "Am I to take your words as the apology?" Her tone was not angry or mocking, which was an improvement on their recent exchanges.

He shook his head. "I understand that for you to believe I am truly contrite and fully accept that I was mistaken at the assembly, I must do more than that. I must know you enough that I can truly feel and assert that I do not believe what I said of you that night. That is what you told me." She nodded slowly. "I do not know how to go about it, but I would like to earn your forgiveness."

"This is quite an alteration from our last conversation," she said. "How do you explain it?"

He was certain if he touched his cheeks, his fingers would burn. "Perhaps I am not used to people telling me their honest opinion of my comportment. Since more than one person has informed me that I have not acted as I should, I would be a fool to overlook it, and once I admitted they were correct, what sort of person would I be if I did not seek to remedy the consequences of my actions?"

"Are you referring to my father? I know about him calling on you. I did not ask or expect him to."

"It never occurred to me that he was there because you—Though, I suppose you had every reason to be upset and to want a public apology." He paused, holding up a palm facing her. "I am beginning to babble. It was not just your father, to answer your question."

"I doubt you are capable of babbling, Mr Darcy." She smiled, her eyes bright with amusement, and he felt something inside him shift, acknowledging that it was not the first time he had experienced the sensation of late. He did not know what it meant, and this was hardly the time to sort it out.

He said, "I feel like I am, because I do not know what to say to you. Indeed, I am simply glad and grateful that you are speaking to me at all. Bingley. It was Bingley who also told me he thought I could be…more amiable. I do not know whether you are aware that his mother was from Hertfordshire."

"Jane mentioned it lately. Near St Albans, if I recall

correctly. That is where you have been these last few days, is it not?"

He nodded. "I ought to have known he would have told your sister. They *do* enjoy each other's company." He chuckled lightly and awkwardly. "Bingley finds it easy to make friends. *I* do not."

Miss Elizabeth coughed, and he had the impression it was to hide a laugh.

"None of his mother's family lives there now, so Bingley did not care where in Hertfordshire he found an estate, but being here is important to him. It was something his father had planned to do. I refer to residing in the county, at least for a year or two, but he never did. His own people—and his business, while he still owned it—are in Yorkshire, and I suppose it was difficult to leave." Darcy shrugged; with both of his parents dead, he understood the desire to do whatever was necessary to remember and honour them. In his case, he still saw both his father's and mother's relations regularly; the Bingleys knew only those of their father. Darcy also had Pemberley and the many memories of happy times they had spent there.

"I value Bingley's friendship, and I understand I...did not present myself well at the assembly. I must apologise to you," he said again, "but first I must know you. Only then would I be able to tell everyone who is aware of my remarks that I was mistaken, that my words then do not reflect how I view you. When we were at Lane Park, I was shocked that Mr Edward Best—who was not in attendance that night—knew of it, to say nothing of his willingness to speak of it to you." He could not keep the anger from his voice. The impudence of the young man, the sheer thoughtlessness to refer to an event that might have, probably had, injured her was astonishing.

Miss Elizabeth gave a light laugh. "Since he fancies himself half in love with me, we must consider ourselves fortunate he did not challenge you to a duel. Though I have reason to hope he now believes he never had tender feelings for me and will leave me alone."

He gaped at her and was on the point of asking whether she was serious when she again chuckled. "I am joking. I…do. Maybe more than I should. I tease and take pleasure in ridiculing the silly things we all do or say upon occasion."

"I suppose you have laughed at me?"

She tilted her head to one side and gave him a pointed look that asked whether he genuinely wanted her to answer.

He did not and instead cleared his throat and said, "This is my dilemma. If I am to earn your forgiveness and that of the good people of the neighbourhood, I must first become more familiar with you. However, your father has forbidden you to be near me, and because of that, I cannot know you better." He lifted his hands in a gesture that asked what he was supposed to do under these circumstances.

"I understand your predicament. I told my father he was taking the entire affair too seriously, but I have not seen him like this since I was a young girl. He has said nothing to indicate he has become less adamant that I avoid you."

Darcy averted his gaze and did his best to suppress a

sigh. He had hoped Mr Bennet was beginning to think better of him, between the meeting they had both attended, his connexion to Frederick Darcy, and his behaviour at Lucas Lodge. His disappointment must have shown, and compassionate young lady that she was, she sought to alleviate it.

"I suppose we might happen to see each other upon occasion," she said. "We met by chance this morning, for instance. There might be opportunities when we are at the same evening party, times when my father is not present or is distracted enough not to notice. Oh, but others would, and word would get back to him. I shall think on it further. What I mean to say is, perhaps we can find a way to speak a little. Enough that you can apologise in a manner that satisfies him."

Satisfies *him*? Was she suggesting it was Mr Bennet who had decreed what would make a genuine apology? Darcy had believed it was Miss Elizabeth who would decide whether he had done enough. He set aside the question of whom he must please in order to take advantage of the time she was currently willing to give him. Thus, he said, "I have begun the task of using whatever means are at my disposal and have discovered several things about you since we met in October—or did not meet, if you prefer. Today I learnt you are kind to animals—which I greatly admire—you are fond of walking, you play and sing charmingly—"

She laughed. "There is no need to flatter me, sir."

"I do not understand."

"I am sure you have heard far more skilful performers. I never practise as much as I should."

"Whatever mistakes you might make while playing the pianoforte, I assure you, they are adequately compensated for by…the way you approach music. I do not know how to describe it, but I was serious." The words that came to mind—the joy and almost fearlessness with which she sang, the feeling she somehow imbued in the notes—seemed too intimate to express. Leaving aside the issue, he continued. "In my quest, I have eavesdropped on your conversations with others upon occasion. In this undignified manner"—she laughed, as he had expected she would—"I found out that you like to read. May I ask what sorts of books you prefer?"

"As a young lady, am I permitted to say anything other than novels and poetry? Would it damage your opinion of me if I admit I enjoy reading about scientific discoveries?"

"Not at all. I encourage my sister to read whatever interests her. She is particularly fond of history."

Miss Elizabeth asked about Georgiana—how old she was, where she resided, and the like—saying, "I have a strong interest in sisters. Whatever their flaws, I dearly love mine, and I believe everyone ought to have at least one, if they can manage it."

They spent several minutes speaking of Georgiana, then she surprised him by saying, "Thank you for what you said about my family the other night. At Lucas Lodge. You must wonder why the Bests were so quick to disparage us."

Of course he was curious, but it was none of his business. "I did happen to notice their behaviour towards you was remarkably different from what it was when we all met at Lane Park."

"The reason is simple enough, and I shall tell you since they involved you in it. I asked my father to tell the Bests that I shall never have…a particular interest in Edward." As though not wanting to discuss it further, she quickly added, "I had no notion my father and your cousin were friends. That is…shocking."

"It is proof that Darcys and Bennets can be friends," he said, earning him a smile. "I wrote to him and recently received a reply. I hope to discuss it with Mr Bennet." Before she remembered she was not supposed to be speaking to him, he enquired, "Apart from walking, reading, and music, how else do you like to pass your time? Do you draw?"

She gave a hearty laugh, causing Budge to briefly wake from his nap. He gave a soft bark and looked up at her. Once she had patted his head and told him all was well, the dog again buried his nose in his paws and began to snore. Earlier, Darcy would have been embarrassed; at present, because Miss Elizabeth gave no hint of thinking less of Budge—or him for having such an animal—he was not.

"I cannot so much as draw a circle without assistance," she explained.

It was Darcy's turn to laugh and smile. "I am no better, though my sister is. I would still like to know what diversions you enjoy. Say, if you are confined to the house because of bad weather, what do you do?"

"You are attempting to get to know me." It was a statement not a question, yet he confirmed it. "With four sisters—to say nothing of my parents—there is always someone to speak to or do something with, such as play a game. I have recently begun learning duets on the pianoforte with Mary, and my father has asked me to help Kitty—Catherine, that is, though I suppose that is obvious—and Lydia practise their currently rather lacking French skills." She blushed, but he was not sure why unless it was because she had said more than she had intended to. For his part, he did not mind at all.

"And now, I really ought to go." She patted Budge and murmured a few words to the dog before giving Darcy a long, contemplative look and saying, "Good day, Mr Darcy."

As he had done before, Darcy watched her walk away. It had been the most congenial conversation they had ever had, and he fervently hoped it would not be the last—and not only so that he might apologise properly.

*She is…uncommon, though why she strikes me as such, I cannot say.* Whatever it was, he knew he liked her. He liked her very much indeed.

## CHAPTER SIXTEEN

Elizabeth walked away from Mr Darcy, her head swimming with confusion and other feelings she could not identify. Hearing him speaking to his dog, his tone a mix of pleading, exasperation, and fondness, made her giggle.

"Come on, Bud. We must return to the house, and you are too heavy for me to carry all the way. You are not a puppy any longer, and I am not Georgiana. I promise, I shall let you sleep by the fire all afternoon."

How much had happened in the last quarter of an hour! She supposed it might have been twenty minutes or longer; she could not tell how much time had passed while she had been pleasantly—how could *that* be?—with him. It was more than just this one interval that added to how unsettled she felt; there was what her father had said to her after the Lucases' party. Was she really so stubborn that she refused to alter her first impressions of people? And she must add her past encounters with Mr Darcy, including the last time they had unexpectedly met while she was walking alone. Today, what had most struck Elizabeth was the added element of humbleness in his comportment. He had seemed embarrassed by Budge—which he had no cause to be; the dog was very sweet—and truly desirous of correcting the mistakes he had made. When he had first apologised to her, it had been done in such an offhanded manner, clearly something he felt compelled to do without meaning the words he spoke, which is why she had refused to accept. Could it be that he was sincere? Did he genuinely feel he had disappointed himself and his friend?

"What is certain is that he *is* trying to know me, just as I said he must," she murmured. It was important for her to hear the words to truly believe them, so unexpected was the sentiment. But perhaps it should not be, not after how he had spoken of her family to Mrs Best and her son.

Elizabeth decided the only possible course was to see how Mr Darcy acted towards her and others in the coming days. At the very least, she might accept that his behaviour in October had been unusual for him, that her animosity was the result of an unfortunate introduction to the gentleman because she had not seen him as he truly was. Why his mood had been so bad that it led him to be arrogant and insulting was puzzling—and he ought not to have been amongst others during such a period—but it would be wrong of her to be unwilling to forgive it if he proved that was not a reflection of the person he commonly was or wanted to be.

And perhaps the task might be more easily undertaken given Mr Darcy's...attractions. She could not deny that he was handsome, and his trim, athletic form only added to his appeal. As did him having a lazy dog with a silly name whom he evidently spoilt.

Elizabeth saw Mr Darcy again while she was taking a walk before breakfast two days later. She could not entirely call this encounter accidental because she had acknowledged to herself that she very well might see him—especially since she chose the same path upon which their previous meetings had happened. He was alone and explained that Budge had been immovable in his refusal to accompany Darcy on a long ramble through the countryside.

"He truly is the laziest dog I have ever known," he said. "He would have been better suited to be Georgiana's companion, but..."

"Would you think me fanciful if I say I believe dogs and cats have a sense of who needs them? Not all of them, to be sure, but since Budge has chosen you, it must be because he believes you need him."

Mr Darcy gave her an incredulous look and seemed unwilling to answer her question.

"He might feel you need to slow down, enjoy your life more," she continued. "Are you often rushing about, not taking the time to sit and relish whatever you are doing without jumping into something else?"

"Sleep the day away as he does?" His tone was humorous, and she laughed, after which he added, "I shall not comment on your...interesting view, but I have decided to add an entry to my list of things I know about Miss Elizabeth Bennet."

There was nothing in his voice to suggest he was ridiculing her, no hint that he considered her silly, and she was rather pleased. She suspected that he was reserved by nature, which she could not fault, but that he could be livelier under the right circumstances. *He needs practice and not to feel that people would judge him.*

"What is it, sir, or is it to be a secret?" she asked.

"You like to laugh." He regarded her, one eyebrow slightly higher than the other, as though daring her to deny it.

"I do! I find it lightens the spirit. I know I always feel better if I can laugh at some misfortune or, if not *at* it, then something close to it. For instance, I might not joke about a fall that resulted in badly scraping my hand, but I would laugh at how large the bandages make my hand look."

"While I hesitate to mention that evening, I thought you might have laughed at what I said. About you, I mean."

Elizabeth took a moment before responding. They were managing to speak without arguing, and she might even be willing to say that she liked his company, if the right person asked at the right time. It was no hardship to speak to him—he was interesting and knowledgeable, and his voice seemed to warm her, like a thick blanket on a cool evening. Since she had last seen him, she had spent a considerable amount of time reflecting on how quickly her view of him was improving. She did not want to do anything to disrupt their growing accord by saying the wrong thing.

"I believe I did," she said slowly. They had stopped walking and stood facing each other, a field in which cattle grazed on one side, a stream on the other. Between the noises from either side, she and Mr Darcy were being treated to a unique concert. Her eyes were on his, her head tilted slightly to the left. He encouraged her to speak freely, and she admitted, "I do not know whether I was bothered by what you said at first. With everything that has happened afterwards, I might be misremembering my sentiments. I do know that I ceased to find it amusing once I realised how many other people were talking about it, some who appeared too pleased that you had slighted me—which says nothing good about their characters. Upon occasion, I have wondered whether my father treating it as seriously as he did made the entire situation more...*more* than it would have been had he treated it as a joke, as I had anticipated he would."

Mr Darcy lowered his eyes and nodded his head several times, giving the appearance that he was carefully contemplating everything she had said. "It *was* a serious matter, and Mr Bennet was right to tell me so. It has taken me longer than it should have to admit that, as you know." He sighed. "If a gentleman had spoken of my sister in that manner, I would be every bit as angry as your father was."

She gave him a quick smile and gestured that they should resume walking. "I should thank you."

"For what?"

"You see, I have long been my father's favourite daughter. He was affected by knowing you had looked at me and found me lacking, and—"

"Miss Elizabeth—"

She unconsciously touched his arm to stop him from assuring her he regretted his behaviour at the assembly, as she assumed he meant to. "Do not forget what I said earlier. I have a tendency to tease. People, that is, not animals. You need not worry about Budge, should I be fortunate enough to meet him again." He chuckled, and she continued. "A consequence has been that my father is spending more time with my younger sisters. All of us, really, but I believe they need the most attention. I told you the other morning that I was learning duets with Mary and helping Kitty and Lydia with their French studies. It is all at the request of my father. He hopes they will improve." Suddenly, she was alarmed that she had told him, of all people, such a personal thing about her family. Feeling hot and cold at once, her voice was rough as she said, "I have said enough about it. Really, I ought not to have mentioned it at all. Pray forgive me. I- I should—"

He interrupted her before she could say that she would leave him. "Think nothing of it. Truly, Miss Elizabeth. If it helps, I shall vow to forget the last few minutes of our conversation."

"Thank you." She took a deep breath, slowly exhaling it until she felt the pounding of her heart ease. "Will you tell me something about yourself?" She hoped he would understand her need for a moment to fully regain her composure. If he did, she would add it to the list she was beginning to make of reasons to like him. He had given her the idea by talking of keeping a similar one regarding her.

"I despise dancing. That might be overstating it, but not by much. I find it marginally more agreeable when I know my partner well, and I do dance when I feel it is my duty—such as with Bingley's sisters at the assembly—but I do not enjoy it."

"That must be difficult, given how frequently dancing is involved in our entertainments. I imagine it is even more common in your circle." She wanted to know whether there was a reason for his dislike, but it would be rude to ask.

He made a noise of agreement. "I do not believe I ever looked forward to it. Even as I was learning to dance, I did not find it diverting, but as I entered society as a young man, and especially after my father's death, I grew to hate it. I always feel as though I am being closely observed and spoken—gossiped—about, not without reason. You might wonder why I am telling you this. I do *not* do it to excuse my behaviour at the assembly, but it might help explain a part of the reason why I was unconsciously uncivil. We had not been there a quarter of an hour before I heard people talking about my estate, annual income, and connexions. I do not know how word of them seems to spread so quickly."

"I can explain, at least for that occasion. Mrs Hurst. A lady asked about her brother's friend. I was nearby, and while I did not hear everything she said, I learnt quite a bit." Elizabeth laughed awkwardly, worrying she had again said too much and that, if he was offended, he might argue with Mrs Hurst or his friend. "Perhaps I ought not to have told you!"

"No, no," he interjected, sounding unconcerned. "I am glad to know. It does not surprise me all that much. If I had bothered to guess, I would have realised she or her sister was the most likely source."

They lapsed into silence for a while until he asked her what pieces she and Mary were practising on the pianoforte. Through their subsequent discussion, she discovered that he knew a great deal about music, although he played no instruments and claimed his singing was best described as 'awful'. They continued on this topic until it was time for her to return to Longbourn. She had almost suggested that if he apologised, she would accept, but she could not bring herself to speak the words. It took most of the morning for her to realise it was because he might no longer feel the need to spend time with her once the deed was done. Having someone new to speak to was always appreciated, but that it was *him* was wonderful. She assumed he would not remain in the neighbourhood much longer, but while he did, why might she not enjoy his company?

There was one reason: her father's demand that she should have nothing to do with the gentleman. But she would deal with that complication when it became necessary. At present, Elizabeth preferred to anticipate seeing Mr Darcy again.

# CHAPTER SEVENTEEN

The following Monday, Jane received an invitation to spend the day and take dinner with Mrs Hurst and Miss Bingley; the gentlemen would not be there, having received their own invitation from Colonel Forster. Elizabeth was happy for her, because Jane liked the ladies; she was also glad the invitation had not included *her*, because she did not, although she could not explain why. Then again, with her thoughts full of Mr Darcy, she had not tried to understand, particularly as she found her occupation increasingly less frustrating and more pleasurable.

"It is too bad you will not see Mr Bingley," Mrs Bennet said when Jane raised the possibility of accepting at breakfast. "I have had an excellent notion! It is sure to rain, and if you ride, Miss Bingley will have to ask you to stay the night, and then you will see him."

"No, my dear wife, Jane most certainly will *not* ride to Netherfield in some sort of plot to speak to Mr

Bingley for a few minutes," Mr Bennet said with exaggerated patience.

What followed was akin to scenes of an unfamiliar play. Her father calmly shook his head while her mother pleaded the case for her proposed scheme. A month ago, Elizabeth would have expected him to roll his eyes and let his wife arrange matters however she liked. She was developing a strong preference for this version of her father, and she prayed he would not go back to his old ways.

He turned to Jane and asked, "Do you wish to go?"

"Yes, but…but only if I may have the carriage." Jane glanced at Mrs Bennet, her cheeks pink, telling Elizabeth she was conscious of disappointing her. "I am sure I shall see Mr Bingley soon."

Mrs Bennet sighed heavily but made no argument. Jane went to Netherfield Park soon after breakfast and was safely returned to Longbourn before it began to rain heavily.

DARCY HAD FOUND THE EVENING WITH THE officers agreeable. He had refrained from spending every minute thinking of Miss Elizabeth, though he had collected a number of diverting anecdotes to share with her and imagined the sound of her laughter and how her eyes would dance with mirth when he did. The colonel was a decent chap, interesting enough to have a conversation with during dinner, and some of his officers were likewise amiable. Apart from knowing the evening would give him an easy subject to discuss with a certain lady whose company he wanted much more of, what Darcy most enjoyed was the return to ease between himself and Bingley. It was not in his friend's nature to cling to resentment and anger; thus it was not a surprise that he gave every appearance of having forgotten his recent disappointment with Darcy. That alone was one reason he valued Bingley's friendship; he was caring and loyal, and, having been betrayed again and again by his former close companion—George Wickham—Darcy greatly desired having people about him that he could trust.

At Netherfield, they found Mrs Hurst and Miss Bingley in the drawing room. Hurst immediately poured himself a large glass of wine and went to sit with his wife.

As Bingley prepared drinks for himself and Darcy, he asked his sisters how they had spent the afternoon. "Did you ask anyone to visit you?"

He had previously suggested that they do so to establish connexions in the neighbourhood. Bingley believed their recent excursion to St Albans had improved his sisters' opinion of his having leased Netherfield. Darcy suspected it would take more than that, given their long-standing fondness for everything they considered fashionable—especially people—and disdain for what was not.

Exchanging a look with her sister, Miss Bingley said, "Jane Bennet was here for a few hours. We gave her a fine dinner and sent her back to Longbourn."

"Miss Bennet was here?" Bingley said with a touch more enthusiasm than he had displayed since they entered the room. "Did any of her sisters accompany her?"

"Which one would we invite? Really, Charles, think about it. The youngest three should not be out in society, and Miss Eliza is intolerable," Miss Bingley said, glancing at Darcy.

"I like Miss Elizabeth," Bingley said, his tone sharp. "She is amusing, kind, and excellent company. What I do not like is you speaking meanly of our neighbours."

This led to a short argument between Bingley and his sisters during which Hurst rubbed his forehead and Darcy counted the number of yellow flowers in a large painting.

"Enough," Mrs Hurst stated. "Our opinions of Miss Eliza will never be the same. You are free to converse with her as much as you like, Charles, but Caroline and I are equally free to find her disagreeable."

"She has a conceited independence that is disgusting to me," Miss Bingley added.

"How can you say that?" Bingley interjected. "I have hardly ever seen you speak to her—"

"But I have heard her talking to others. It is enough for me," Miss Bingley asserted. "Miss Jane Bennet is sweet, I grant you, if a little…too accustomed to life in the country. But her family! Brother, you cannot have failed to notice that the Bennets are not the most respectable people."

"How so?" Darcy enquired, the sound of his voice surprising himself as much as anyone else.

Miss Bingley regarded him as though uncertain she had understood the question, leaving Mrs Hurst to respond. "I cannot criticise Miss Bennet, but the behaviour of her sisters and mother is deplorable, and Mrs Bennet's connexions are all in trade. Her brother-in-law is the town's attorney! Need I say more?"

Her sneering tone, her words, or a combination of both made something intangible shift inside Darcy. A month ago, he would have agreed with her at once, but at present, having been forced to confront his arrogance and having learnt more about Mr Bennet, spent time with Miss Elizabeth, and heard her speak of her mother and sisters, he was uncomfortable and even felt vaguely sick to hear Mrs Hurst disparage the Bennets. Briefly, he debated whether he should remain silent; but what did it say of him if he did not defend them, and was that better or worse than possibly quarrelling with Bingley's sisters?

The image of Miss Elizabeth on their recent walk—her eyes bright, cheeks rosy, and lips turned up in pleasure as they spoke of poetry—made the choice easy.

"I like the Bennets. I hope to know them better while I remain here, and especially that I can earn their forgiveness for my rude behaviour last month. Mr Bennet and my cousin Frederick were friends in their younger years, and my cousin writes highly of him. That is good enough for me."

"Well said, Darcy!" Bingley cried, while his sisters' countenances reflected their disapproval.

"Your cousin and Mr Bennet, you said?" Hurst asked.

Darcy nodded and explained the connexion further. Fortunately, neither lady added to the discussion, but he noticed them yet again exchanging looks. He held such wordless conversations with his two male cousins that were closest in age to him—Viscount Bramwell and Colonel Fitzwilliam, the children of his uncle the earl—and knew it was the result of knowing them so intimately that you always understood how they would view various situations.

"We ought to entertain," Bingley said, shifting the topic. "Other than having callers and you asking Miss Bennet here today, we have not hosted our neighbours yet. Caroline, you ought to be eager to do so. You spoke about it as a benefit of living with me in the country. What ideas do you have?"

Darcy bit his lips together to avoid laughing at the expression that flashed across Miss Bingley's countenance. Bingley could be credulous to the point of naivety; probably he truly believed his sister would leap at the chance to welcome their neighbours to Netherfield despite her dislike of them. Possibly, Bingley simply believed that if he refused to acknowledge his sister's mean-spirited sentiments, she would keep them to herself. Unfortunately, she did not.

"All the fuss and money for those people?"

"Caroline," Bingley admonished.

Mrs Hurst, who Darcy had noticed was usually protective of her younger sister, said to Bingley, "I suppose it is necessary since you are intent on making connexions here. Be sure you are not making the wrong sorts of connexions, however."

"What do you mean by that?" Bingley asked.

Darcy finished his drink and wished he had another;

he believed he could guess how Mrs Hurst would answer, and his friend would not appreciate it.

"Everyone can see that you favour Miss Bennet," she said.

"I do," Bingley agreed. "I like her a great deal."

Miss Bingley sighed loudly, and Mrs Hurst said, "She would not be a suitable wife—"

"Oh, good Lord, Louisa," Bingley interjected. "First, she is a gentleman's daughter, so yes, she would."

"The situation of her mother's people—" Miss Bingley began to say, but her brother was quick to interrupt her.

"Is not unlike our own. I shall not speak of it again. And before you say she has no dowry, I happen to have more than enough money. I do not care about adding to my fortune. I never have, as you know. Enough about Miss Bennet. I have not known her a month, and it is too soon to think of marriage. Finally, I shall remind you that whom I marry is a matter for *me* to decide, not either of you. Now, let us return to the topic of how we shall thank our neighbours for their warm welcome."

Darcy wanted to applaud. Too often, Bingley had let his sisters do and say whatever they liked, even if he privately admitted to Darcy how much he disagreed or disapproved.

Miss Bingley's lips pursed in evident disgust, and after a brief pause, she said, "Very well. A card party. That is easy enough."

Bingley's features twisted into doubt, and he shook his head. "No, it should be something grander than that. I was thinking of a ball."

"What?" Miss Bingley exclaimed, while Mrs Hurst said, "A ball?"

Bingley nodded eagerly. "I was speaking to some of the ladies when we were at Lucas Lodge, and they told me that Netherfield's owners used to host balls regularly. It is the only house hereabouts with a ballroom. It will be wonderful! We can even ask some of our friends from town. I can hardly wait!"

It took some insistence—and a long enough discussion that Darcy almost fell asleep—but finally it was agreed. The Bingleys would host a ball at Netherfield before the end of the month.

To Darcy's astonishment, his first thought was that he longed to talk to Miss Elizabeth about it. He wanted to see her delight, and—even more astonishing—he wanted to ask her for a set. *It is only right. It will be the dance we ought to have shared last month.* In his heart, he knew it was more than a duty; he, who hated to dance, desired, even longed, to stand up with Miss Elizabeth Bennet.

Before retiring a while later, Bingley announced that he planned to call at Longbourn the next day. He did not say it was to see Miss Bennet, but anyone who thought otherwise was a fool.

"I shall go with you, if you do not mind," Darcy said. "I wish to talk to Mr Bennet about my cousin's letter."

Bingley grinned and assured him that his company would be most welcome.

## CHAPTER EIGHTEEN

Bingley chatted incessantly as they rode to Longbourn the next morning, though Darcy only half listened. He felt unaccountably anxious about seeing the Bennets again, especially Mr Bennet and Miss Elizabeth. It was a ridiculous sentiment—was he not an adult, one with an enviable position? He liked to think of himself as a person who was used to confronting difficult situations with resolve and authority. But there it was; he was nervous. Perhaps it was knowing that Mr Bennet had been an intimate friend to his cousin Frederick, a man Darcy looked up to as an uncle, partly due to the difference in their ages but also because his father had often said that Frederick was like the brother he had never had. It might also be because Mr Bennet stood between Darcy and his wish to know Miss Elizabeth better. At first, that had been a necessity, but, more and more, he realised that he relished spending time with her regardless of his desire to earn her forgiveness. It had become vitally important that she thought well of him. His actions had placed him in a difficult, even shameful, position, and thanks to her, he had taken steps to become a better man. To be sure, Bingley and Mr Bennet had played a part, but Darcy preferred to think of only Miss Elizabeth having such a pivotal role in his life. He did not question why; that was a matter for another day, after they had known each other for longer than a few weeks.

That was, if he was given the opportunity to know her further.

Arriving at Longbourn, they were shown into the drawing room. He immediately looked for Miss Elizabeth; their eyes met briefly before she averted her gaze. Darcy was almost certain she had given him a quick smile and that she was pleased to see him—as well as hesitant to show that to her family. With luck, after he spoke to Mr Bennet today, the gentleman would loosen his restrictions on him and his daughter conversing.

The two youngest daughters and their father were absent, but Mrs Bennet's enthusiastic welcome more than made up for any they might have contributed. Her attention was chiefly for Bingley, but Darcy was not forgotten.

"So kind of you to call on us," she said. "Jane was honoured to receive your sisters' invitation, Mr Bingley. Naturally, she would have liked to have seen you as well. Is that not true, Jane? But here you are. Please, do sit. Mary, ring the bell for refreshments. Jane, I am sure Mr Bingley would like to know how you enjoyed your day at Netherfield. Oh, Mr Darcy, so good of you to accompany your friend, I am sure. We can have no objections, not after the other night. You know what I mean. Naturally, Mr Bennet spoke to Mr Best about it—you can be sure his set-down was every bit as sharp as the one he gave —" She stopped abruptly and tittered awkwardly before continuing. "Mr Bennet says I should forget about what that horrible, gossiping woman said."

"And so we should, Mama," Miss Elizabeth said, glancing at him. "Mr Darcy *was* kind to speak so favourably about us, but I suspect he is the sort of gentleman who would prefer not to receive too many thanks."

"Miss Elizabeth is correct," he said. "I did only what was right, and I hoped to ensure that she—and others—did not have the mistaken impression that I would listen to people disparaging your family or anyone else so wholly undeserving of such cruelty."

Miss Bennet and Bingley were sitting together, already lost to the rest of their party, and Mrs Bennet indicated a wing chair she evidently thought Darcy might prefer. It was close to her, suggesting she meant to entertain him and leave her eldest daughter to the gentleman who gave every sign of developing a *tendre* for her. Bingley would be an enviable match for Miss Bennet; thus Mrs Bennet's actions might be an attempt to secure a wealthy gentleman. In other words, she was being mercenary. But could he criticise her for it? Was her behaviour really so different from that of many others with young ladies to settle in marriage, including those in his social circle? Acknowledging he would not have considered the situation in this light a month ago—no doubt dismissing Mrs Bennet as scheming and vulgar—he silently thanked Miss

Elizabeth. She had inadvertently forced him to see the people about him in a kinder light. It was one of the many reasons he was finding to appreciate knowing her.

Miss Mary had returned to her seat and picked up her needlework. To Darcy's relief, Miss Elizabeth took the place next to her mother on an old-fashioned settee.

"Mama, I have heard that Mr Darcy's estate is in Derbyshire. Does not Aunt Gardiner have a connexion to that county?" she said. She was turned slightly towards her mother, but she frequently glanced at him. It allowed her to be involved in the conversation—perhaps even direct it—without speaking to him and disobeying her father.

"Is it?" Mrs Bennet said. "Now that I think of it, I *do* recall hearing that. And yes, you are correct, my sister-in-law does have a connexion to Derbyshire. How clever of you to recollect that detail, Lizzy." She patted Miss Elizabeth's hand and turned to him as she continued. "My Lizzy is a particularly clever girl. Everyone says so. That is why she is Mr Bennet's favourite. Not to say he does not equally love our other girls, or that they lack intelligence, it is just that—"

"I am sure Mr Darcy realises that," Miss Elizabeth said softly. "Do you recall where my aunt resided?"

The matron dabbed at her cheek with a lace handkerchief before responding. "It has been some time since I last heard her speak of it, but my brother did say they were thinking of travelling to Derbyshire next year or the year after. Or perhaps they would go to the Lakes. How lovely it must be to travel! My husband is not fond of it, you see, and I do not suppose I would find it easy to spend quite so long in the carriage, but I would like to go to the seaside."

Her voice had slowed and become quieter as she evidently slipped into a day-dream, which Darcy found amusing—especially when the twitching of Miss Elizabeth's lips indicated she agreed. She regarded her mother with fondness, and he wished that someone would look at him in a similar manner. In truth, he was almost certain he wished for *her* to look at him with affection—and more.

"Derbyshire," Miss Elizabeth whispered, leaning closer to her mother.

Mrs Bennet started. "Oh yes, of course. Let me think... Madeline—my younger brother's wife, you understand, Mr Darcy—did spend some years of her youth in Derbyshire. It was a town whose name begins with an L. Lipton? Langston?"

"It would not be Lambton, would it, madam?" Darcy asked.

She grinned at him, and it struck him that she was a handsome woman. As a girl, she must have been as beautiful as Miss Bennet, though he doubted she had ever been as reserved. Like her eldest daughter, she was fair haired with bright blue eyes; in Darcy's opinion, dark-haired Miss Elizabeth was just as lovely, and he had never seen eyes that could capture one like hers did. Indeed, if he was not careful, he would become lost in them immediately, and that would be both inappropriate and embarrassing.

"That is it exactly!" Mrs Bennet cried. "Do you know it?"

"I am indeed familiar with Lambton. It is but five miles from my estate."

For an interval, he told them about the neighbourhood around Pemberley and listened to Mrs Bennet talk about her brother, his family, and the business of some sort he owned in Cheapside; she was unable to give a clear description of it. Refreshments in the form of tea and lemon cake were served, and he complimented her on both.

"I would have expected nothing less after the excellent dinner I was so fortunate as to enjoy here last month. I do not believe I adequately thanked you for that evening."

Miss Elizabeth regarded him, her brow arched and eyes dancing. He interpreted her look as saying that she understood he was trying to win over her mother, who had justly despised him, but she thought he was being too obvious about it. Yet, he had judged that Mrs Bennet would not see it that way; she would accept his compliment as her due and be delighted by his flattery.

She thanked him, saying, "Without doubt, we have the best cook in the neighbourhood. Mr Bingley might have brought a French cook from town, I suppose. I do not know, but you would. Has he?" Darcy confirmed that he had, and she continued. "Lady Lucas envies me my cook, and Mrs Best—that horrible woman—has tried to convince her to leave Longbourn and work at Lane Park! Can you believe the audacity to try to steal my cook from me?"

Darcy soon found himself stuck in a conversation about servants and the competition between houses in the neighbourhood to secure the services of the best ones. Nothing Miss Elizabeth could do would distract Mrs Bennet into a new topic, and he did his best to attend to her politely. Fortunately, after about ten minutes, Mr Bennet entered the room and rescued him by inviting him to his book-room.

Taking the chair across from Mr Bennet, an old walnut table between them, Darcy sat as still as possible while the older gentleman examined him. Despite feeling that he should speak, he was not sure what to say. Instead, he surreptitiously studied the room while he waited for Mr Bennet to begin the conversation. There was plenty in it to interest him beyond the shelves full of books, such as souvenirs that looked like they had come from abroad. It was not nearly as large as the library at Pemberley, which was hardly a surprise, but by all appearances, Mr Bennet had an excellent collection. Given how much Darcy valued books, it made him like Mr Bennet even more. That, in turn, made him wish to improve the gentleman's view of him.

"I have been attempting to decide whether I am surprised, possibly even affronted, that you are here," Mr Bennet said.

"Sir?" he managed to say despite how his throat muscles tightened.

"Oh, I know you came to dinner not long after that… what shall we call it? Unfortunate incident at the assembly? I only agreed to you being part of the invitation under duress. In short, my wife and daughters—Lizzy chief amongst them—assured me we could not ask Mr Bingley and his family without including you. You know that I told my girls to have as little to do with you as possible, and Lizzy to avoid you entirely?"

Darcy nodded glumly; this was not going well at all.

"I wish to protect them from those who would injure them. I do not believe you would physically harm them, but words can be damaging."

"I deeply regret my behaviour that night," Darcy interjected.

Mr Bennet tilted his head to the side in a manner that reminded Darcy of Miss Elizabeth and peered at him for a long moment. "I think I might believe you. Thus, my surprise. When we spoke the morning after the assembly, I was convinced you would never be willing to accept you might have been wrong. Observing you of late, I begin to think perhaps you have. Certainly, how warmly you spoke of my family at Lucas Lodge gives that impression."

Good Lord, Darcy thought. Could he be any more uncomfortable? Perhaps if he were sitting here seeking permission to marry one of the man's daughters. Miss Elizabeth's image came to mind, and he swatted it away; it had no place here, and really, he could hardly be thinking of her in such a manner, not after so short an acquaintance, especially when they had passed most of it at odds.

"I do not like to hear people disparage others unless they have genuine cause to," Darcy said. "Perhaps the situation would be different if the other person had cheated them or something such as that. I recognise the irony in my statement, given how I spoke of Miss Elizabeth. It was plain to me that Mrs Best expected me to agree with her, and I could not." It had also been an opportunity for him to subtly apologise for his behaviour at the assembly to everyone present, and he had grabbed at it.

Mr Bennet offered him a slow nod and a glass of sherry. Darcy accepted, and, after taking a fortifying sip, said, "I had hoped to see you today, sir. I wrote to my cousin about meeting you, and he has replied."

Darcy showed him the part of the letter in which Frederick Darcy had expressed his delight in hearing news of his old friend and his request that Darcy discover whether Mr Bennet would agree to receive a letter from him—in short, whether he would be willing to renew their correspondence. Therein followed a relatively pleasant interlude in which the two gentlemen spoke about Frederick Darcy and Mr Bennet's memories of their friendship and time at Oxford. Darcy could not be completely at ease; he felt he had only earned a sliver of Mr Bennet's trust, and it would vanish if he said a wrong word. Their interview ended with Mr Bennet claiming a hope that he and Frederick would not only write to each other but that they might meet in town or elsewhere.

When the older gentleman indicated they should return to the drawing room, Darcy was satisfied with how their time together had passed. Their conversation had been friendlier than any they had previously had. It was excellent progress, although he felt a lingering sense of disappointment. Mr Bennet had said nothing about Darcy being permitted to speak to Miss Elizabeth or forgiving him the terrible nature of their first meeting. Darcy would be satisfied if he agreed to overlook it, should forgiveness be too much at present.

## CHAPTER NINETEEN

Bennet was doing his best to live up to the promise he had made to himself to be a better father and husband. Fortunately, the endeavour was becoming easier with each passing day, no doubt helped along by seeing improvements in his ladies. This was especially true regarding Kitty, Lydia, and even more so Mrs Bennet. He could also point to encouraging signs in Mary, and, after Mr Darcy's recent call, he thought it possible Elizabeth could be added to his list. He was much mistaken if his darling girl had not taken to heart his words about not clinging to her initial assumptions about people. When he and Mr Darcy had returned to the drawing room, Lizzy had not spoken to the gentleman, but she had looked at him frequently, and there had been no disapproval or dislike evident in her expression. If anything, Bennet would say he saw the opposite. And he further believed that Mr Darcy had often turned his gaze to Lizzy.

The implications of them stealing glimpses of each

other, of seeming to listen to hear what the other was saying, were not ones Bennet was entirely comfortable with. Indeed, if Mr Darcy did not have a connexion to someone he had once valued as a close friend, and if he had not seen that the young man was genuinely attempting to ameliorate his deportment, he would be tempted to warn him off.

It did not escape Bennet's notice that both he and Mr Darcy had been forced to improve how they dealt with others. It was possible that made him feel a kinship to him.

*I shall say nothing of it to Lizzy. She has seen that I am willing to treat him as a friendly acquaintance, and now I wish to observe how she acts towards him—and he towards her.*

He had an opportunity to see the couple together soon after, when they met at a card party held by the Gouldings at Haye-Park.

Elizabeth was at a table with Mr Darcy. Declining to play cards himself, Bennet stood with several other guests who likewise did not wish to take part, and he watched Elizabeth for signs of distress. There were none; if anything, had he not known their history, he would have thought she was speaking to a friend. She smiled and laughed, did not avoid looking at him, and listened closely as he spoke. It was all exceedingly interesting; so much so that twice one of his companions had to repeat themselves because he had not been giving them his attention.

As soon as Elizabeth stepped away from the card table, he pulled her aside. "Are you enjoying yourself?"

"I am, Papa. I do like a rousing game of cards, and I

assure you, there was a sufficient amount of intrigue to cheer even the most curmudgeonly amongst us." She smiled, and her eyes drifted towards Mr Darcy.

"I find it difficult to imagine what intrigue might occur under the present circumstances," he said.

She laughed. "There was a question of Mrs Stuart having the great luck of securing nearly perfect hands two games in a row—not that anyone would outright accuse her of cheating—and Mr Simms was seen winking and contorting his features in a most odd manner, as though he were attempting to communicate some hint about his cards to his partner, but he claimed there was a lash irritating his eye."

Bennet chuckled and shook his head. "I would believe Mrs Stuart but not Simms. He has always been willing to do whatever was necessary to win, even at something as inconsequential as a game of cards in a neighbour's drawing room." Hoping to surprise her into saying what first came to mind—and was thus the most truthful—he quickly added, "You and Mr Darcy appear to be on better terms."

His trick did not work. She regarded him for a long moment before saying, "He was polite, amiable even."

"Is that enough to overlook his misdeeds?"

She glanced towards the gentleman. "Do you object? You demanded that he apologise to me, and he cannot do that if we never speak."

"Should he not be able to do the deed in under a minute?"

The colour in her cheeks deepened. "When he first spoke to me—in the churchyard, if you recall—I told him he needed to know me before he could genuinely say he was mistaken about what he said of me. For that to happen, we must have a little conversation."

Bennet pursed his lips and considered his next words, including what might be influencing him either in favour of liking the young man or continuing to dislike and distrust him. "I grant you, he has been more polite this last fortnight or thereabouts, but is that enough? Do you wish me to tell you I no longer require you to avoid him, that you are free to chat to him as you would any other new acquaintance?"

"I suppose I would say yes and yes. I would like to forget the whole thing ever happened. If everyone sees that Mr Darcy and I can speak together easily, that we do not avoid each other or scowl whenever we meet, they will cease to remember what happened at the assembly, and I shall be happier for it."

Slowly, Bennet nodded. "Very well. But I shall continue to keep a close watch on him. Now, let us find something to drink. Do you think we shall be able to depart soon? I am beginning to long for my book and slippers. These shoes your mother made me wear have never fitted properly."

THE FOLLOWING TUESDAY, ELIZABETH AND HER sisters walked into Meryton. The day was pleasant, given it was mid-November, but the breeze was chilly, leading Kitty to complain more than anyone appreciated. Lydia teased her about it, resulting in the pair squabbling, Mary sighed disapprovingly, and Jane attempted to bring peace to the group, going so far as to promise them all some small gift at their favourite shop.

Elizabeth admittedly did her best to overlook all their talk and instead take in the scene around her. She found her thoughts often drifted to Mr Darcy; an event that was increasingly frequent. It was just over one month since they had met. That night, she had been certain she would despise him for the rest of her life. Currently, her feelings were a jumble. She would readily admit that she liked him, but it was an odd sort of liking; it seemed different from how she viewed Mr Bingley, for instance. She had known the two gentlemen the same length of time, and as much as she found the latter amusing and easy company, Mr Darcy was…*more*. She could think of no other word that fitted quite as well.

*I shall only sort it out if I spend time with him.* That was not a disagreeable prospect, and she could use the excuse that she had to speak to him whenever the occasion arose so that he might properly apologise. Not that anyone apart from her father had yet asked her why she did not mind talking to the man who had spoken so meanly of her in public. It was a little strange that Jane had not, but she was caught up in her budding romance with Mr Bingley, and Charlotte had not seen Elizabeth and Mr Darcy together enough for her to question the matter.

Soon they were entering the market town. Having made up their disagreement, Lydia and Kitty walked ahead of their sisters. At the other side of the street, Elizabeth saw a soldier, his red coat standing out against the white and grey buildings; with him stood another man whom she did not recognise.

Lydia pointed and cried, "I think it is Mr Denny! Who is with him? Come, Kitty."

"Lydia, you are not to run after the officers. What would Papa say?" Jane said in a low voice, glancing about to see whether she was in danger of being overheard.

Lydia stopped walking to turn to Jane. "Papa is not here."

"Very true," Elizabeth said. "But you can be sure that I shall tell him if you do not comport yourself as a young lady."

Lydia stamped her foot and muttered a few words Elizabeth was glad she did not hear; the most likely outcome was a row and a quick return to Longbourn. It was enough that Mary murmured, "You are such children," evidently meaning her two younger sisters, who had begun whining that they were never permitted to have any fun.

Jane, ever seeking to appease, said, "Since we know Mr Denny, and since I see that he and his companion are approaching us, we may speak to them for a few minutes."

Mr Denny greeted them and introduced his friend, Mr George Wickham, who had lately come to Meryton to join the regiment. Elizabeth was struck by Mr Wickham's good looks and his open expression, which indicated he was pleased with everything he saw—from the town to, if she was not mistaken, the young ladies he had just met. With Mary silently standing beside her,

Elizabeth spoke to him; Jane remained with their younger sisters and Mr Denny, who had lately returned from a brief trip to London.

"Have you known Mr Denny long?" Elizabeth asked.

"Oh, some years." Mr Wickham smiled at her before his eyes again examined the street. "I must say, Meryton looks exactly as he described it. Excellent shops and agreeable proprietors, I hope."

Elizabeth and Mary exchanged a glance; it was an odd comment, and she found his lack of attention a little rude. "Does it?" she said.

"Wh—? Oh, forgive me, ladies. Meryton appears to be a charming town. Really quite charming." His eyes swept over her features and then Mary's. "Denny and I happened to see each other a day or two ago. He told me how glad he was that his regiment was stationed here. After that, it took little convincing for me to agree to accompany him on his return. I have wanted occupation, you see, and the militia will provide it. I am quite alone in the world, and belonging to a company, a band of brothers so to speak, was an attractive notion."

"I pray you will find the sense of fellowship you desire," Mary said.

Elizabeth was on the point of asking him where his family had been from, when she caught a glimpse of horses approaching and was distracted by realising it was Mr Darcy and Mr Bingley.

## CHAPTER TWENTY

"Miss Bennet," Mr Bingley cried, pulling his horse to a stop and quickly dismounting. "How good it is to see you."

Elizabeth heard nothing else he said. Under other circumstances, she would have been happy to speak to Mr Bingley, even expect that she, her sisters, and the two newly arrived gentlemen would spend an interlude talking together, exchanging a few commonplaces, ascertaining why they were all in Meryton, and introducing Mr Wickham to them. But she had a strong suspicion Mr Darcy and Mr Wickham already knew each other. Mr Darcy all but glared at him, his chin barely lowering enough to call it a nod. It was difficult to tell in the bright daylight, but she believed Mr Wickham's complexion had paled.

"Miss Elizabeth, Miss Mary," Mr Darcy said, removing his hat. "I hope I find you both well."

"V-very, thank you, sir," Mary said, the slight stammer informing Elizabeth that her sister had also noticed the uncomfortable greeting—or rather, lack of—between the men.

Mr Darcy met Elizabeth's eye. She furrowed her brow slightly, intending for him to read a silent question in her expression, and was almost certain he answered it with a slight shake of his head.

"Denny, we-we should not take up any more of the Miss Bennets' time," Mr Wickham called to his friend.

"Oh, but Mr Wickham, we have not had a chance to talk at all!" Kitty said.

"I know!" Lydia exclaimed. "You must come to my aunt's house tomorrow evening. Mr Denny has been invited, and she will not mind if you are there too, Mr Wickham. Say you will."

Jane attempted to stop her, but she was not equal to the task, not when both Kitty and Lydia insisted Mrs Philips would be desolate if she learnt she had missed out on hosting the newest member of the regiment before anyone else could. Mr Wickham agreed that if Mrs Philips extended the invitation to him, he would attend her gathering. Elizabeth had the impression he had largely conceded so that he and Mr Denny might depart.

"I shall go directly to my aunt and demand she send Mr Wickham a note at once," Lydia stated as soon as the two officers were gone. "Come along, Kitty."

Seeing that Jane was occupied with Mr Bingley and had not heard, Elizabeth said, "No, you will not. We shall remain together, all five of us." Turning to Mr Darcy, she said, "I apologise for my sister's behaviour. I do not believe she, or Kitty for that matter, have even acknowledged that you are here." Kitty turned pink and murmured a greeting. Elizabeth worried her own complexion would take on a noticeable amount of colour, such was her embarrassment, but that was forgotten in a moment because Mr Darcy smiled at her.

Lydia let out a loud, not entirely polite noise, which Elizabeth would have overlooked had her sister not also said, "How can you tell me what I am not to do when you are speaking to Mr Darcy even though Papa said you are not permitted to? I do not see that him saying something kind about us to Mrs Best, who everyone knows is a horrible gossip and is only angry because you made Papa—"

"That is enough, Lydia," Elizabeth interjected. "Mr Darcy, again, I apologise for my sister's poor manners."

"Shall I take her and Kitty to the shop?" Mary asked. "Will you and Jane be far behind us?"

Elizabeth agreed, first impressing on Kitty and Lydia that they were to obey Mary else the five of them would return to Longbourn without Jane's promised treat. Lydia stamped away, leaving a red-faced Kitty chasing after her and Mary struggling to keep up with them without running. Elizabeth sighed and briefly closed her eyes, opening them at the sound of Mr Darcy's voice.

"How are you this morning?" he asked, his gaze on her.

"After *that* display? Lydia is headstrong, but I hope age—and vigilance by my parents, sisters, and me—will make a difference. Apart from being mortified, I am well." When she looked into his eyes, she momentarily felt light-headed and kicked herself for being so stupid—

both for having prattled on about Lydia and for being so affected by his presence. "And you?"

His eyes flickered in the direction Mr Wickham had taken, and he shrugged. "I am afraid Bingley and I cannot keep you and your sisters company while you are in Meryton or return to Longbourn with you. We have business at Purvis Lodge, but we could not ride by without spending a few minutes with you."

"While *you* might be able to withstand the temptation, I am sure Mr Bingley could not." She tilted her head to gesture towards where he stood with Jane, the couple speaking animatedly.

Mr Darcy chuckled, which somehow made him even more handsome, a feat Elizabeth would have said was impossible. "I agree so far as Bingley is concerned, but as to what you said of me, I shall assume you were teasing."

She grinned, and for a minute or two, they exchanged what little news they had. She was curious about his connexion to Mr Wickham, but to her surprise, she only remembered their awkwardness once she and Mr Darcy had separated; while they were together, she had been caught up in their conversation, even though they had not touched on any serious subjects.

When saying goodbye to them, Mr Bingley added, "I hope we shall see all of you, and your excellent parents, soon. Very soon." The Netherfield party was engaged elsewhere the following evening and would not be at Mrs Philips' soirée.

"I am sure an occasion to meet will arise before long," Mr Darcy said. "Perhaps the day after tomorrow."

He was looking at Elizabeth, and she wondered whether he hoped they would see each other during an early morning walk; he might even be hinting that he desired to meet in the only way open to him at present. As she walked farther into Meryton with her sisters, Elizabeth reflected that he might want to talk to her about Mr Wickham, and she knew she would do her best to be on those paths where they had encountered each other before and at about the same time.

Mr Wickham attended Mrs Philips's evening party, presumably having received the necessary invitation. Elizabeth did not speak to him at first, but she did study him. There was no doubt that he was a good-looking man, perhaps one of the most handsome she had ever seen, and he spoke easily and warmly to everyone he met. In short, he was charming, and given the strange behaviour she had witnessed in both him and Mr Darcy the day before, she was perplexed; indeed, she had spent far too long reflecting on it and was ever more anxious to speak to Mr Darcy.

It was only after she had been at her aunt's house for about an hour that she spoke to Mr Wickham. She had been talking to friends, but when they left her—and before she could join Charlotte in another corner of the room, as she had intended—he was beside her.

"Miss Elizabeth, I am glad to finally have a moment to get to know you better. I began trying to catch you almost as soon as I arrived, but each time I thought I might, someone has prevented me," he said, giving her a lopsided smile. "Everyone has been so friendly, even more than I expected from what my fellow officers said."

"We are always glad to welcome new people, but I suppose that is usual in small towns. We are forever running the risk of becoming tired of each other's company."

He laughed more than her small joke deserved. "I have tried to make my way to you several times, but someone always stopped me."

She wondered at him repeating himself. Did he particularly want to know her? It was flattering, she supposed, given his good looks and happy manners. If she had not seen the way he and Mr Darcy acted towards each other, she might have found him engaging. *If there was no Mr Darcy, or if I still clung to my hatred for him, I probably would be rather pleased with Mr Wickham's company. But now...I wish* he *were here instead!*

There was nothing she could think of to say to Mr Wickham, so she smiled and sipped from her cup, hoping he had not noticed that it was already empty.

"I spoke to your younger sisters—Miss Catherine and Miss Lydia. Such lively girls. Delightful company." He paused as though waiting for her to respond, so she thanked him. "They told me that your family lives at Longbourn and have for some generations."

"That is true. The Bennets have occupied the land for well over a century."

"I look forward to seeing it, and to meeting your father. I regret that he was not able to attend tonight."

So was Elizabeth; she was interested to know what her father would think of the young man, given his evident intention to make friends with everyone he met—perhaps especially the young ladies. Mr Bennet had not yet found any of the officers agreeable except for Colonel Forster, and that, she suspected, was because he had lately married. This evening, Mr Bennet, Sir William, and several of the other neighbourhood gentlemen were occupied with a meeting whose purpose she could not recall. She understood it was the same one Mr Darcy and Mr Bingley were attending.

"He will be happy to make your acquaintance," she said politely. "You must not expect too much from Longbourn. Although I love it dearly and think it is everything it should be, it is hardly a grand estate. It is nothing to Netherfield Park, which is the largest property in the neighbourhood."

"Ah." He nodded and took a long drink from his glass of wine. "That is the one Mr Bingley has taken. He has not been here long, I believe?"

Would he mention Mr Darcy too? Mr Wickham must know that he was staying with his friend. "Only since Michaelmas. He is here with his sisters and the husband of the elder, Mr Hurst. Do you know them?"

He responded by shaking his head. "I have met Mr Bingley once or twice. Informally, you understand. I do not believe we have ever said more than two or three words to each other. As for Darcy… Well, you must have seen that he was *not* pleased to discover I am nearby."

"I take that to mean you are more familiar with him than Mr Bingley. I had presumed as much," she admitted, keeping her tone even so as not to betray her wish for him to tell her everything about their connexion, despite it being unconscionably rude and intrusive.

He chuckled. "We are not friends, which an intelligent young lady such as you must also have noticed immediately. I should say we are no longer friends. I understand you and he are not either." He leant closer and lowered his voice. "Denny, you see. He told me about my old friend insulting you. I wish I could say I am surprised."

Elizabeth felt a flash of annoyance and was certain it showed in her countenance.

Before she could say anything, he continued. "Oh, not because of *you*, I assure you. The moment we met, I was struck by your loveliness, if you will excuse my boldness, and any fool would see that you are a delightful young lady, one any man would be pleased to know and dance with as often as possible. Darcy, however, is a fool—an arrogant, impossible to please fool. I am sorry you had the misfortune to encounter such a man, and I pray he has done you no lasting injury."

"No, not at all. I ought to—" she said, intending to make an excuse to leave his company; she was suddenly uneasy. She hated him referring to the assembly—and hated hearing him insult Mr Darcy even more. If only she could deliver a set-down such as the one Mr Darcy had given Mrs Best! But she was wary of saying too much, of drawing attention and creating gossip, especially when everyone else was finally beginning to speak less of *that night*. Her feeling of protectiveness for the gentleman was shocking in its strength, and she was determined to question herself about it later.

To her regret and irritation, Mr Wickham interjected and spoke as though he had not heard her. "I have known him all my life, and he has always been a proud, disagreeable fellow. Thus, he was as a boy, and thus he remains. His father liked me, even preferred me. As a child, I wondered why, but now, I see it was because he approved of my character and could not like his son's. I am a simple man, Miss Elizabeth, with simple desires—good friends, pleasant conversation, and a laugh or two." He chuckled sadly. "To earn my way in the world respectably. Darcy has always been jealous of me. The end of it was that he robbed me of the inheritance his father wanted me to have, which included a valuable living in Derbyshire. Instead of being a poor soldier with an uncertain future, I should even now be living near where I grew up. I do love Derbyshire, and I would have loved to be a parson, to be settled in that fine county, and be doing some good for the people there. Oh, I am extremely glad to have a place in Colonel Forster's regiment—excellent man, I could see that at once—but it is not what I had dreamt I would be doing with my life."

"I am sorry for you, Mr Wickham, but I am glad you are satisfied with your present situation." Her speech evidently pleased him, and before he could say more, she succeeded in excusing herself, truthfully claiming a need to speak to Lydia and Kitty, who appeared on the point of arguing with each other yet again.

She quickly dealt with their petty disagreement and spent the remainder of the party with them or Mary, having lost interest in idle chitchat. Mr Wickham continued to delight everyone, and she heard more than one person express how glad they were to have met him. Elizabeth kept him in her sights all evening, mostly to ensure he stayed away from Kitty and Lydia, who she suspected would quickly decide they liked him above all other officers simply because he was better looking.

Elizabeth considered talking to Jane about what Mr Wickham had said, but she decided against it. It was possible there was some truth in what he had disclosed, but she wanted to believe better of Mr Darcy. A month ago, she certainly would not have; she would have considered Mr Wickham's portrayal of him exactly what she expected of the gentleman she had encountered at the assembly. But after witnessing how much effort Mr Darcy was putting into rectifying the errors he had made that night, seeing what an admirable gentleman he was, she could not. Briefly, she wondered how Mr Denny had come to tell his friend about the assembly—he had not been present, after all. She supposed he was aware that the two men knew each other and, having heard the gossip—and plenty of people were still talking of *that night*—had thought it an amusing story to share.

Elizabeth fervently hoped that people would forget the assembly had ever taken place! If they must, they should think only of meeting Mr Bingley. If he and Jane fell in love, as they seemed set to do, it might become a romantic tale of how they had met and known at once that they were destined to spend their lives as husband and wife. What the neighbourhood needed was another event that they could speak of enthusiastically, recounting details again and again because they were so delicious. She did not know what form this event might take, but in her dreams, it was one in which there was no discord, only endless moments of pleasure and cheer.

At Longbourn, Elizabeth retired immediately, assuring her family that she was well, just excessively tired. In truth, she was still vexed with Mr Denny and Mr Wickham and anxious to see Mr Darcy. Silently, she prayed that they would meet the next morning and that she might convince him to tell her more of the newest member of the militia.

# CHAPTER TWENTY-ONE

Two days after seeing the Miss Bennets in Meryton, Darcy went for an early morning ride hoping he would encounter Miss Elizabeth as he had previously. As soon as he had seen Wickham, he had been overtaken by a twin yearning to kick him and pull her away in order to protect her, determined that he would not fail her as he had Georgiana. This strong desire had faded into a more reasonable decision to advertise something of his history with the scoundrel so that the Miss Bennets and other young ladies would be on their guard. He would begin by speaking to Miss Elizabeth and then Mr Bennet or some other gentleman.

He coaxed Budge into joining him, believing Miss Elizabeth would be pleased to see him again. When the ridiculous dog had been unwilling to leave his comfortable spot by the fire, Darcy had stooped to whisper that he might see her if he did. It had to be coincidence that Budge had then stood and shaken himself, making his white fur look even more unkempt than usual.

"Well, there is nothing for it," Darcy had said, scratching his faithful companion's ears. "Fortunately, she is not the sort of lady whose feelings for you depend on your looks." It was yet another of her admirable qualities; he was discovering that there were a great many.

Any attempt to make Budge more presentable might be the difference between meeting Miss Elizabeth that morning or missing her. It was important that he speak to her before Wickham had a chance to spread his usual lies. He would have liked to have done it sooner—immediately—but circumstances had not permitted it. Darcy hoped he had done enough that people would find it difficult to believe the worst of whatever his former friend said, though it was always possible, even probable, that Wickham would make up ever more outrageous stories in his quest to ensure he was loved and Darcy was hated. Although he did not want anyone to think poorly of him, the person whose opinion most mattered was Miss Elizabeth. What had begun as a wish to make her think better of him had altered into something far greater, and it was increasingly difficult to overlook that he liked her more than any other lady of his acquaintance.

Sure enough, when they were about halfway to Longbourn, Budge barked several times and ran off; Darcy found him with Miss Elizabeth a moment later. Once again, she was crouching, giving the dog the attention he apparently desperately needed—as suggested by his frantically wagging tail and enthusiastic attempts to lick her face.

"Mind your manners!" Darcy cried; he tried to pull Budge away from her, but she only laughed.

"How could I object?" she asked. "I am seldom greeted so gleefully. You will spoil me, noble Budge, and make me think entirely too well of myself." She kissed the top of his head and accepted Darcy's offer of a hand to help her stand.

They strolled, the exercise necessary in light of the November chill and the shaded path they were on. He listened with growing anger as she told him of her conversation with Wickham at her aunt's house the previous evening. Sure enough, he had told her the usual lies. *If he feels she did not believe him, at the next opportunity, he will add that I gamble excessively and have been known to prefer less than respectable company.*

"I do not know that I can even call it a conversation," she said. "I was a most unwilling participant, I assure you, but I had the impression he had information he wished to convey, and nothing would stop him."

"You must wonder whether any part of it is true," he said, keeping his gaze forwards, despite being tempted to glance at her. She walked beside him, and he was nervous that he might see suspicion in her eyes, but the tone of her voice gave him reason to hope she felt none.

"I suppose I am curious what the basis for his tales is. I do *not* believe you are a reprobate, as he was clearly suggesting, but do not exaggerations or lies often begin with some element of truth, some little thing the teller bends and twists to suit their purposes?"

Darcy shrugged. "From what I can discern, the only truthful elements are that we have known each other all our lives and were raised in Derbyshire. My father, who was his godfather, was fond of him, I admit. Wickham's own father was Pemberley's steward. He was an excellent man, and I know that my father believed George would grow up to be just like him." He had once expected the same, and disappointment at what had happened momentarily robbed him of speech.

Miss Elizabeth touched his arm and said, "But he did not?"

Shaking his head, Darcy went on. "My father never saw the signs that father and son were as different as could be, though I did. I was never jealous of George. If anything, he was jealous of me, of my position in life and especially my wealth. I have often thought that the differences between us and what that meant for our futures became more apparent to him as we went through adolescence, and with it, he grew to despise me. My father found him amusing and took an interest in him. He provided Wickham with an education and promised him a valuable living if he chose to go into the church. It is completely untrue that my father liked him more than me. My father *liked* him, but he *loved* me. It was me that he taught to ride and fish and shoot, me he took with him wherever he went, and for whom he bought the finest gifts. Confided in and sought comfort from during his final illness."

He fell silent, remembering those difficult months. Miss Elizabeth slipped her arm around his. She must have sensed that he would find it more soothing than words, and he appreciated her quiet support.

After a brief pause, he continued. "My father and I

travelled during the brief period it was safe, almost a decade ago now, and when we returned, I saw at once how Wickham had changed. He had made new friends in my absence, ones that encouraged him to…live a more dissolute life, which he was able to keep hidden from our fathers. He was enraged by the terms of my father's will—chiefly that he had only been left one thousand pounds rather than the thousands he apparently feels were his due." He went on to tell her that Wickham had disclaimed any interest in the church and had been paid three thousand pounds in place of the living.

"So much money!" she cried. "He told me he was poor. How can he now have nothing?"

Darcy could only shrug again. "Living beyond his means, and I understand he is excessively fond of gambling. He has a tendency to leave debts behind him wherever he goes." He would have to ensure the local shopkeepers knew not to give Wickham credit—and to protect their daughters from him. "I am sorry. I have perhaps said too much. I do not wish to distress you."

"You need have no concern for me. I can see it distresses *you* to recall it. I wish I had discouraged you from doing so."

He ran a hand over his face, accidentally knocking his hat from his head. As soon as he stopped to pick it up, Budge lay down and rested his head between his paws.

Miss Elizabeth giggled. "He is a silly thing. Adorable but silly. Shall we let him rest?" She gestured to a large rock at the side of the path that was in the sun, and when he nodded, they sat.

Neither of them spoke for a while, and he found the

quietness peaceful; it was only disrupted by Budge's soft snores and the rustling of wind through the trees. The strength of his wish to tell her everything surprised him. Did he trust her enough? When the words poured from his mouth and he explained what had happened at Ramsgate the previous summer, he had his answer: he did.

Her shock was everything he knew it would be—as was her anxiety for Georgiana. "Your poor, poor sister. How she must have suffered. She was only fifteen? That is Lydia's age! I pray she is well now, though if you say she remains affected, I would not be surprised."

"She is doing well, quite well, from what my aunt tells me. My sister is staying in the country with my mother's brother and his wife. One of their sons is Georgiana's other guardian. There are times I believe I have taken Wickham's betrayal to heart more than she has. But we *were* friends. I believed we always would be. I rejoiced when my father spoke of reserving the Kympton living for Wickham because it is so close to Pemberley. He and I would always live near to one another. There would be no impediment to our friendship, our children would grow up together as he and I had…" He sighed heavily. "Instead, he became a man I could not like or respect, one that I would wish never to see again—and that was *before* he attempted to use my sister to revenge himself on me."

"And this all happened just weeks before you came to Netherfield," she said gently.

Darcy turned to face her, his eyes meeting hers.

"Please do not excuse how I acted then. It is true I was in a foul mood. Even Bingley noticed it. I believe he said I was insufferable, or he might only have implied it. I was angry and betrayed, partly because I could do nothing about what had happened. Which authority could I tell that would have made a difference, that would stop Wickham from treating another young lady as he had my sister, or injuring some other man who had considered him a friend? What could I do that would not risk Georgiana's reputation?"

"Those are questions to which I do not have answers, but I do not believe you expect me to. Very well, Mr Darcy, I shall not excuse you. Indeed, I did not intend to, but it does provide an explanation, especially when added to knowing you overheard people speculating about you, which you have said you hate, as most people would."

They remained where they were a while longer. Darcy almost told her about the ball Bingley had decided to hold and requested that she reserve a set for him, but he should first ask Mr Bennet for his permission. It was ridiculous to do so for a dance, but it would show the older gentleman respect that he might appreciate, given their unusual situation. Mr Bennet must have seen him and Miss Elizabeth speaking at Haye-Park during the recent card party, but that did not mean he would approve of them standing up together for half an hour. Bingley was planning to go to Longbourn that afternoon to deliver the invitation to the ball, and Darcy determined that he would go with him. He would speak to

Mr Bennet about Wickham and the ball, and, if granted permission—as he expected he would be—he would ask her then.

# CHAPTER TWENTY-TWO

During the brief moment Bennet had between being told that Mr Darcy and Mr Bingley were at Longbourn and them actually entering the drawing room, he had decided to keep his attention on the latter to study how he and Jane were together. It might soon be time to have a serious discussion with the young man, and he supposed he ought to speak to Jane as well to discover what her feelings were. His eldest daughter was a sweet, gentle person, and Bennet believed he saw signs that she was falling in love with Mr Bingley. Given her nature, she would suffer greatly, and for a long while, if he did not return her regard. What sort of father would treat that possibility lightly?

When Mr Bingley announced that he had brought an invitation to a ball at Netherfield, Bennet almost wished he was elsewhere. How could the ladies be anything other than thrilled, and in that enthusiasm, excessively loud? It left him feeling as if knives were piercing his eardrums.

"A ball? Did you hear that, girls?" Mrs Bennet said. It was hardly necessary; all five of them were already talking about it. Lydia and Kitty were demanding answers to various questions about the arrangements and who else would be invited—such as the officers, who interested them far too much for Bennet's liking—Mary and Lizzy had their heads bent together, Lizzy's bright and eager expression radiating how pleased she was at the prospect of a private ball, and Jane was once again showing her value by managing to listen to her mother while also attempting to calm Lydia and Kitty and smile at Mr Bingley and thank him for the invitation.

"Sir, I wonder whether I might speak to you alone."

He startled and turned to see that the quiet voice belonged to Mr Darcy, who stood beside him. Bennet nodded and led the way to his book-room.

"Please, sit." Bennet gestured to an armchair. "Would you care for a drink?"

"I would, thank you. I am afraid that what I have to tell you is unpleasant. A subject I would rather avoid."

"And some strong wine would help," Bennet stated. Studying the younger man, he saw obvious signs of strain—shoulders slightly slumped and a heaviness about his eyes. Handing him a glass and choosing a chair near him rather than across his desk, Bennet added, "I cannot imagine what has happened, but if there is anything I can do to be of assistance, I shall try. I hope it is not bad news from your family."

"No, no." Mr Darcy shook his head and took a sip of wine. "It is about one of the new officers. I happened to see him in Meryton the other day, standing with your daughters. Mr Wickham. You see, he is known to me."

Over the next few minutes, Mr Darcy explained their history and Mr Wickham's dissolute behaviour, claiming he was a danger to young women—high and low born—and that he always accumulated a great deal of debt, both of business and honour. Mr Darcy's serious mien and his offer to supply proof assured Bennet that he spoke the truth.

"Thank you for warning me," he said. "I do not see why he would be interested in my girls. They have no fortune or connexions, as I assume you are aware, gossip being what it is." He wanted to ensure Mr Darcy knew, because that would mean that his friend did too; it would not come as a shock should Mr Bingley eventually decide he wanted to marry Jane.

Mr Darcy nodded and said, "Unfortunately, Wickham's jealousy or hatred towards me—whatever emotion is strongest in him at the moment—means that all he needs to know is that I am on friendly terms with your family. He has already sought to injure me by using my sister. If he would do that, seek to harm a girl he has known since she was an infant, he would not hesitate to use one of the Miss Bennets."

Bennet pressed his fingertips to his forehead and rubbed it vigorously. He did not want this added complication to a life that was already keeping him away from his usual pleasures more than he liked. Although, upon reflection, he could not say he *disliked* spending time with his ladies at present. His efforts with them were yielding the results he had hoped for, which was satisfying and the encouragement he needed to persist.

"That is most disturbing, as you must realise, not being a fool. Lizzy would tell you to take that as a compliment. I often think ninety percent of the people about me are fools." He shook himself. "Forgive me. I am aware I currently sound like a fool myself. I shall certainly ensure this Mr Wickham never enters Longbourn, and we must find a way to inform my wife and daughters and neighbours. Do you agree?"

Mr Darcy nodded. "Though I would prefer to keep my sister's part in it quiet."

Bennet was quick to agree. "I would not dream of telling anyone. Miss Darcy has surely suffered enough for her youthful indiscretion. Having five daughters, I have seen how easy it would be to flatter them into doing what they should not. That your sister's companion encouraged the connexion— Well, I am heartily sorry you and she had to experience such a plot against you, and I thank you for confiding in me. It has given me a clear understanding of his character and what we must do. It has lately come to my attention just how close an eye a man must keep on his family."

"I know that I am part of the reason," Mr Darcy interjected. "I genuinely regret my own behaviour in October, and I assure you, I have learnt a valuable lesson from it and hope that I shall never forget it."

If the gentleman made a similar pretty speech to Elizabeth, Bennet wondered, would his dearest girl see beneath Mr Darcy's reticence to what he suspected was a rather honourable, caring, undoubtedly intelligent young man? Setting aside such reveries, he said, "Now, what shall we—or I, if you prefer—do about this?"

They spent the next minutes determining the steps they would take. Their plan involved speaking to Colonel Forster and several men who would pass on the message to others. Their aim was to ensure people knew to be cautious but not ostracise Mr Wickham. Bennet wanted him to have the opportunity to make a success of his new position, so long as he did it honestly and left the neighbourhood and all of its inhabitants no worse than they had been when he arrived. Had he not recently discovered that a man *could* change, given sufficient motivation? Perhaps Mr Wickham had experienced something of late that had encouraged him to want to amend his manner. His charity would not extend to admitting him into his or his family's company, however.

Once that was decided, Mr Darcy cleared his throat and awkwardly said, "I would like to ask your permission to dance with Miss Elizabeth at the ball. I am not generally fond of the exercise, which I suppose I did not need to say, but I would like to dance with her. If-if nothing else, it would show everyone in attendance that I do not think she is unworthy of my attention."

Bennet sat back in his chair and sipped his wine. *And is there* another *reason you would like to spend more time with my girl?* "As you are aware, I made Lizzy promise to avoid you. This was when the whole unfortunate business first occurred." Mr Darcy nodded and blushed, which Bennet found diverting, though he managed not to smile or laugh.

"I am, sir, and I have come to appreciate that you told me how reprehensibly I acted. I have been attempting to be a gentleman that my family, including my late parents, would be proud of."

Bennet experienced an odd feeling in the region of his heart. He was not exactly sure what it was, but it struck him that his opinion of Mr Darcy had improved a great deal—far more than he had realised. If he showed this aspect of himself to Elizabeth, she would find herself liking him—and perhaps more. "I am sure they would be. You may ask Lizzy to dance with you." He took a large mouthful of wine and attempted to banish the notion of his daughter living so far away as Derbyshire; it was much too soon to worry about it. "Enough of that. Tell me, you are five- or six-and-twenty?"

Mr Darcy's brow furrowed, showing the change of subject surprised him. "Seven-and-twenty."

"Have you been fortunate enough to travel abroad? You would have been old enough during the last time it was not inadvisable or, dare I say, foolish to do so."

Mr Darcy briefly chuckled, which Bennet thought was kind. His quip was not that amusing.

"My father and I did when the Treaty of Amiens was in place. We left in June 1802 and came home early the following year when my uncle sent word that we must return at once, that it might not be safe to remain out of the country much longer."

"Your uncle the earl? He would have had early intelligence on the matter, I suppose." Mr Darcy nodded.

"Useful to have such connexions—or know someone who does." *And now I know you!* Bennet added to himself.

They spoke about travel for a while. He had visited all the usual countries and seen all the usual sights to complete his education as a young man, and it was agreeable to discuss it again with someone who would appreciate it. Elizabeth always liked to hear about his adventures, as she called them, and she often said she hoped to one day explore more of the world herself. Bennet would never play matchmaker—it was a solemn vow he had made to himself—but he could not help but speculate about his dearest girl and the young gentleman sitting across from him. *I am afraid they might be exceedingly well matched, and, if anything comes of it, I believe I would be pleased for them both.* A little more time to know Mr Darcy would give Bennet added confidence in him, and he determined to take it where he could.

# CHAPTER TWENTY-THREE

Elizabeth attempted not to let her curiosity show when her father and Mr Darcy entered the drawing room, but she was positive everyone could see that she was burning with it. Why had Mr Darcy asked to speak to her father alone? Was it about her? Perhaps a request that he permit them to spend time together?

A more reasonable assumption was that it had to do with Mr Wickham, which meant it could be of little interest to her. She had already determined that she and her sisters must avoid the man as much as possible—a situation that made her laugh since it had grown from a conversation with a gentleman whom she *had* avoided, and no doubt Mr Wickham would tell her she had been right to. How could it not be amusing to think that a gentleman she had once disliked told her another was unworthy of her attention, and she believed him? It had not occurred to her for even a second to question Mr Darcy's intelligence. She had believed him immediately

—known even as she was speaking to Mr Wickham that he was not trustworthy—and that was interesting in and of itself. So much had altered in her connexion with Mr Darcy without her realising it. Would the next days and months bring about yet more changes?

Both men approached her, and she willed herself not to blush and her eyes to remain steady on her father, despite how quickly her heart was beating; she could not look at Mr Darcy.

"I believe Mr Darcy has something to ask you, Lizzy," Mr Bennet said. "You have my permission to accept. Or not, as you like." He clapped Mr Darcy on the shoulder and went to sit by her mother. Only once he was across the room did Elizabeth turn to Mr Darcy.

"What did you and my father talk about?" she asked, surprised that the first question was not about what he wanted to say to her.

He lowered himself into the chair beside her, and, watching him, she was struck by what a handsome man he was, far handsomer than any other man she had ever seen. And he was *good*. She had been dreadfully mistaken about him when they first met. It was not without reason, to be sure, but everything she had learnt of him lately made her value knowing him. She liked listening to him speak of things he enjoyed: books, his home, and his family, whom he clearly loved. The situation with his sister and Mr Wickham demonstrated how protective he could be, and that was particularly attractive to her. Glancing towards her father, she supposed it was because she had often felt unprotected by him. She had contemplated the matter a fair bit of late. While she had no doubt her father would always have done what he could if confronted with an obvious threat, such as a fire in the house, he would only act if it was absolutely necessary, and for too long he had neglected many more subtle threats, those to her ease and happiness—her mother and younger sisters' lack of proper decorum, for instance. She gave him credit for his efforts over the past month, but it would take longer for her to believe he would remain resolved to be a better father and husband.

By comparison, what she had seen of Mr Darcy suggested that he had only lost his way for a short while. When confronted with his less-than-gentlemanly behaviour, he had soon admitted it and was doing his best to make up for it. That, in addition to his other characteristics, made him, in a word, admirable.

Keeping his voice quiet enough that no one else would hear, he said, "I wanted to tell your father of my history with Wickham. He needed to know about the man's less-than-honourable behaviour, and I wanted his advice on how to ensure people in the neighbourhood are not taken in by him. He can easily make friends, but regretfully, I cannot say he ever deserves them."

"Have you and my father devised a plan?"

He nodded. "We hope that people will be on their guard around him, not trust him too readily, yet I cannot be absolutely certain that he has not reformed. It is a ridiculous hope, but perhaps what happened this past summer, using Georgiana as he did, forced him to acknowledge how low he has sunk. I do not believe it is so, but for his father's sake, I wish it were. It would make no difference to me—he and I could never be friends again—but..." He shrugged. "He might genuinely want to make his new career a success and live an honest life."

Elizabeth detected a subtle longing in his tone and knew he not only hoped Mr Wickham had reformed; he *wanted* his former friend to become the man he knew he could be. It might only be because he knew it would please his and Mr Wickham's fathers, it might be because of his memories of them as boys, but it would gratify him, and for his sake, she wished it would come to pass. She smiled and nodded to show that she understood and decided a change of topic was in order.

"My father said there was something you wished to ask me. I admit, I am impatient to know what it is."

He chuckled and glanced at her but did not seem able to keep a steady eye on her. "Will you dance with me at the ball? I-I thought perhaps the first set?"

She bit her lips together to stop the words that wanted to burst from between them. They would have been a combination of astonishment and a hasty agreement; both would have left her feeling equally as silly, especially once she considered that he might be asking as part of his quest to ensure everyone who knew about his insult at the assembly saw that he regretted it. If that was the only reason he wanted to dance with her, she would just as soon decline. They might spend the evening in conversation instead. That was an activity she knew they would both enjoy.

"But you dislike dancing," she said.

He swallowed audibly and fixed his gaze on hers. "But with you, I do not believe I shall find it so disagreeable. I know you will keep me sufficiently amused."

She laughed, feeling flattered and consequently awkward. "How exactly do you suppose I would do that? Since you hate the exercise, I imagine the task would be difficult and almost certainly beyond my skills."

Still keeping his eyes on hers, he shook his head. "All we need do is have a conversation similar to those we have had of late. Speak to me of more than how lovely the flowers are, do not hint that you would like to befriend my titled relations or question how many bedchambers there are at Pemberley."

Hastily covering her mouth to muffle her exclamation, she needed a moment before she could respond. "Do ladies actually do that?"

He pressed his eyes closed and nodded, letting out a weary sigh. "And worse. I shall give you no names, but I have encountered some ladies who all but invite themselves to stay at my estate, others who encourage me to call on their fathers or brothers who, naturally, want nothing more than to be the best of friends—and more. One even hinted that I could do her brother a great deal of good if only I would give him a thousand pounds."

"Oh, how wretched. And unfair! With such experiences, I am surprised you attend balls at all."

"If I could avoid it, I would. My cousins and aunt—perhaps I ought to use names so that you know of whom I speak. I have several cousins and people I call aunts. I am referring specifically to Lady Romsley and her sons. These particular cousins seem to feel I should enjoy flirting with every young lady I meet, as they do, and my aunt believes I should be looking for a wife and am sure to find her only if I dance with every eligible lady in town."

"Do you ask their fathers for permission to request a set?" She did not restrain her grin at the picture he painted of his life, intending to teach him to find the humour in it, if she could. Understandably, he would find his family's coaxing him to behave in ways contrary to his nature extremely disagreeable, despite the current lightness of his tone.

He rubbed the back of his neck and momentarily averted his eyes. "No, but under the circumstances, I thought I should. He did not seem to mind that we spoke together the other evening, but a card party at Haye-Park is not the same as dancing together at a large ball. You have not answered my question."

"No, I have not. Let me do so now. Of course I shall dance with you, sir. Thank you. I am greatly anticipating it." She spoke cheerfully, seeking to ease the seriousness she heard in his voice. Soon, he would apologise again, she would accept, and her next task would be to make him leave their unfortunate beginning in the past. *But that makes it sound as though I expect our…acquaintance to last longer than the week or, if I am fortunate, two he is likely to remain in the neighbourhood. I ought not to think that way. It will only result in disappointment.* Surely, Mr Darcy's visit to his friend would end soon, and while she and he might see each other again if Mr Bingley remained at Netherfield Park or if he and Jane married, whatever friendship the two of them were beginning to establish would be over. Until that happened, however, there was no reason she should not relish every minute of his company.

His expression softened, and she felt her cheeks warm when, in his deep, smooth voice, he said, "I, too, am looking forward to it."

## CHAPTER TWENTY-FOUR

It began to rain later the same day, but the weather did nothing to diminish the happiness of six ladies as they spoke of the forthcoming ball. Vital questions, beginning with what they would wear, then moving on to whom they would dance with, whom they wanted to ask them, and returning to their costumes, were debated again and again.

"I shall be cowering in a corner of my book-room, not to be disturbed unless it is absolutely necessary," Mr Bennet said on Sunday morning. "Recall, I shall never have a useful opinion on what gown suits any of you best."

Only on Monday, the day before the ball, did the rain begin to ease, though the sky remained covered with clouds and the air felt heavy. Nevertheless, at breakfast, Mr Bennet announced his intention to take the carriage into Meryton.

"I have business at the bookseller's," he explained.

Sitting beside him at the table, Elizabeth was able to

see the tightness of his jaw and suspected he simply needed an excuse to be away from the house for a short while. She did not blame him; she hated being confined indoors for so long and felt the want of fresh air and exercise. Besides, he had been uncommonly good over the last few days, sitting with his family far more than he would have previously; he did not tease any of them for being silly or stupid, no matter how much they chatted about the ball, or ridicule Kitty and Lydia's more and more outlandish predictions for what would happen —including several proposals, at least one indecent, and the exposure of an illicit love affair. Where they had got the notion that any such occurrence was probable eluded Elizabeth, and she hoped they did not find the ball too tame for their liking. At the least, if they found it dull, she prayed they would not attempt to liven things up in some inappropriate way. She had been worried enough about it that she had mentioned it to her father the day before, and he had promised to keep a close watch on them.

"But Mr Bennet, it might begin to rain again at any minute," her mother said, alarm in her voice. "What if you fall ill? You must be well enough to escort us to the ball! Netherfield may well be Jane's home one day soon—"

"Mama," Jane said. Her protest was not sufficient to stop her mother, but her father's was, to Jane's evident relief.

"Oh, very well, I shall not speak of it. But the carriage wheels might become stuck in mud. How would we get to the ball if you break some crucial part of our only vehicle?" Mrs Bennet asked.

"Nothing evil will befall me. I am determined to go," Mr Bennet said with a sharpness Elizabeth had not heard in weeks. Speaking more gently, he added, "I shall be well, my dear. The roads between here and Meryton are excellent, and if it begins to rain again, I shall take shelter at the inn until it passes."

His eyes flickered to Elizabeth, and she knew he had guessed that she would request to go with him, which she did, already suspecting what would happen and having a plan in place to get her way.

"No. Absolutely not, Lizzy," her mother said. "I cannot stop your father from risking his life—"

Before she could continue, Elizabeth said, "But if I accompany Papa, I can ensure he is being careful, and I can go to the haberdashery and anywhere else you or my sisters need. Have we not all mentioned various items we would like for tomorrow? Mary, you wanted new pink ribbons for your gown, and Kitty, one of your gloves is stained."

With this inducement, her mother approved of her going and, along with her sisters, wrote a shopping list for Elizabeth to take with her. She insisted they organise it into two categories—what was absolutely necessary and what was only desired—else she would need all afternoon, and her father would not agree to such a long excursion.

Once they were in the carriage, he rested his head against the squabs, closed his eyes, and said, "It is good to be out of the house. I do not even care that we may not be gone for long. I trust you understand my feelings."

He patted her hand, she assured him she did, and he rested quietly for the short ride into Meryton. She almost told him that she was proud of the efforts he was taking with her mother and sisters but expected he would not like her to draw attention to the changes he had made; it was a reminder of the ways he had *not* been the man they had needed. He had helped her too. His caution about refusing to rethink her first impressions had been invaluable; without it, she might never have let herself know Mr Darcy, and her life would have been poorer for it.

Once in Meryton, they went their separate ways to see to their errands. Elizabeth had just selected a new pair of cream-coloured silk gloves that would perfectly match Kitty's gown when the door to the shop opened. To her delight, Mr Darcy entered. She smiled broadly; he returned the gesture with a more restrained one. Given he did not demonstrate his feelings as easily as she did —she had noticed that about him some time ago—she felt free to believe he took as much pleasure in their meeting as she did.

"Miss Elizabeth, how do you do? I am surprised to see you here, given the threatening clouds." He bowed.

"I am well, sir, and I might say the same to you. My father and I leapt at the first opportunity to be somewhere other than at home for a short while. He is at the bookseller's while I find a few last trinkets my mother and sisters insist they need for tomorrow. I am to meet him there once I have finished."

During her speech, he had come to stand next to her and acknowledged the shopkeeper with a polite nod.

"I, too, was glad for the chance to leave Netherfield for an hour or two, though I cannot claim any particular reason to do it other than a desire to see something different. I thought I might go to the bookseller's and was on my way there when I spied you through the window."

"Are you on your own?"

He nodded. "I believe Bingley wanted to accompany me, but his sisters requested his assistance as they make final preparations for the ball."

He chuckled in a way that suggested he had found the entire business rather fatiguing—not that Elizabeth supposed he had any direct role in it. Knowing how much her mother fussed over the arrangements for a dinner party, she could imagine that Mrs Hurst's and Miss Bingley's conversation was centred on the decorations, refreshments, supper, music, and guests—to say nothing of their own costumes—all of which were unlikely to hold his interest. His next words showed that she was right.

"I understand it is a large undertaking, and neither lady has had much occasion to host such an affair before. Naturally, they want everything to be as close to perfect as possible. I admit, I have been a little shocked by how much care Miss Bingley is putting into it." After ensuring no one was listening to them—the shopkeeper had gone to assist another customer—he added, "From the beginning, Bingley's sisters made it plain that they wished he had taken an estate in a more...fashionable county. It has taken them time to recognise Hertfordshire's charms. I believe it was only after we went to St Albans that their view of the neighbourhood began to change, especially for Miss Bingley, who is too young to remember their mother."

Again, he looked about them before continuing, this time lowering his voice to little more than a whisper; he leant closer to her. "I have not known whether I should say anything, but I think I should. Forgive me if I am mistaken. Bingley is growing rather fond of Miss Bennet. I am afraid his sisters…" He fixed her with a look that made it seem like he was begging her to understand and save him the awkwardness of saying the rest.

She let out a heavy breath. "They believe he could do better, such as a lady who would bring connexions and a substantial fortune to their marriage?"

He nodded. "Bingley has told them that such things do not matter to him, and I do not anticipate that they will change his opinion, no matter how stubbornly they insist he would be acting imprudently in pursuing your sister. But Miss Bennet should be aware that she should exercise caution in befriending them, although I truly believe they like her. Bingley's sisters love him, and with time, I expect they will accept that he will not take their opinions into account when it comes to something as important as choosing his wife. I do not say he has decided—"

"I understand, Mr Darcy," she interjected. "They have hardly known each other a month. It is too soon for either of them to have determined they would suit."

They gazed into each other's eyes for a long moment,

and Elizabeth was sure her heart stopped beating. Were they speaking only of Jane and Mr Bingley? Did he also feel that the same held true for the two of them? Could he possibly like her enough to think that their friendship might become so much more?

Fortunately—or perhaps unfortunately—the shopkeeper then returned to them and asked whether Elizabeth had decided on the gloves. Tearing her eyes and thoughts away from Mr Darcy, she added the pair to several other items she had already selected and concluded her purchases. She then invited Mr Darcy to go with her to meet her father, and they proceeded to the bookseller's, neither speaking. For her part, Elizabeth felt too much and needed the short interlude to gather her thoughts and set them aside until she was alone and could freely contemplate her evolving sentiments for the fine gentleman who was increasingly occupying her mind and heart.

# CHAPTER TWENTY-FIVE

As soon as her father saw Mr Darcy, he grinned.

"Well, Mr Darcy, this is a coincidence. Did you also experience a desire to run away from your home—albeit a temporary one, in your case? I cannot imagine you felt as confined as Lizzy and I did, given how large Netherfield is."

Mr Darcy glanced at her, making her wonder whether he was unsure how to answer. He said, "I did not wish to distract the ladies from their preparations. They impressed upon Bingley and me that there is a great deal for them to do in advance of the ball, and while they have not hesitated to demand their brother assist them, they would hardly be so free with me."

"Please, Papa, try not to tease Mr Darcy. He is not used to your ways," Elizabeth said.

Mr Bennet chuckled. "Or yours, my dear. You are almost as capable of teasing someone as I am. Very well, I shall not allude to you possibly being uncomfortable at Netherfield, Mr Darcy, and I shall refrain from sharing my next joke, which was about finding it small compared to your own estate."

His eyes held a mischievous twinkle; that, combined with his words, told her that he liked Mr Darcy. It gladdened her, and as she had done before, she marvelled at how quickly their opinions had all changed of each other. In response to her father, she rolled her eyes, and Mr Darcy shrugged, which she took as him agreeing with the statement; Mr Darcy's expression was one of good humour, and Elizabeth could see that her father approved.

For the next while, they spoke of books. Her father sought Mr Darcy's thoughts on several of the bookseller's latest finds, which led to them asking each other whether they owned or had read certain volumes and what their opinions had been. Elizabeth participated when she felt like it, but she was content to listen and observe.

There was no denying she was attracted to Mr Darcy in a way she had never felt before. To be sure, she had experienced one or two infatuations when she was younger, but they had never lasted long. What was it about *this* gentleman that inspired her tender feelings? She appreciated his good looks, he had an excellent mind, and spending time in his company was agreeable and remarkably easy, but there was more to it she had yet to sort out. Was it seeing how he treated Budge, that he clearly cared for the little creature, despite also finding him embarrassing? She suspected it also had to do with his willingness to admit his faults. He had listened to the censures of his friend and her father, and

—instead of dismissing them or simply leaving Meryton—he had stayed and demonstrated that he could do better, which took an inner strength that was worthy of praise, as did being so open about how Mr Wickham's betrayals had affected him. Or maybe it was all of this plus an indefinable something that created a certainty in her that he was worth knowing.

More and more, she felt lighter, happier, and oddly fuller in his company. The way he kept glancing at her gave her ample reason to believe he returned her feelings, and that his recent attentions had not all been about apologising for insulting her. Although less than six weeks had passed since then, she felt like she had known him for years.

Having concluded his business, which involved purchasing three books, Mr Bennet said, "What say we go to the inn and take refreshments before we return to our respective abodes? We can avoid all the talk of the ball a little longer."

Mr Darcy and Elizabeth agreed, and soon they were sitting in a small parlour. Plates of cheeses and meats and soft fresh bread and tea covered the oak table. Her father mentioned that he had lately written to Mr Frederick Darcy. "I hope to hear from him soon. Perhaps it is old age creeping up on me, but I have found it rather… enlivening to think of seeing a friend from my youth once again."

"You see friends from your youth all the time!" Elizabeth said.

He waved his hand, dismissing her comment. "Goulding, Best, and the lot of them do not count. They are men with whom I was thrown together because we happened to be born in the same corner of Hertfordshire. Frederick Darcy is a friend I chose. The situations are entirely different." Turning to their companion, he continued. "You said he has a daughter about Lizzy's age, did you not? What is she like?"

After taking a sip from his cup, Mr Darcy returned it to the table before replying. "My cousin Rebecca is twenty. I do not know how to describe her other than to say she is a lovely person. Actually, I believe she reminds me of Miss Elizabeth." He blushed, and his gaze fell to his plate; he busied himself slicing a piece of cheese into bits small enough for a mouse.

"Does she?" Mr Bennet said, looking at Elizabeth and quirking an eyebrow. She gave him a stern head shake, begging him to say nothing further.

"You mean, I suppose, that she likes some of the same things I do—taking walks, reading, avoiding practising the pianoforte as much as she should, occasionally teasing people. And dogs, especially those with uncommon names," she said.

Mr Darcy regarded her and chuckled. "Yes, more or less. She enjoys being in the open air, walking but also riding. She claims her fingers are incapable of finding the right keys on a pianoforte so does not play at all, and she is fond of books, particularly those about travel and exotic locations. She tolerates Budge."

"What is a Budge?" her father asked.

Answering that meant having to explain that she and Mr Darcy had met on several mornings. She had worried how her father would take the news, but he bore it well;

indeed, she did not think he minded at all. She credited that to her admission that she had been reluctant to speak to the gentleman at first—which Mr Darcy confirmed—and telling him about the role Budge had played in encouraging her to listen to him, which made him laugh and tease Mr Darcy for his choice of dog and Elizabeth for only liking him because of Budge.

After completing their repast, they agreed they had best depart, having been absent from their family and friends long enough. They said their farewells in the street, standing by their carriages, which the innkeeper had called for.

"Thank you for including me in your excursion," Mr Darcy said, bowing his head politely.

Elizabeth curtseyed and was about to reply, but her father spoke first.

"Think nothing of it! Plenty of people will have seen us, and since gossip is the most popular sport in the neighbourhood, everyone will know we spent an agreeable couple of hours together. That will surely give them the impression that you do not look down on my daughter or family."

Elizabeth was too shocked to say anything, while Mr Darcy spluttered, "That is not—I assure you, sir—"

Mr Bennet laughed and slapped him on the shoulder; it was not the first time she had seen him do it, and it was yet another sign that he liked him. "If you are to be our friend, we shall have to teach you to recognise a joke! Come along, Lizzy. I swear I can hear your mother and sisters' anxious remarks drifting in the wind, wondering where we are, or more to the point, where the trinkets you bought for them are. We shall see you tomorrow, Mr Darcy. Our regards to your friends."

Not knowing what to say to Mr Darcy, especially with her father beside her, Elizabeth only smiled at him. She was more than satisfied with the look he gave her in return.

Bennet spent the short trip back to Longbourn studying his daughter. Uncharacteristically, she remained silent and looked out of the window, although there was nothing noteworthy to see. He was glad they had happened upon Mr Darcy. To think that he had loathed the man just a few weeks ago and would have been glad never to see him again. He had even wished Mr Bingley had not leased Netherfield. At present, Bennet was quite glad events had unfolded as they had. Thanks to it, he felt a sense of pride in himself he had not experienced in years because he had been willing to undertake the task of improving the lives of his family, all in an effort to ensure their respectability and that no one would dare to insult his daughters again. He also had the prospect of seeing his old friend again, and had he not met the young man, he doubted it would ever have occurred to him to seek out Frederick Darcy.

*It is as well that we shall renew our connexion, because I have a strong notion that our families will be tied together by more than simple friendship one day soon.*

It had been surprising and amusing to learn that Elizabeth and Mr Darcy had met during her early morning walks—and that she had kept it secret. It helped to explain why he had noticed a degree of familiarity between them that went beyond what was expected after only meeting at a few evening parties. Bennet liked Mr Darcy more and more and believed Elizabeth did as well. It was almost painfully evident that the gentleman's appreciation for her fine qualities was growing. If their connexion continued to deepen and reach its natural conclusion, would he be a good husband to his dearest girl? If Jane and Mr Bingley also married—and he was almost certain they would—the girls would be pleased to know their husbands were close friends.

*Stop, you old fool! You are in danger of sounding like your wife. Let the young people sort themselves out. And prepare yourself to give over care of your two most deserving daughters to other men.*

# CHAPTER TWENTY-SIX

Several times—by which he meant closer to several dozen—Darcy asked himself what was happening between himself and Elizabeth. It was nearly impossible to remember what he had thought when he saw her at the assembly and spoke those fateful words. At present, no matter what he was doing or where he was, he was reminded of her again and again. Miss Bingley had made a remark about longing to be in London and attending 'truly elegant entertainments', and he had spent the next interlude reflecting on everything Elizabeth had said about being in town and her opinions of the city. He compared her sentiments to his own: both preferred the country, though her feelings were stronger than his. He supposed that might change when—*if*—he showed her *his* London, if she was able to experience it the way he did rather than from the more modest way her aunt and uncle lived. Strolling on the terrace at Netherfield one morning, he had heard a bird sing—a robin, he guessed—which brought to mind the conversations they had

had about the environs of Hertfordshire and Derbyshire, which had led to speaking about travel.

Was it possible that he was falling in love with her, that *she* was the lady he had been waiting for, the one who would be his life's companion? Was it possible to deny what his heart already knew to be true?

*I must think about this rationally.* He was not a man who acted in haste, and as much as part of him wanted to tell her of his burgeoning affection, he knew it would be better to wait a little longer. They should be friends for more than a brief time before such things were spoken of; if Bingley said that he intended to tell Miss Bennet that he was in love with her, Darcy would advise caution solely based on their short acquaintance, and the couple had not had to overcome the same initial dislike he and Elizabeth had. Although, really, had he ever *disliked* her? He had not appreciated her willingness to dismiss his so-called apology at the church, but in retrospect, she had been correct, and he had come to value the lesson she had imparted that day.

Entering the house after his visit to Meryton, Darcy was glad he had gone—not only because he had seen Elizabeth and her father but because he had escaped the busyness at Netherfield. Servants were rushing back and forth, carrying pieces of furniture or cleaning tools. One young girl almost ran into him as he made his way to the stairs; she looked mortified and apologised, saying, "The mistress says we are to clean the green parlour again. It weren't done good enough."

Miss Bingley appeared and scolded the girl, who scurried away. Darcy planned to seek her out later and

## THE ART OF APOLOGY

give her a coin in recompense; he did not like the harsh tone with which his hostess had spoken to her.

"It is impossible to find good help in the country," Miss Bingley complained. She tucked her hand around his arm and led him towards the large drawing room the family preferred, apparently unconcerned that he had been going in another direction. "You must tell me how you deal with it at Pemberley."

"We seldom have any problems. My butler and housekeeper do an excellent job guiding the younger servants and teaching them to do their work properly, and I support them however I might." His hopes that she had taken his meaning were dashed by her next words.

"Ah, but that is what comes with being in a superior neighbourhood. I am glad, truly I am, that Charles took Netherfield. He can have the satisfaction of knowing he fulfilled my father's wishes, and it was agreeable to go to St Albans. I do not even dislike Meryton. A few of the people are...acceptable, I suppose. But between us, I look forward to my brother quitting the place and finding an estate elsewhere."

To his surprise, rather than enter the drawing room, she continued past it, he assumed to extend their walk. He knew she had once hoped that their connexion would be more than that of friends, but he had believed—and mostly still did—that she understood that he did not view her with particular interest. Still, knowing what her wishes had been, he was uneasy being alone with her for so long and listening to her confidences.

"Should we not join the others?" he said. "Is your brother in the drawing room? There is something—"

"In a minute or two. I must beg your indulgence, Mr Darcy. It is so refreshing to speak to someone other than Louisa, and Charles refuses to admit I am right. I know *you* will understand my sentiments. You are so discerning that you are bound to agree with me." She gave him no time to respond before continuing. "I shall be very glad when the ball is behind us. It is such a lot of work, so many details to see to, and no one to help at all! I *thought* Louisa was going to, but everything has to be decided by me. I ask for her opinion, and she says she does not know, what do I think. I request that she sees to this or that little thing, and if I am fortunate, she does not refuse, but then she leaves it half undone or done so poorly that I end up having to correct it."

"I am sorry to hear that," he murmured when she paused and looked at him expectantly.

"You are most kind. To be sure, Louisa is a willing assistant, and if I tell her exactly what I want, I can trust her to see to it." With a great sigh, she repeated, "I shall be glad once the ball is over!"

Not sure how else to escape the awkward conversation, Darcy claimed a desperate need for a drink, and they made their way to the drawing room. Before entering, Miss Bingley excused herself, promising to join him shortly. Opening the door, Darcy heard Mrs Hurst speaking to her husband, who was the only other occupant.

"I shall strangle Caroline if she does not stop all her useless fussing about and changing her mind every other minute, and if she does not stop treating me like a child. I know more about arranging parties than she does, but will she listen to me? Of course not! *She* knows better than anyone else."

Darcy deliberately made enough noise to alert the couple to his presence; he acted as though he had not overheard, but he was not sure they believed it. After pouring himself a glass of wine, he took a seat, and they sat in silence. Bingley and Miss Bingley walked into the room at almost the same moment.

"Darcy, I am glad you are back," Bingley called. "Glad, too, that it has not rained again. I thought you were wrong to risk it, but, well."

Bingley laughed. It sounded a bit false and too hearty, which Darcy better understood a couple of minutes later. His friend served his sisters and brother-in-law drinks, then sat next to him, leant close, and whispered, "If you care for me at all, make an excuse for us to leave the room and go elsewhere, just the two of us."

Naturally, Darcy did as requested, and they made their way to the library. As he had before, he regarded the mostly empty shelves with dismay and contemplated presenting Bingley with a collection of books as his thanks for having him to stay and his honesty in pointing out how tiresome he was becoming.

"Thank you!" Bingley said as he dropped onto a sofa. "You are a good friend, Darcy."

Darcy chuckled and took a place across from him. "If telling your relations a small lie is all it takes…"

"I am sorry. I know how little you like to deceive anyone, but I believe the good you did to my sanity makes up for it. Caroline and Louisa's behaviour is intolerable! I am happy for you that you took yourself away from it for a while. If only I had gone with you! I am serious. Do not be surprised if you find me running through the house without a stitch of clothing on. Thank God the ball is tomorrow. If I had known what they would be like, I would not have insisted on it."

"What has happened?"

"My sisters are, in true sisterly fashion, constantly in one dispute or another and over the most ridiculous things." His brow furrowed. "Do you suppose the Miss Bennets squabble as much as Louisa and Caroline do? I spoke as if all sisters are like mine, but that cannot be."

Seeing the question was not rhetorical, Darcy said, "I understand Miss Catherine and Miss Lydia do, but they just as quickly get over their differences. It is impossible to imagine Miss Bennet arguing with anyone."

Bingley smiled at the mention of the lady he admired. "No, she would not. She is the loveliest, most gentle lady I have ever met." He fell silent and only continued when Darcy pointedly cleared his throat. "My sisters, however, are spirited, to use a polite word. They insist everything must be perfect for tomorrow evening, yet they feel the effort will be wasted on the people of this neighbourhood—given they are too unfashionable to know the difference between a well-managed ball and a poorly managed one. They have both said as much, yet they go on to assure me that they no longer hate Meryton or think meanly of its residents." He rolled his eyes. "Even worse, they keep complaining to me that the other is not only doing nothing to help but is actually making the task more difficult."

"What you need is a wife," Darcy said, in part to see how his friend would respond. "Then balls and all other amusements would be her responsibility and hers alone." He did not add that Bingley might need to remind his sisters of that, especially Miss Bingley who seemed fond of calling herself Netherfield's mistress, based on the number of times he had heard her say it.

As expected, Bingley's expression softened, and he once again smiled to himself, quietly muttering, "That is not a bad notion."

Darcy left him to his reveries for a moment, after which he told Bingley about seeing Mr Bennet and Elizabeth in Meryton.

"I am glad to see that whole...business so happily concluded," Bingley said. "Furthermore, I have thought that you have been in a better mood of late—other than the day we saw Wickham, which is understandable. Am I mistaken?" Darcy shook his head, and Bingley asked, "Is there any particular reason?"

When Darcy only shrugged, Bingley shook his finger at him, and to forestall further questions, Darcy said, "Let us *not* speculate, if you please. How long do you think we can safely seclude ourselves in here?"

# CHAPTER TWENTY-SEVEN

As Darcy dressed for the ball, he resolved not to hold any expectations of what the night would bring. He had dreamt of dancing with Elizabeth, how he might talk to her whenever possible throughout the evening, how she would laugh and smile at him, and he would drink in her loveliness, impressing everything about her onto his memory. It would sustain him when they were separated. He had determined that he would be wiser not to imagine speaking to her of wishing to deepen their connexion.

Or would he? He needed to return to London soon, but how much should he say to Elizabeth and her father of his growing affection for her before he left? Need he say anything at all, given Bingley's residence in the neighbourhood, which gave Darcy an excuse to return and see the Bennets? It was also probable he would encounter them as Mr Bennet and his cousin Frederick rebuilt their friendship. Surely, he would know what to say and when, if he stopped thinking about it so much and letting his anxiety grow. The easier he was, the less likely he would be to misspeak or struggle to find the right words.

He went downstairs to wait for the guests with Bingley, his family, and the friends from town who had made the trip to attend the ball. Shortly before the first carriages arrived, Miss Bingley pulled him aside.

"Do you approve?" she asked him, peeking up at him through her lashes.

He wondered what exactly she meant—the friends they had invited, the decorations about the house, her attire, the dinner they had enjoyed earlier? "I am anticipating an agreeable evening."

She giggled and playfully slapped his arm. "It is unlike *you* to joke, sir, but I appreciate your attempting to rid me of my nerves."

"I do not take your meaning." He looked over his shoulder to Bingley, hoping to catch his attention and signal that he needed his assistance. But he was occupied with some of the gentlemen.

"I know you dislike both dancing and large parties," she said. "It is good of you not to complain. I would have been happy not to go to all the bother, but Charles had his heart set on a ball, and I am sure I have done my best. He will be happy, at least." She sighed, and he wanted to as well; he had heard her say the same thing countless times. "I hope he agrees to return to town soon. The Festive Season will be upon us before we know it, and I should like to spend it there, amongst my friends. Besides, I worry that he is spending too much time with a certain lady."

"Miss Bennet?"

She dipped her chin in agreement.

"I regret you do not approve. I had thought you liked her."

"I *like* her, but that does not mean I consider her an appropriate wife for him."

This also was not news to Darcy, but unsure how else to respond, he said, "I am afraid we shall have to disagree on that point. If you will excuse me." Darcy stepped away, forcing her to either relinquish his arm or draw attention to her unwillingness to do so. She chose the former, and he went to stand with Bingley.

Before long, there was a steady stream of people entering the house. Darcy kept an eye out for the Bennets and was quick to greet them.

"Oh, Mr Darcy," the matron said. "It is very good to see you. My goodness, Netherfield does look quite the thing, does it not? So many flowers. Mary, you like flowers. Have you seen those white ones? What are they?"

Mrs Bennet took Miss Mary's hand and pulled her towards the blossoms she was curious about. Darcy and Elizabeth exchanged smiles; seeing her left him feeling light, free from worry, and confident that this evening would be one he looked back on with especial fondness for the rest of his life. Bingley came and took Miss Bennet away; he said something about introducing her to his friends that Darcy only half heard.

"Kitty and I are going to see which of the officers are here," Miss Lydia said. "We do not want to stand about like this. It is too—"

"Lydia," Mr Bennet interjected. The young lady

immediately fell silent, though it looked like she was struggling not to speak. "Kitty, you may take your sister to speak to Charlotte and Maria. They are by the window." He pointed in the direction he meant. "I remind you both that if you do not behave with decorum, I shall take you home at once."

"Yes, Papa," Miss Catherine murmured, looking abashed.

Mr Bennet, Elizabeth, and he watched the pair go, and the older gentleman sighed. "Tell me it will be easier with time, Lizzy. Even at your worst, you were never as headstrong as Lydia is."

"Papa! What a thing to say." Elizabeth laughed, giving Darcy yet another reason to value her. Few ladies would treat such a statement with good humour. "You would not want to make Mr Darcy think ill of me, would you?"

Mr Bennet glanced from one of them to the other and back again. He then pinched her cheek, said, "As if anything could," and left them alone.

"Your father has an…interesting sense of humour," Darcy said. He would like to ask the meaning behind Mr Bennet's last remark, but he did not know how. If he had to guess, it seemed like the gentleman recognised that Darcy's interest in his daughter was changing, which led to another question: How did he—and more importantly *she*—feel about it? He *thought* she liked him, but might her sentiments be more than those of friendship?

Once again, Elizabeth laughed. He was growing to love the airy, musical sound she made when she was truly amused or happy. Who was he deceiving? He already did.

"I suppose for someone who is not accustomed to it, it might take getting used to. I know some people are unable to tell when he is teasing or is slyly hiding an insult or criticism in his words despite the length of the connexion. I assure you he was teasing. I believe he finds it amusing that we disliked each other so greatly and hardly a month later, we are…"

She blushed, and he assumed it was because she did not know how to describe what they were to each other. He rejoiced at this sign that she thought well of him and might also believe that 'friend' was too weak a descriptor but 'lovers' was too much. *For which I have only myself to blame. If I had acted as a gentleman should last month, we might now be as close as Bingley and Miss Bennet are.* There was not a doubt remaining, not even a tiny speck. Any pretensions he had once held about the sort of lady he would make his wife—that she would be titled and rich, as his mother was—had been tossed on the rubbish heap. He wanted to marry for affection and friendship and mutual comfort, and he knew with absolute conviction that he and Elizabeth could share the deepest love and happiest of marriages. He only prayed she also believed it, or that he would be able to convince her to see their future the way he did.

To alleviate the awkwardness of the last few minutes, he said, "Friends. I hope you consider me one, at least."

Their eyes met, and, slowly, a beautiful smile overtook her expression. Hardly more than whispering, she said, "I do." The colour in her cheeks became darker, and she averted her gaze.

"Well, my friend," he said, "shall I introduce you to the guests who came from town? They are chiefly ladies and gentlemen Bingley knows well, but I am acquainted with them all, and they are pleasant."

She agreed, and when he held out his arm to her, she readily accepted it. From then until the first set formed, they remained with others, including some of the local residents such as the Miss Lucases, or spoke to a few of the officers who were there. Wickham was not amongst them, naturally, and the Best family had also been excluded. After Mrs Best insulted the Bennets publicly, they had found themselves unwelcome by many, including Bingley.

The first set passed so quickly that Darcy almost did not believe it when the end came. It was remarkable for him, given how little he liked dancing. However, as he was learning, many situations were notably different—and always for the better—when he was with Elizabeth. They had explored several subjects, mostly diversions. She wanted to know how he liked to pass his time when he was in London and at his estate. In turn, she shared more about what she was used to doing in various seasons in Hertfordshire and places she had been in town when visiting her aunt and uncle.

Darcy acknowledged that he could not keep her by his side throughout the night. It would be unseemly; she was asked to dance by other gentlemen, and he had responsibilities to other ladies. Whereas previously he might only have asked Miss Bingley and Mrs Hurst to dance, tonight he stood up with others, including all of Elizabeth's sisters and Miss Lucas. He attempted to approach Miss Maria, although he had seldom spoken to her, but he knew the Lucases and Bennets were intimate friends. However, she ran away from him, and when he mentioned it to Elizabeth, she assured him it was only because the young lady was exceedingly shy. This conversation took place during one of the intervals, and it resulted in him telling her more about Georgiana, who also was excessively reserved amongst strangers.

Just before the supper set, for which they were both engaged with other partners, he asked whether she would dance with him again later in the evening.

"I would like that very much," she said. As had happened earlier, they spent a brief moment simply looking at each other and smiling. In Darcy's opinion, it had been an extraordinary evening already, and the remainder of it promised more delightful moments for him to recollect when they were parted. He was silently drawing plans for the coming months, notably ones that would keep their separation brief.

An image of her father suddenly came to mind. "I wonder whether we should ask your father?"

She furrowed her brow and said, "I do not think it is necessary, but if you would prefer to, we can." She did a half-hearted survey of the crowded room before continuing. "I do not know where he is, but if you were to join us at supper, you might ask him then. He has insisted that my family sit together."

Darcy did his best not to grin or exclaim aloud at her suggestion. He supposed they should take supper with the people they would attend during the forthcoming set, but he was willing to make an exception to be with her. His partner was the sister of an acquaintance; she was engaged to another of Bingley's friends and was unlikely to object to him leaving her with her brother and betrothed. As for Elizabeth, she would be escorted by one of the young Mr Lucases, and her demeanour told Darcy that he would not care that she sat with her family rather than him. Thus, satisfied that no one would be insulted, he agreed.

# CHAPTER TWENTY-EIGHT

It had been impulsive to ask Mr Darcy to sit with her and her family during supper, but Elizabeth was glad that she had. She was having a wonderful time, and it was entirely due to him. Her feelings for him had changed so quickly that it left her dizzy and occasionally questioning whether it was real or she was caught up in a dream. At present, there was nothing about him she did not like. She was wise enough to know that it was unrealistic to view anyone as faultless. But she was not a simpleton. She acknowledged that one of her flaws was a tendency to quickly sketch a person's character and refuse to admit she might be mistaken. In October, Mr Darcy had left more than her with a very poor view of him, and it was possible she would have clung to it forever no matter what he did or said if it had not been for two interventions: her father's warning and Budge, and she was grateful to both. It was meeting the little dog and observing Mr Darcy with him that struck the initial blow to her resentment and dislike. Since then, each time they were together, she found more to admire in him.

*I think he feels the same for me,* she told herself as she moved through the steps of the supper set with Mr John Lucas. Reprimanding herself, she attempted to pay attention to the young man standing across from her, not the one farther down the line. She must not let herself believe she understood Mr Darcy's sentiments; if she was mistaken, her disappointment would be acute. Until he said something, gave some hint that he hoped their connexion might become more than it currently was, she must guard her heart. Given her nature, doing so would be difficult, but she would try. *And pray he gives either Papa or me an indication of his feelings sooner rather than later!* Once he did, the tumult of her emotions would settle down, and she could allow her affection for him to fully blossom.

Supper was as agreeable as the rest of the ball had been, despite Elizabeth having to share Mr Darcy's attention with her family. Jane was not there; Mr Bennet had given his leave for her to sit with Mr Bingley. The crowd being what it was, it took Elizabeth some time to see where they were, but once she did, it was evident that her sister was happy. His younger sister and several of his London friends were with Jane and Mr Bingley, and they appeared to be having a lively conversation.

Mrs Bennet welcomed Mr Darcy warmly and immediately told him about a recent letter she had received from Mrs Gardiner. "I wrote to her about you being from

Derbyshire, and she recalls your family. Not you, exactly—she moved in rather different circles—but she knows of you and used to see your mother and father when they would go to Lambton." She paused to take a sip of wine. "She said that knowing we have met you has made her wild to return to her childhood home again. I shall tell her to convince my brother to take her as soon as he can manage it, but he is an excellent husband and is likely already planning to do just that. Whatever can bring her pleasure, he will do."

It was not only Mrs Bennet who wanted a portion of Mr Darcy's attention; her sisters did as well. Kitty and Lydia wanted to talk about London, and since they had learnt that he had a younger sister, desired to know all about her, especially what her wardrobe was like. He could not answer those questions other than to say, "Her clothing is very pretty, just as yours is." Hearing that Miss Darcy loved music interested Mary, and he was asked about her favourite composers and the like.

"Girls, you must allow Mr Darcy to eat his supper," Mrs Bennet said several times. "Everything is delicious and so well prepared, but I would expect nothing less. When Jane and Mr Bing—"

"Mrs Bennet," her husband interjected, speaking softly but firmly. Elizabeth knew he had forbidden her mother from speculating on their marriage prospects.

She regarded him, her lips formed an 'o', and she nodded. "As I was saying, the food is delicious. Instead of asking him so many questions, why do you not talk amongst yourselves or-or tell him what music you like,

Mary. Kitty and Lydia, you have been reading those books your father gave you. You can tell him about them."

"But quietly, please. There is more than enough noise in the room as it is," her father said.

Elizabeth met Mr Darcy's eye, trying to silently enquire whether he minded her sisters demanding all his attention, and received a slight but decided head shake in response. Nevertheless, she did her best to make sure they did not vex him. Her mother had turned to her neighbours—several other matrons—and remained occupied with them.

"I think you can stop worrying about Mr Darcy, Lizzy," her father whispered to her part way through the meal. "He is made of stern enough stuff to cope with the three of them, now that they have become less silly, and if he is not and he intends to continue to partake of our society, he had best find a way. Are you enjoying yourself?"

"I am. Are you?"

He slowly inclined his head. "I would rather be at home, where it is quieter, and I do not believe there will ever be a time I say otherwise, but it is not so bad. I have had to correct your sisters less than I expected, which I take as a victory, and I do like seeing you, your sisters, and your mother looking so lovely and happy."

She kissed his cheek. "That was a very kind thing to say, Papa, and I thank you on behalf of us all. As for your other remark, I *would* consider it a victory. I am grateful for what you are doing, and they are—or will be—too."

Again, he nodded. "I have noticed that you and Mr Darcy have often been together."

She did not know what to say to that statement so chose not to address it. "He has asked me for another set. Do you object?"

This time, her father shrugged. "I do not see that it has anything to do with me. If you have not grown fatigued of his company, I suppose you ought to accept."

Feeling heat creeping into her cheeks, she busied herself with her glass of wine. At an opportune moment, she informed Mr Darcy that they had her father's permission, news he greeted with such a look of satisfaction that anticipation for what lay ahead swelled in her chest. She did not know what it would be, but before she returned to Longbourn that night, *something* between them would have altered; she was convinced of it, and that it would make her even more joyful than she currently was.

When at last they danced together again, she found Mr Darcy to be distracted, but in a subtle manner she would not have been able to describe if pressed to explain. He continued to look at her a great deal, and it would have taken a much better imagination than her own to discover any hint that he was displeased or disapproved of spending time with her. Yet, it was apparent his thoughts were heavy.

"Is something worrying you?" she asked, knowing it was unlikely the other dancers were interested in what they said to each other, even if they could hear it over the music, the footfalls on the wooden floors, and the voices filling the large ballroom.

"I-I beg your pardon. My mind was elsewhere."

She offered him a polite smile that suggested it did not matter, but it was a blow, albeit a small one, given how great her earlier enthusiasm had been. Even if she was not the cause of his distraction, her company was not enough to make him set aside his cares for half an hour. Curiosity, seeking to assure herself she had done nothing wrong—or that he had witnessed her family behaving in a manner he found distasteful—provoked her to ask, "May I enquire what has you so lost in thought?"

There was a pause before he answered. He looked about them and waited until the pattern brought them closer together, then whispered into her ear, "You."

She gaped at him; a shiver ran down her spine. They completed the set in silence, and as soon as she had curtseyed and he had bowed, he took her hand and drew her into a quiet corner of the room. Her heart thudded in her chest, and her mouth was too dry to permit speech. All she could do was wait with as much patience as she could for him to relieve her curiosity by explaining himself.

"I was a fool the night of the assembly. More than a fool. An idiot. How could I ever have looked at *you* and let such hateful words pass my lips? I might be rewriting what happened in my memories, but I believe I knew they were false even as I said them. You, Miss Elizabeth Bennet, *are* handsome enough to tempt me, more than beautiful enough for even the most fastidious of men, and even a quarter of an hour in your company would provide the stupidest man with a long list of attractions that would have them stumbling over their feet in their haste to earn your approbation."

She laughed and blushed and shook her head, but he was not finished yet. Surreptitiously, he lightly clasped her fingers.

"You are intelligent and curious and charming and caring, and"—he exhaled audibly—"you tempt me as I have never been tempted before. To slight you, a man would have to be blind—in spirit if not physically—and so I was. I could see you, but I refused to *see* you. It was not until you insisted I apologise properly that my eyes began to open. You have made me view the world about me and the people in it with greater clarity, and I shall forever be grateful, especially because it means I have had the chance to know you."

"Oh, Mr Darcy," she whispered, almost too overwhelmed to say more. "I would say you have learnt to apologise properly. You have exceeded every expectation I ever had." Her last statement encompassed more than how well he had delivered his words of contrition; she wondered whether he knew that or whether she would ever be brave enough to tell him.

He chuckled and pressed one of his hands to his chest; the other was still wrapped about her fingers, which she curled as much as possible, hoping he felt the pressure of her grasp.

"There is so much I want to say to you," he said. "I feel the words knocking at the back of my teeth. But my rational self tells me it is too soon. There is no rush, and if I ask too much of you, I would be acting foolishly once again. I suspect you, your father, perhaps even I, would be more comfortable with a delay—a slight delay—before I...make my wishes for our future plain."

Her free hand flew to her mouth, and tears filled her eyes. She managed to nod and say, "A part of me wishes to disagree, but I know you are right."

He pulled her hand to his lips and kissed it. "Then we shall postpone the rest of *that* conversation."

"And take the time to relish this period," she said, silently adding, *the one in which we continue to fall in love and dream of what our lives—our life together—will be.*

The colour of his eyes deepened. "I intend to savour every moment. Earlier, I was trying to determine how we might see each other as often as possible in the coming weeks. I must return to town soon, to see my sister and relations."

"Miss Darcy must be missing you. I would not ever want to keep you from her." She would be displeased with any man who attempted to separate her from her sisters. Mr Darcy liked her family and would never limit her intercourse with them; she would extend the courtesy to him in return.

A bubble of joy made her warm and a little dizzy. He *did* feel as she did. She would not leave Netherfield an engaged woman that night, but in the not-too-distant future, he *would* propose, and she would accept. "I hope I shall be able to meet her soon."

Her hand was still in his, and he gently pressed it. "I have had an idea or two about that. I must consider it a little more, but we shall speak of it in a day or two, if that is acceptable."

"Of course it is. Would it be too bold of me to say

that all that matters to me is that we shall have more time together?"

He grinned—she did likewise—and had just opened his mouth to speak when they were interrupted by one of his acquaintances.

# CHAPTER TWENTY-NINE

It was all Darcy could do not to whisk his Elizabeth away to where they could be alone. He supposed he should not call her *his* Elizabeth yet; he had not proposed—as tempted as he had been to do so—but regardless, she was his, and he was hers. He was content to wait for the day when their understanding would be a formal one—so long as that day happened within the next two months. Ideally less.

But they were at a ball, and other people had a right to their attention. He did not dance again, since he could not ask her a third time. She had already accepted a request for a set, and while she was with her partner, Darcy sought out Mr Bennet. He had no particular purpose other than having grown to appreciate his company and wanting to be on good terms with the man who would become his father-in-law.

"Ah, Mr Darcy. I do not see Lizzy. Have you lost her?" Mr Bennet said.

"She is dancing with Captain Farmer. I trust your

remark was not an indication that you believe I have been spending too much time with her. If you have any such concerns, I beg you would speak to me of them."

Mr Bennet pursed his lips and shook his head. They were standing near a window—fortunately open to let some much-needed fresh air into the room—and Mr Bennet was turned towards the crowd, not Darcy. That, and the dim candlelight, made it difficult to see his expression.

"I am glad the two of you are on better terms. Since discovering that my old friend is your cousin, I have often reflected that, had we not let our correspondence lapse, you and Lizzy—and my other girls—would have known each other since childhood. It is an interesting notion, is it not? I wonder what difference it would have made to your lives."

"I suppose we shall never know." He did not find it helpful to reflect on what might have been; he had done enough of that after Ramsgate. Wickham being in Meryton was one of the issues he needed to sort out in making plans for the coming weeks. He had been considering speaking to Bingley about bringing Georgiana and her companion to Netherfield at Christmas, but he would only do so if he was confident she would not have to see the reprobate. Perhaps he would speak to Mr Bennet about it—and Elizabeth, naturally.

"True. I have been hearing a fair bit of gossip this evening. Recent events have taught me to pay attention to such things."

When Mr Bennet paused and regarded him out of the corner of his eye, Darcy said, "Oh?"

"About you."

"Me?" Darcy exclaimed, alarm shooting through him. What had he heard, and what effect would it have on his relationship with Elizabeth and her family? And why was it taking Mr Bennet so long to tell him?

"There is no doubt. Some of it was said to my wife, and she was quick to mention it to me. I do not know who approached her, but I have heard the same sentiment from several people, and they specifically mention your name." The gentleman gave him an amused smile. "How happy they—meaning you and my Lizzy—seem together, and what a handsome couple you make. Oddly, my wife had not considered the possibility that you might develop...well, let us just call it an interest in Lizzy. She still has not, as incredible as that sounds. I believe it is a combination of her attention being on another couple and her understanding that we wanted to correct the notion that you found Lizzy lacking. Mrs Bennet was happy to assure me that now no one will ever remember that horrible assembly, as she called it, and although I was not there to witness it myself, I suppose I would give it the same name too. My wife thinks that you and Lizzy are very clever for how you are acting. I found her ignorance—which I shall correct soon—quite diverting, though not for all the gold in the world would I laugh at her." He made a rueful noise. "I would not *now*. I believe you and I have both learnt to be more careful with our words, and I know I am much improved for it."

He continued before Darcy had a chance to devise a response. "Then there was Sir William, who said to me that you seem to find my daughter handsome and more tolerable company now. I shall not speak to him for at least a week for that. I would prefer not to hear that word for a decade. It is becoming too much of a joke in the neighbourhood, and it has never been and never will be at all diverting. He also went on about the pair of you taking an interesting—his word, not mine—path to liking each other, and that it reminded him of something from one of his wife's novels. How, I ask myself, does he know what is in the astonishingly silly books I know Lady Lucas and my wife both enjoy so much?" Mr Bennet turned to face Darcy directly. "What do you have to say to all that?"

Darcy considered making a quip about not being familiar with Mrs Bennet's reading habits but thought better of it. "I suppose it will be an entertaining tale to share with future generations."

Mr Bennet grinned and patted his arm. "I look forward to sharing it with them, with an embellishment or two just for fun."

Darcy chuckled, and they returned to observing the dancing.

Two days after the ball, Mr Darcy called at Longbourn. He brought Mr Bingley with him, but—as much as Elizabeth liked him—it was not his company she desired at present. Without doubt, it was the opposite for Jane. The sisters had shared confidences regarding the gentlemen during a long conversation the previous day. Jane had been surprised at Elizabeth's disclosure regarding her feelings, chiefly that she had been wholly unaware of how much her connexion with Mr Darcy had improved. Elizabeth learnt that, like Mr Darcy, Jane's beau had hinted that he hoped to propose soon.

"I believe he wanted to know whether I would be receptive to receiving his offer," Jane had said.

"And will you?"

The look of joy on her sister's face had been answer enough, not that Elizabeth had needed one. For above an hour, the sisters had dreamt of the future, beginning with a double wedding and ending with many exquisitely happy years in which they, their husbands, and their children were the closest of families and friends.

Mrs Bennet fussed over the callers, and there was a general discussion of the ball—the Bennets expressing their gratitude to Mr Bingley yet again. Kitty and Lydia were especially fervent with their thanks, and they promptly asked him when the next one would be.

"Girls!" their mother cried. "You must not be greedy. You have no notion how much work is required to host such a large party, or how much money. I am sure Miss Bingley has no wish to go through it all again. An opportunity will arise sooner or later. Perhaps when there is something *particular* to celebrate, Mr Bingley will consider hosting another."

"You mean when he marries Jane?" Kitty said, only to be immediately told to hold her tongue by Mrs Bennet, while Mr Bennet proclaimed it an excellent moment for Kitty, Lydia, and him to talk about something else in another room.

A short while later, Elizabeth and Mr Darcy were at last able to speak on their own.

"I wanted to come yesterday," he explained. "But with the guests from town delaying their departure until well after breakfast, it proved impossible. By the time I was able to discuss a few matters with Bingley, it was too late to call."

Elizabeth dismissed his implied apology. "You would have found us all insipid company, me especially. No matter how late I retire, I always wake up early, and I felt half asleep all day."

Mr Darcy regarded her with undisguised fondness, and it thrilled her to know that their period of hiding their mutual affection from each other was at an end. "First, I shall never find your company insipid, and second, I am the same way. I believe I nodded off during dinner, which was most embarrassing. I think Hurst had to kick my foot to wake me up at one point."

She giggled. "I would have liked to have seen you yesterday, and I know Jane feels the same about Mr Bingley, but I understand. Have all Mr Bingley's friends left?"

"They have. Bingley considered going with them to attend to some business matter, but I suggested he delay a day or two so that we could go together. I wish I could be here and in London at once, but I cannot, and since I have been here longer than originally anticipated, it would be wrong of me to extend my time further. My sister is expecting me, as I believe I told you the other night, and my relations, who have been in the country, are now in town. I am referring to my aunt and uncle

Romsley—my mother's brother and his wife—and their two sons, with whom I am good friends."

"Eventually, I shall understand the construction of your family, but at present, all I know is that you have more relations than I do."

This earned her another smile, after which he said, "My cousin, your father's old friend, is also there, with his family. I have reason to see them all, beyond those of love and duty." He gave an impatient head shake. "I am not explaining it well. I have a scheme in mind, and Bingley has agreed to it. I would like your opinion, and, if you approve, I shall speak to your father."

Elizabeth's eyes opened a little wider. "I am curious what you might need both my father's and my approval for." Other than a proposal of marriage, that was, and she knew he was not thinking of that.

"I asked Bingley whether he would be agreeable to me returning and bringing my sister and her companion to spend Christmas at Netherfield."

"Did you?" she exclaimed, suddenly far more eager for the Festive Season. She always enjoyed that time of year, but knowing Mr Darcy would be amongst them—along with his sister, whom she longed to meet—left her wanting to immediately begin planning amusements and as many excuses as possible for them to spend hours together every day.

He nodded. "He considers it the most wonderful idea he has heard in months, though I suspect he was exaggerating." They shared a laugh, and his demeanour grew more serious. "My only hesitation in bringing Georgiana here is Wickham."

"Oh, of course," Elizabeth said, instantly sobering and touching his hand briefly. "But surely they would not see each other? I suppose they might accidentally, such as in Meryton, if Miss Darcy wished to go there one morning. He is not welcome at Longbourn or in the homes of those we customarily see, so there is no danger there."

"I had hoped you would help me determine how I shall keep Georgiana from having to see him, and already, you have alleviated most of my concern. I can now see that it will be easily accomplished. Georgiana is not yet out, but I and my cousin, with whom I share guardianship, permit her to attend some functions. If she returned to Meryton with me, I would hope to take her with me to smaller parties—here or at Netherfield, certainly, and perhaps some others. There would be no chance of an encounter then. I told you that she is shy, and while I do not fear she would be excessively distressed at seeing him, she would be embarrassed, and it would rob her of the good cheer I know she will otherwise experience here."

This mark of his care and goodness, and knowing what it signalled for her own future, made Elizabeth's eyes sting with tears; she blinked them away. "Could you not ask Colonel Forster when Mr Wickham will not be out and about? That way, we could arrange to visit Meryton one day. I am sure my sisters would like to show Miss Darcy the shops, even knowing they are not as fine as those she is accustomed to. It is diverting for us, and I assume another young lady would be equally as glad to sort through ribbons and such to pass the time."

"She would," he said, sounding pleased with the suggestion. "We could arrange to take refreshments at the inn, as we did with your father."

They spoke of several other ways they might amuse themselves. Elizabeth told him that Mr and Mrs Gardiner would almost certainly come to Longbourn, which would add to their festivities. He gratified her by saying how much he anticipated meeting them. Mr Darcy then raised another matter.

"As I said, when I am in town, I shall be seeing my family. Lady Romsley has a Twelfth Night ball every year. I am required to attend. She would not speak to me for a year if anything other than grave illness kept me away."

She laughed, delighted with his increasingly obvious sense of humour; she supposed it was easier for him to show it since he was more comfortable with her and her family.

He continued, "Would you be able to return to London with Mr and Mrs Gardiner so that you might go with me? You and Miss Bennet both. I would like to dance with you at it."

"Truly?" For a few seconds, she was light-headed. He wanted to take her to his aunt's—a countess's—ball in London. Although she knew he had titled relations, she had not before considered that they would become her own if—*when*—they married. "Would she invite us? I assume Mr Bingley is attending." Even meeting an earl and countess was beyond what she had ever expected to experience. But she was confident enough in her worth not to cower or be fearful, and her enthusiasm to go to such a grand event was already growing.

"He is, and yes, if I ask it of her, she would. She would include your aunt and uncle, of course, as your chaperons."

Surreptitiously taking a deep breath to clear her head, Elizabeth said, "My aunt and uncle are always happy for us to stay, but I shall write to them at once to ensure there is no reason it would be inconvenient. My father could inform you of their response, if you agreed." She did not think he would object to corresponding with her father, but it was courteous to enquire.

Their solitude was soon interrupted, but Elizabeth was resigned to sharing him with her sisters and parents, all of whom appeared to have forgotten how much they had initially despised him. Either that or they were willing to never speak of the night of October 18, 1811 again. In time, they might all succeed in forgetting there had been an assembly on that date. Though why should she wish it? After all, it had been the day she and Mr Darcy first met, and, as Shakespeare said, 'all's well that ends well'.

Before the gentlemen departed, Mr Bingley explained that he had errands to see to in London, would leave the following day, and anticipated an absence of no more than a week. Mr Darcy would be gone longer—perhaps up to three weeks—but he vowed to see them all before Christmas.

# CHAPTER THIRTY

The following Tuesday, Jane received a note from Miss Bingley, announcing that she and the Hursts had gone to London.

> *We are anxious to be amongst our friends after so long an absence. Despite what our brother said about soon returning to Netherfield, Louisa and I agree that, once reminded of the delights of being in town, he will not want to. We imagine that, even now, he is thinking of writing to urge us to join him.*
>
> *I shall always be so grateful that we were able to learn something of Hertfordshire and that Charles can be satisfied that he has fulfilled our father's wish. Your company and the warm welcome extended to us by your family and neighbours has been most appreciated.*
>
> *With fond regards,*
> *Miss Caroline Bingley*

Jane had come into Elizabeth's chamber to show the missive to her. They were sitting on the bed together, and having read it, Elizabeth folded the fine paper and tossed it onto the small painted table to her side. She looked at Jane, who was nervously nibbling her bottom lip, and rolled her eyes.

"You do not think she is correct, do you?" Jane asked. "That Mr Bingley might change his mind about coming back."

Elizabeth took hold of her hands. "No, my dearest sister, I do not, and I do not believe you do either. Has Mr Bingley given you any indication that he could be so fickle?"

Jane shook her head. "It is just that...I *do* care for him, and my heart would break if he did not."

Elizabeth linked their fingers together. "Mr Bingley adores you, as he should. Mr Darcy has also promised to return, and I have complete confidence in his word—just as you ought to in Mr Bingley's. Unfortunately, his sisters are not as fond of the neighbourhood as he is. I also suspect they hope to separate him from you. I am sorry to say it because I know you think of them as friends. As kind as they were"—*to you,* she silently added—"I have reason to think they want him to purchase an estate in a county they find more acceptable and to make a brilliant match—one that will assist with their social ambitions. Fortunately, Mr Bingley is wise enough to know that he should choose his home and his wife to please himself, with his happiness in mind." The source of her information was Mr Darcy, but she would not disclose it without his permission.

Jane lowered her eyes and frowned. "I thought the ladies liked me."

"I believe they do. Who would not?"

"Their disapproval will disappoint Mr Bingley. *If* he decides to propose to me."

Elizabeth laughed. "You know he will. *I* know he will. *Everyone* who has seen you together knows he will. Mrs Hurst and Miss Bingley will resign themselves to his decision, and I shall think them despicable creatures if they do not grow to love you and admit that he was right to settle on you within two years of your marriage. We shall see your Mr Bingley very soon—by Thursday, or perhaps Friday—and then you must pity me. Mr Darcy will not return for another fortnight or longer."

True to her prediction, Mr Bingley was once again ensconced at Netherfield Park by the end of the week. He was unconcerned about his family's departure when Mrs Bennet mentioned it to him, saying only that, "I understand they received several invitations they did not feel they should refuse, including from Hurst's family," and that he was unsure when they would be in Hertfordshire next.

He spoke more freely to Elizabeth and Jane when the three of them walked into Meryton together several days later. The afternoon was as warm and fair as it was right to expect in early December, and Mary, Kitty, and Lydia formed a trio ahead of them. Their purpose in going was to search for small Christmas gifts for Mr and Mrs Bennet and the Gardiners.

"They talked a lot of nonsense," Mr Bingley said, sounding exasperated. "It was nothing I had not heard before. I *like* Meryton, to say nothing of the people I have met here." There was a pause during which Elizabeth pretended not to see the affectionate looks he and her sister exchanged. "I told them I was fixed at Netherfield for...well, I do not know how long. In part, it depends on the owners. They were not interested in selling the estate when Darcy and I enquired last summer, but I do not know whether they will hold to that or when they will wish to return. In any event, this is where I choose to be."

"How could they ask you to stay in town when you and Mr Darcy had already agreed that he would bring his sister here for Christmas?" Jane said. "It would be going back on your word."

"Which I would not do," Mr Bingley said with a firm nod. "I would never want to disappoint Darcy, who has always been a good friend to me. I had the impression my sisters did not believe he was serious about spending Christmas here or thought that he would change his mind now he is in London." He turned to Elizabeth. "I have forgotten to give you his message. He begged me to tell you that everything is arranged, and he will be in Hertfordshire on the twentieth, unless the weather delays their journey."

"Their? It is certain that Miss Darcy will be coming with him?" Elizabeth asked.

Mr Bingley nodded. "I knew Darcy liked you, but his actually requesting that I pass on his assurances... You have made a conquest, Miss Elizabeth, and I can name a dozen young ladies who would be wildly envious if they knew."

All three of them laughed. Mr Bingley mentioned that his friend had spoken to his aunt about invitations to her ball, assuring her and Jane that, "He has arranged all that, too, and either you will receive Lady Romsley's card in the post or he will bring it with him." To Jane, he added, "You *will* be able to accept?"

Jane smiled serenely and nodded. "My aunt wrote to say that they would be very happy to take us to town with them after Christmas and accompany us to the ball."

Peeking around the gentleman to her sister, Elizabeth said, "I believe you and I have gowns to shop for. Do you think Mr Bingley would object if we spent a short while—no more than two hours—looking at fabric?"

Their laughter was hearty enough that Mary, Kitty, and Lydia demanded to know what was so amusing.

IN HER OWN WORDS, GEORGIANA WAS delighted to hear that Darcy had met a special lady. That is what he had called Elizabeth when he informed his sister what had kept him away so long. His happiness was such that he had told her almost as soon as he had arrived at his town house. She had also sounded surprised, for reasons he did not understand, but her eagerness to meet Elizabeth had only grown the more he described her. She had readily agreed to spend Christmas in Hertfordshire, even when he had warned her of Wickham's presence in the neighbourhood.

Furrowing her brow and sounding shocked at the notion that it would disturb her, she said, "What do I care about *that*? When will you propose? Do you think she will like having me as a sister? Did you say she has four others already? What are they like? What are their names and ages?"

They were in her apartment, and once she had voiced her final question—not even waiting for him to respond—she rose from the sofa and went to her writing table, saying, "I must begin to make preparations for our departure." She listed items she must remember to pack, notes to send to friends she had intended to see in the coming weeks, and purchases she wished to make.

"We shall not leave for some time," he reminded her.

Her back was to him, and thus he could not see her expression, but she shook her head.

"There is so much to do," she said. "You cannot imagine, Brother. If I am not confident I have seen to it all, I shall be nervous when I meet her. She might be my sister! I hope she will be. She sounds perfectly lovely. She must be since you are so much happier than you were when you went away. I do not want her to hate me because I am flustered when we first meet."

Darcy wondered whether her rather exaggerated notions were a common occurrence amongst young ladies of her age. He did not know enough about them to make a comparison, but Elizabeth might have some valuable insight.

"Georgiana," he said. She made a noise that indicated she had heard him. "It has lately come to my attention that I was in a particularly disagreeable mood last summer. I am sorry for it."

He watched as her body stilled, and, after a pause, she slowly turned to face him. Her voice was small when she said, "You owe me no apology. It was my fault."

"No," he said firmly, shaking his head in emphasis. He had wanted to acknowledge his poor behaviour, which must have affected her as it had Bingley, Elizabeth, and many others, and he was glad he had; it told him that she had blamed herself, and it was important that she realise he and he alone was responsible for his actions. Beyond that, it was Wickham who was the cause of his unhappiness, not her. He attempted to explain that he had been angry with the man he had once considered his dearest friend and disappointed in himself for failing to do his job of protecting her adequately. That led to a longer conversation about Ramsgate and his recent history with Wickham, and he told her a little of what had happened when he had first arrived in Meryton. Part way through, she returned to her former place near him.

"I am even gladder that you met Miss Elizabeth," she said. "She *has* made you happier, and I shall love her for that alone. Is her father really an old friend of Uncle Darcy's?" She was as astonished by the coincidence as he had been.

"He is, and they are both desirous of renewing their connexion. I shall call on him in a day or two, if you would like to come with me. Aunt Darcy and Cousin Rebecca will wish to see you."

She said that she would, then asked whether she might return to her preparations. "I still want to hear more about the Bennet girls, but perhaps you can tell me at dinner. I shall talk to Mrs Annesley as soon as she returns from her errands. I am sure she will be agreeable to going with us to Meryton since she had not planned to see her family until the spring. Oh, I just remembered something I must add to my list!"

After attempting to speak to her of her activities since he had been away or anything other than Elizabeth and Hertfordshire and receiving no reply, he left her to her task.

# CHAPTER THIRTY-ONE

Darcy's discussion with his relations went as well as expected. He called on the earl and countess and his cousins Viscount Bramwell and Colonel Fitzwilliam the following day, and once they had shared recent news, he told them that he had met a lady he intended to marry.

"Are you engaged?" Bramwell said. "Before me? I am three years your elder."

"Which is a sure sign that you had better stop amusing yourself and get serious about settling down," Lady Romsley said in a reprimanding tone. "We all know you have found your lady. I shall refrain from asking when you will propose—for now."

Before the conversation became about his cousin's romantic life or anyone mistook his position, Darcy explained, "No, I have not yet proposed to her, but I am confident that I shall. For her sake, I thought it would be better if we knew each other a little longer. There are... reasons."

"Oh?" Lord Romsley said, fixing a stern eye on him. "I take this news to mean you have given up any notion of marrying Anne. It would be an excellent match for both of you, uniting the Darcy and de Bourgh fortunes. Who is this lady who has captivated you? Tell us about her. Everything we need to know, if you please. I do not want to discover some important fact later." He, like the countess, was a caring person, but both he and his wife took their responsibilities to the family's reputation and future seriously.

"Sir, you know I was never especially interested in marrying my cousin, no matter how prudent a financial decision it would be." The earl made a gesture that signified reluctant acceptance, and Darcy proceeded to tell them about Elizabeth, being sure not to hide what they might find difficult to approve of, chiefly her lack of connexions and fortune and the situation of Mrs Bennet's relations. He also emphasised everything admirable about her—her character, Mr Bennet's intelligence and friendship with Frederick Darcy, and their family's long history as landowners.

"You are happy when you are with her?" Lady Romsley said.

Darcy blushed, which embarrassed him and made him feel like a child, only serving to make his cheeks grow hotter. "I am."

His cousin Fitzwilliam laughed. "It has finally happened! You, the most stoic, fastidious man I have ever known, have fallen in love."

Everyone responded in one fashion or another. Bramwell called the comment harsh, but nevertheless laughed, while the earl and countess reprimanded Fitzwilliam for being cruel.

Darcy said, "I am not fastidious." He *had* been, but he was finding life was far more agreeable if he judged people by how they acted and not who their parents were or the size of their fortune. Having rightly earned Elizabeth's disdain and that of many others, he understood how unpleasant it was to be dismissed as unworthy of their attention. At the same time that he was beginning to view people more generously, he learnt to want them to see him as more than a wealthy, well-connected gentleman with a large estate and titled relations.

Lord Romsley demanded they be serious. "I admit I am concerned, Nephew. You hardly know this girl. I am relieved you have not yet committed yourself, but the whole business seems unlike you. Too impetuous."

"I understand why you feel that way, but I assure you, I know with everything that I am, *she* is the lady I am meant to marry. She will be an excellent wife to me and sister to Georgiana."

"And you are happy when you are with her," Lady Romsley stated, giving her husband a rather pointed look. "Once, long ago, your uncle claimed to know within a day of meeting me that I was the lady for him."

"Perhaps old age is robbing him of his memory," Bramwell said, trying but failing to appear sombre. Sitting beside him, Fitzwilliam sniggered.

"That is enough from the pair of you," the earl said. Regarding Darcy, he sighed. "It is true that emotions can lead you where sober reflection might suggest you should not go." Darcy opened his mouth to interject, but Lord Romsley held up a finger to stop him. "I do not say that Miss Elizabeth Bennet would be an unwise choice. I only meant that she does not seem like the sort of young woman any of us expected you to marry."

"Unlike Anne?" Fitzwilliam asked.

Bramwell added, "He would never have been happy with her, and I do not believe she wants to marry him any more than he does her."

"And before anyone proposes it, I shall not marry her either," Fitzwilliam said. "Lady Catherine would not approve, and Anne and I would suit even less than she and Darcy."

Lord Romsley scowled at his sons, but before he spoke, the countess did, addressing Darcy.

"I share your uncle's trepidation, but I am looking forward to meeting her and forming my own opinion. Will she come to town soon?"

"I am hoping you will agree to invite her to the Twelfth Night ball. She has relations in London with whom she is accustomed to staying, and she is certain they would welcome her after Christmas. Her elder sister would accompany her."

He explained Bingley's interest in Miss Bennet and that he would appreciate the Gardiners also being included. As expected, his description of Mr Gardiner's place in the world was greeted with dismay, especially by the earl and countess, though they did a good job of masking it because of their love for and trust in him. Lady Romsley looked at Lord Romsley, giving the impression that she wanted to know what he thought before deciding; after a brief pause, he gave a slight nod.

"Very well," she said. "I shall ask all four of them to attend. Mr Bingley and his family are already on my guest list, as you know. Before you leave today, please give me the necessary directions."

Darcy went to kiss her cheek. "Thank you." Upon returning to his seat, he raised the question of Lady Catherine. "I can at last tell her that I have found a lady I want to marry. She has told me often enough that she will not cease to promote her daughter as an appropriate bride until I do. I have been wondering whether I should go to Kent to inform her before returning to Hertfordshire. What is your opinion, sir?"

The question was directed at Lord Romsley, though both of his cousins said he must be mad to consider it, as any visit to the de Bourghs was only likely to vex him and thus result in him returning to Elizabeth ill-tempered and irritable.

"She would send you packing at once," Fitzwilliam said.

Little did his cousin know that she was well aware of how horribly he could act and had seen past it. If he was in a bad mood because his visit to Kent had gone poorly, Elizabeth would do everything in her power to cheer him; just being with her would do the trick. With Lady Catherine in his thoughts, he realised that having Elizabeth with him would make visiting Rosings much easier to bear, which would be a good thing for his connexion to his aunt. Not that she would see it that way; if anything, she would be horrible to Elizabeth, in which case, Darcy would avoid seeing his aunt and cousin again.

"Miss Bennet is made of sterner stuff than that," he said.

"I am glad to hear it," Bramwell said. "She will need to be to tolerate you."

"And you two," Lady Romsley said to her sons.

Lord Romsley's advice was that Darcy should not go to Kent. "Wait until you and Miss Elizabeth have settled things. Even then, I suggest writing to my sister about her. Once you are married—supposing that is what the future holds for you—you can present her to Catherine as Mrs Darcy. She is more likely to treat her respectfully, then."

"Mind that he said 'more likely'," Fitzwilliam said. "We all know Lady Catherine will despise any girl who marries you who is not Anne."

"I propose we worry about that only when we must. Perhaps Catherine will surprise us all," Lady Romsley said. "Now, tell us more about Miss Elizabeth."

Mr Darcy returned exactly when he said he would, and Elizabeth was almost overwhelmed by all she felt upon seeing him again. It was as though his brief absence had made her believe that she liked him less than she did—and she knew it was a great deal—but then, as soon as she saw him, she was so happy that tears filled her eyes. There was only one word for what she experienced: love. True, ever-deepening love.

"Mr Darcy," she said, her voice softer and holding

more meaning than she had intended, given they were surrounded by her family and several others—Mr Bingley, a girl who must be Miss Darcy, and a genteel, middle-aged lady whom she took as the companion. Yet, she found she did not care who realised she had learnt to admire him.

"Miss Elizabeth," he said, his tone similar to hers, and she felt like rejoicing. As much as she had not expected their separation to change his sentiments, here was confirmation that it had not—not just in the full, warm manner of his speech but in the expression in his eyes and apparent unwillingness to look away. "It is very good to see you again."

"For me too." She had no time to say more before their attention was required by their companions.

The Darcys had arrived with a variety of treats, "for my friends in honour of the Festive Season," he explained. There were confections, wine, several books sure to appeal to more than one Bennet, and a thick letter from Mr Frederick Darcy for her father.

Reading it, Mr Bennet announced, "He has invited us all to visit his estate in Shropshire next summer. Listen to this, my dear. He writes, 'It is time for us to reestablish the close bonds of friendship that once existed between us'. Handsomely expressed, do you not agree?"

Elizabeth was glad for her father; he was genuinely pleased at the thought of meeting his old companion again, and it was wonderful to see him so happy. With the new peace in their family that arose from his growing supervision, to say nothing of the prospect of her and Jane soon being married, which delighted her mother, it was a fine interlude for the Bennets.

Miss Darcy was a charming girl, and, although shy, she gave every indication of desiring to know and love Elizabeth and her sisters and be loved by them in turn. Elizabeth was confident that they would soon be intimate friends, should she and Mr Darcy marry—and she would be heartbroken if he changed his mind and did not propose. Given his open preference for her, it seemed exceedingly unlikely, and, while she agreed that becoming engaged in November would have been too soon, she hoped he did not intend to wait much longer before making her the happiest woman in the world by asking her to be his wife. *If he is not quick enough about it, I shall have to resort to hints and tricks. More likely, Mama will do it for me. She is anxious to have the business settled, as she has said.*

To no great surprise, the Hursts and Miss Bingley did not return to Hertfordshire for Christmas. Mr Bingley informed them that they would spend it with Mr Hurst's relations in London.

"It was what they preferred, and I was hardly going to beg them to be here if they did not like it. We shall see them at Lady Romsley's ball." He nodded to Jane and Elizabeth. "Mr Hurst's father is some distant relation of the countess's—a cousin thrice removed, perhaps. Darcy would know better than I."

"I do not," Mr Darcy said. "It means she feels she must invite the Hursts, and as a courtesy, she includes Miss Bingley. It would be unfair not to, given her brothers and sister will attend."

## THE ART OF APOLOGY

That was the most any of them said of Mr Bingley's relations. Elizabeth was not looking forward to seeing them again, and neither was Jane, from what she had said.

"But I am determined to treat them with kindness and openness," Jane had told her one evening when they were alone. "If they are to become my sisters, I would like us to be on good terms."

Elizabeth was glad such difficult relations would be Jane's lot and not hers; her elder sister was far more capable of being patient with disagreeable people.

On December 23, the Gardiners arrived and added to their merriment, and the following days were busy indeed. Throughout it all, Elizabeth spent as much time with Mr Darcy and his sister as possible, and when they were necessarily kept apart, she spoke to Jane about romance and love and Mrs Gardiner about Derbyshire, which her aunt assured her she would find delightful. On the final day of the year, the Darcys, Mr Bingley, the Gardiners, Jane, and Elizabeth boarded their carriages and left for London.

"I expect you to write to me the moment either of them proposes!" Mrs Bennet told her daughters in the minutes before their departure.

"Their young men might have other plans in mind for the moment after securing two of the worthiest young ladies in the country," Mr Bennet said. "Tell them I shall expect to see them both in my book-room, hats in hand, no more than two days later."

Jane blushed and seemed incapable of speaking. Elizabeth laughed and kissed both of her parents, saying, "I shall be sure to pass on your messages, though I cannot promise not to keep every speck of Mr Darcy's attention to myself for a week or more. That is if he decides to propose. I do not take it as a given."

Her father guffawed. "If I thought you harboured serious doubts about him, I would ask the apothecary to examine you for possible illness. Some disorder that was addling your brain."

"Oh, Mr Bennet, do not make one of your jokes now!" her mother cried. "You do not think that he might—?"

"Not to worry, my dear." He patted her arm soothingly, then turned to Jane and Elizabeth, adding, "Off you go. We shall be here, awaiting your excellent news."

In the carriage a short while later, Mrs Gardiner asked Jane whether she was well. "You look anxious. Is something worrying you?"

Jane shook her head, and it was left to Elizabeth to explain what she suspected was the source of her sister's unease: the earlier conversation. "But, Jane, you do not truly doubt Mr Bingley?"

"I do not wish to," she said meekly. "But I know that any number of things might happen to prevent him from proposing. Until a gentleman asks, nothing is secure."

There was truth in her words, but Elizabeth preferred to think only of what made her happy. She would never understand why Jane could not. "Do not borrow trouble," she advised her sister. "It will rob you of your ability to enjoy this period."

Her aunt and uncle agreed, and Mr Gardiner said, "I do not doubt your Mr Bingley, Jane, or your Mr Darcy,

Lizzy, and I refuse to believe that anything will prevent them from proposing. Speaking as a man myself, I promise you that no man would allow himself to appear like a ridiculous moon-calf around a lady unless he was madly in love. For the past week, I have watched both of those young gentlemen tripping over their feet trying to please you two or staring at who-knows-what, clearly dreaming of how glad they will be to become your husbands. You have no need to concern yourself, Jane. Mr Bingley will propose. I would wager within the next week."

"I would not be at all surprised if Mr Darcy ran out of patience and proposed to Lizzy even sooner," Mrs Gardiner said more to her husband than her nieces.

Jane chuckled and thanked them, promising she felt better and would endeavour to banish her nerves.

Elizabeth smiled to herself. Privately, she agreed with the Gardiners. Nothing, it seemed, would stop her and her Mr Darcy from becoming betrothed, and by the spring, she would be Mrs Darcy. Life could not possibly be any better. She spent the greater part of the journey imagining how he might propose. Would it be in the Gardiners' parlour? If it were not winter, she would favour a proposal in the open air where they could be surrounded by the beauty of nature. It would remind her of the walks they had taken during which she had learnt to love him. Wherever and whenever he spoke, it would be the most wonderful, romantic moment of her life.

*It will be such a contrast to the tale of the assembly, and, told together, the two are sure to delight our children and whomever else we share our history with in the years ahead.* Elizabeth anticipated being the one who took the most delight in recounting it, but she liked to think that Mr Darcy would use it as a lesson to any sons they might be fortunate enough to have, just as she would use it to teach her daughters. *You never know where you might find love, and it is best not to risk losing the promise of a joyful future by letting your bad mood or unwillingness to look past a poor first impression get in the way.*

## CHAPTER THIRTY-TWO

The day after they arrived at Gracechurch Street, Mrs Hurst and Miss Bingley called with their brother and Mr Darcy. It was obvious to Elizabeth that the ladies did not want to be in her aunt's parlour, but Jane had told her that Mr Bingley had insisted they come. They were polite but not warm to Jane, and Miss Bingley spent almost the entire length of their visit staring at Mr Darcy and Elizabeth, who spoke chiefly to each other but without completely overlooking their companions. Mr Bingley whispered an apology to Elizabeth as he was saying his farewell.

"I did not think to explain your connexion to her. She has said she gave up her hopes regarding him long ago, but…"

"Think nothing of it," Elizabeth said. "I assure you, I shall not." That was especially true because Mr Bingley was immediately replaced by Mr Darcy, and she was far more interested in enjoying her last moment of the day with him than remembering Miss Bingley.

"I wish we had more time together," he said.

"As do I." The Gardiners, Jane, and Elizabeth were engaged to dine with one of Mr Gardiner's business associates that evening. "Tomorrow."

"Tomorrow," he agreed, surreptitiously taking her hand briefly.

They had already arranged that he would take her and Miss Darcy to call on Lady Romsley. Afterwards, she and Miss Darcy would meet Jane and Mrs Gardiner to do some shopping, followed by returning to his house, where Mr Gardiner would join them for dinner.

Once the guests were gone, Jane announced that she would like to return the ladies' call. "I do not know that we can be friends, but I am determined to be on good terms with them."

"You might feel you need to bend a little to please Mr Bingley by being amiable towards his sisters, but recall that he loves you as you are," Mrs Gardiner said. "A successful marriage requires the couple to learn to work well together. You and he will both necessarily change as you establish your life and family, but do not change who you are in an effort to befriend his sisters."

Fortunately for her, Elizabeth did not need to worry about simply being on good terms with Mr Darcy's relations. His sister was sweet and already dear to her, and, as she met them, she very much liked the earl and countess, their sons, and Mr Frederick Darcy, his wife, and daughter, who Mrs Darcy hinted was on the point of forming an attachment to a certain viscount of their acquaintance. Lady Romsley arranged a family dinner for them all, including Mr Bingley, Jane, and the Gardiners, so that they might become better acquainted before the ball. During it, Elizabeth had a chance to see Miss Rebecca Darcy and Viscount Bramwell together, and it was apparent they were happiest in each other's company. She mentioned his cousins' relationship to Mr Darcy when they were in the drawing room after the meal.

"I do not believe my cousin noticed her a day in her life until last spring, despite having known her since she was a child. Since then, however, he has been trying to earn her regard," Darcy said. "I believe he is succeeding."

"It seems as though romance abounds about us." Their eyes met, and he slipped his hand next to hers on the settee they were sharing.

Leaning towards her and whispering, he said, "I am only interested in one romance. I had not expected we would be so busy."

"Neither had I. I had thought—hoped—we would have fewer demands on our time, especially after how many we had in Hertfordshire."

"I am gratified to hear you say that. It matches my sentiments exactly." He chuckled and added, "I wonder what we might do that would give us the right to insist we be left alone upon occasion."

"As an unmarried lady and gentleman? Nothing I can think of."

He ran his hand over his mouth, and his eyes swept over the room, possibly to ensure they would continue not to be disturbed or overheard. Following his gaze, she thought he lingered on Jane and Mr Bingley. She wondered whether he saw the same thing she did: a couple who were not afraid to show the world that they were in love. Elizabeth did not care who knew of her feelings for Mr Darcy—and everyone present was aware of their situation—but she still felt a need to be more secretive about it than Jane and Mr Bingley were, and Mr Darcy was naturally reticent. In thinking of the matter, Elizabeth had decided her reluctance to display her feelings was because she had spent a greater part of their acquaintance dreading hearing people discuss the two of them—both when she was sure she would hate him forever, then as she began to like him more and more.

Turning to her once again, Mr Darcy said, "Have you ever considered how long two people should know each other, how long they should be friends, before they agree to marry? Bramwell and Rebecca have known each other since she was born, yet I do not believe they spent much time with each other until last Easter, as I mentioned. Nine months later, he still has not proposed. Bingley and your sister have liked each other since the day they met, and I imagine he will propose any day. You and I…"

She offered him a smile meant to show that she understood while also encouraging him not to worry about the past. How far she succeeded, she did not know. "You and I met the same night. We were not introduced then, but I still consider it the day we met. As to your question, I think it depends on the people involved, and sometimes, when you know that the other person is the right one for you…you *know*."

He chuckled. "My aunt said something similar to me recently."

"Is she always so wise?"

He smiled. "She likes you very much, so yes. She told me while we were waiting for you to arrive tonight."

"I like her too," Elizabeth said warmly. "I like all your relations, and they have been so welcoming to me, Jane, and my aunt and uncle."

"You speak too soon. You have not met Lady Catherine or my cousin Anne yet. I suppose Anne is insipid, but there is no real harm in her. My aunt, however, is—I hesitate to use this word anywhere within your hearing—intolerable."

She laughed. "I would find it impossible to go through life without using the words tolerable and intolerable, so I must demand you not act as though there is something evil about them. As to Lady Catherine, I own I am curious."

"I pray a meeting between you will be delayed as long as possible. You will understand why."

During the days leading up to the Twelfth Night ball, Elizabeth's anticipation became almost unbearable—as did her nerves, though she would never admit the last. It would be a night she remembered for the rest of her life, regardless of whether she ended it an engaged woman, as she thought she might. Oddly, she reflected, she had also expected the Netherfield ball would be a memorable occasion, known in her heart it would be, and she had been correct. How often would she date significant moments in her relationship with Mr Darcy to occasions involving dancing? She sensed he was impatient to propose, and it would be terribly romantic if he did it that night, more so than receiving his offer in the Gardiners' parlour. To be sure, she would be overjoyed no matter where they were, but she was so happy—more so than she knew she could be—and when he opened his heart to her fully and she could finally tell him how much she loved him, she thought she might burst with delight. More likely, she would cry and laugh at once. *In which case, the parlour might be better. I would not want to cause a spectacle, as I surely would by crying and laughing and throwing myself into his arms in a public setting!*

The Bingleys' ball had been an elegant affair, as had been the few she had attended when Netherfield's owners were in residence, but a ball hosted by an earl and countess would be an entirely different matter. Despite considering herself full of courage, she was nervous. There was no reason for her anxiety; she would be with people she knew, and she had never found it difficult to be amongst crowds. No matter how she tried to talk herself out of it, there was a growing sense that *something* would go awry that she could not banish despite all her day-dreams of being with Mr Darcy.

The evening began well enough, and she laughed at how silly she had been to worry. Mr Darcy was exceptionally handsome in his evening attire. His blue waistcoat contained thin strands of silver that sparkled in the candlelight, and she was proud to be by his side and for people to see that he favoured her above other ladies. She felt beautiful and desirable, and it had little to do with her gown—which was the loveliest she had ever worn—or the jewels her aunt had lent her. She danced the first set with Mr Darcy, and her subsequent partners were Mr Bingley, Colonel Fitzwilliam, and Viscount Bramwell.

That was when the trouble began.

# CHAPTER THIRTY-THREE

There was not a time in his life when Darcy had been happier, and it was all due to Elizabeth. She was everything—*more* than he had ever expected to find in a lady. He could almost sense his physiology being remade when he was near her, a shift from dour to content, half empty to full and complete. One reason he knew she was the perfect lady for him was the way his feelings for her had grown during their brief separation. Speaking of her to his family had emphasised how much he wanted her with him always, and when he saw her again in Hertfordshire… Each time he thought of it, he recalled exactly what she had looked like in a deep green gown that brought out the richness of her hair and eyes, a wide welcoming smile on her face when she regarded him. The kind, warm manner of her greeting to Georgiana had made him love her even more. The oddest aspect of his present situation was that he knew she loved him too. How could he understand what was in her heart when they had not spoken openly of it? Nevertheless, he did, and he considered it another sign that they were meant to spend their lives together.

Celebrating Christmas in Hertfordshire had been lively and amusing. Elizabeth and her family had made him, Georgiana, and Bingley feel as though they belonged, and the connexions amongst them had become stronger—a joining of their families into a new entity.

Then they had come to town, and here, too, everything was as near to perfect as anyone had a right to expect. It was incredible to him that just a few months prior, his life had seemed dark and dreary because of Ramsgate and its repercussions. He had allowed the least attractive parts of his character—his arrogance and disdain for others—to harden. Darcy thanked God that he had gone to Netherfield and met Elizabeth, who had encouraged him to be a better man. Bingley and Mr Bennet had also played roles, but it was *she* who had been his main reason for improving himself. How soon after meeting her had he learnt to want her good opinion? He would never be certain, but he believed it was a combination of her refusal to accept his insincere apology in the churchyard and seeing her with Budge the first time.

Darcy reflected on all this at his aunt's ball as he watched Elizabeth, who shone like the brightest star. How he wished he could spend every second of it with her! But they were both expected to dance with others. Yet, he did his best to keep Elizabeth in view at all times; he could not do otherwise. Astonishingly, he found he did not care that people were talking of them, speculating about their connexion, even asking him who she was. Six months ago, he would have snarled at anyone who had made so much as an innocuous enquiry about his life, but what did it matter when he was so wonderfully happy?

During an interval in the dancing, Elizabeth and he were standing together, chatting about the evening and the people she had met, contentedly observing the hordes about them. And then a piercing voice rent the air, cracking like a thunderbolt.

"Darcy, what do you think you are doing? Step away from that-that *girl* at once!"

Slowly turning to face the person who had spoken, Darcy stared at his aunt Lady Catherine de Bourgh. Beside her stood her daughter, Anne. Out of habit, he opened his mouth to greet them, but she continued, all but screeching at him. Certainly, she spoke loudly enough for half the room—or more—to hear.

"How dare you flirt with her! Who is she? Has my sister-in-law gone mad to permit such persons to attend her ball? Your mother would be ashamed to see you behaving in this manner."

"I-I did not know *you* would be here, Lady Catherine," he said. His shock at seeing her was receding, and as it did, fury at her words grew. Beyond his aunt and cousin, he saw Lord and Lady Romsley approaching, followed by Bramwell, Rebecca, and Fitzwilliam. Their progress was slow as they had to push through the murmuring crowd that was watching, stunned or delighted or both by the spectacle. The Gardiners, Bingley, and Miss Bennet stood to the side, appearing uncertain.

Lady Catherine announced, "I have come to insist you do your duty and propose to Anne. It is time for us to see to the marriage contract and set a date. What do I find instead? You flirting with some chit I do not recognise, and as soon as I entered the room, I heard people speaking of you being on the point of marriage to another girl. How could you behave in such a scandalous fashion? Everyone knows you are engaged to *my daughter*! You have humiliated me—and Anne—and it will take a great deal for you to make it up to us. You can begin by sending *her* away and apologising."

She used her walking stick to point at Elizabeth, and Darcy was tempted to grab it, pull it from her hand, and throw it away. The possibility of using it to prod her to leave was also appealing. Unconsciously, he held out a hand to his side and felt Elizabeth grasp it. It gave him strength to withstand whatever his aunt did next. Vaguely, he heard the earl and countess protesting about Lady Catherine's presence and behaviour, but he would not leave them to fight this battle for him.

"First, I demand you accord Miss Elizabeth Bennet the respect she deserves as a gentleman's daughter and my dear friend. Second, the only one of us who needs to apologise presently is you—to Miss Elizabeth, your sister and brother, everyone here, and me. If you wish me to accept, it had best be heartfelt. I shall know the difference. Third and finally, I am not engaged to Anne, I have never wanted to be, and I never had any intention of proposing to her, as I have told you many times over the last five years."

"I do not want to marry him either," Anne surprised him by saying. His cousin remained silent more often than not, probably because her mother hardly ever stopped talking. "We never have anything to say to each other, I do not want to remove to Derbyshire or anywhere else, he does not want to marry me, and if you force us to, we would be miserable."

"But you would be mistress of Pemberley, and that would make up for everything else. You will obey me!" Lady Catherine told her daughter sternly. Regarding Darcy, she said, "As will you."

Darcy stared at her for a moment, then turned to Elizabeth and said, "I promise I shall make you a proper proposal when we are alone. For now…Miss Elizabeth, you must allow me to tell you how ardently I admire and love you. Will you consent to be my wife?"

A smile such as he had never seen before lit up her features; joy radiated from her, and he could see that tears filled her eyes. "Nothing would make me happier than to be your wife. Yes, I will marry you."

"This is an outrage!" Lady Catherine cried. "Romsley, insist he rescind his offer and—"

"I shall not," the earl said, the first clear words Darcy had heard from him. It was then he realised that the crowd had gone silent as they watched the scene Lady Catherine was creating unfold before them. If he were not so happy, he would be embarrassed, vexed, furious—any manner of displeasing emotions—but he had Elizabeth by his side, her hand still in his, and he found he did not care what anyone else thought. He pulled her hand to his mouth and pressed a lingering kiss to her fingers, then whispered, "I love you."

"I love you too. I am so very happy," she said.

Next to them, Lady Catherine said to Lord Romsley, "It is not to the children to decide such matters themselves. They have a duty to this family! Darcy has a duty to Anne, and I demand he lives up to it! He cannot marry some unknown creature. She cannot be anyone of note if I have never heard of her. What next? Would you let Bramwell bring such disgrace to the family?"

"I assure you," said Bramwell, humour in his voice, "the lady I intend to marry is no more a disgrace than Miss Elizabeth is. Congratulations, by the way." He nodded towards Elizabeth and Darcy, then turned to Rebecca, who stood by his side. "Since my aunt is already up in arms and causing a scandal, why do we not add to it? Better have it all done at once rather than give her an excuse to renew her complaints later."

Darcy had always liked Rebecca, and he recalled telling Mr Bennet that she reminded him of Elizabeth. She was doing an excellent job of not looking affected by Lady Catherine's antics or Bramwell's perfunctory proposal.

She said, "What are you suggesting? I would like to be sure I know what I am agreeing to."

"Marry me," Bramwell stated.

Rebecca shrugged, but her smile betrayed how pleased she was. "I suppose."

Lady Catherine was, indeed, willing to share her dislike of the match—calling Rebecca and her parents scheming, amongst other insults. It lasted just long enough for Darcy to grow fatigued of her, and he was on the point of leading Elizabeth out of the room, but his other relations had sufficiently recovered from their shock to act. Lady Romsley said something to Fitzwilliam, who nodded and walked away; a moment later, her message became evident when the musicians began to play a lively, loud tune. Meanwhile, the countess brushed past her sister-in-law and congratulated the newly-engaged couples.

"Rebecca, my dear, I am so glad to know you will be my daughter. Bramwell could not have chosen a better wife." She kissed Rebecca's cheek and patted her son's, then looked at Elizabeth and Darcy, her smile fond and approving. "As for you two, oh, Miss Elizabeth, I cannot thank you enough for making my nephew so happy. I anticipate getting to know you, and your charming relations, much better. Welcome to our family." She insisted on kissing both of them.

Lord Romsley, who was holding his sister's arm, nodded at them and said, "I shall return anon. Well done, boys, though I suggest you take your ladies somewhere quieter and tell them you cannot live without them, et cetera. Help them, and yourselves, to forget the brief ugliness my sister has brought to our night." With that, he ushered a spluttering Lady Catherine out of the room. Anne looked as though she did not know what to do, and Lady Romsley went to her, leading her away as she spoke. Darcy neither knew nor cared what the countess intended to do with her.

"My uncle is right," Darcy said to Elizabeth. "Come with me."

Their hands still linked, he led her to an empty alcove.

"Have you lured me here for some nefarious purpose, Mr Darcy?"

Something in her saucy tone made heat course through his body. If he had his way, he would pull her into his arms and kiss her until she felt as on fire as he did.

"Nefarious? No," he said. "But I did promise you a proper proposal, and there is no time like the present."

She chuckled. "You asked me to marry you. Does that not constitute a proper proposal?"

Shaking his head, he said, "It does not. You deserve so much more than that. You deserve to know how much I adore and love you, how overjoyed I am with you, that knowing you has changed my life more than you can imagine. You encourage me, make me *want* to be a considerate, diligent, generous man for you, so that I can be the husband you deserve, one you need never doubt or be ashamed of. You deserve to know that when I look at you, there are times I can hardly breathe. You are so beautiful, truly the most beautiful sight in the world to me, and you are more than I ever imagined I would have in my wife, my partner in life. We could stand here for the rest of the night while I describe everything I find admirable about you—your good humour, quick wit, sympathetic nature. I vow I shall always do everything in my power to never disappoint you—"

His words were interrupted by her suddenly grabbing him by the lapels, pulling him towards her, and kissing him soundly. After a long, indescribably wonderful embrace, she released him enough that she could look into his eyes and said, "Yes, I will marry you, and I love you just as much, and I vow I shall do everything in my power to ensure you never regret your choice—"

Darcy had heard enough and, having discovered how satisfying it was to end a long-winded speech with a kiss, once again pressed their lips together, this time gathering her into his arms and refusing to relinquish her until forced to by the sound of a throat clearing. It was an amused-looking Mr Gardiner, who said he understood but, "there will be time enough for that *after* you are married."

Elizabeth laughed, and Darcy would have been mortified if he was not consumed by love and happiness.

## CHAPTER THIRTY-FOUR

In the small hours of the morning, once all the guests had gone, the Romsleys, their sons, Frederick Darcy and his family, Darcy, Bingley, and the Gardiners and their nieces sat together to discuss the evening and have a final drink before going their separate ways. The ball had continued after the scene caused by Lady Catherine, whom Lord Romsley had ordered to return to Kent and remain there, not contacting any of them, until she was prepared to humbly beg their pardon.

"I said I might also demand she take out a notice in all the newspapers to publicly apologise to everyone who was here," the earl said.

"Oh, it is all my fault," the countess cried, her features crumpled together and chin lowered. Asked to explain, she continued. "I always invite Catherine and Anne. They are family, after all, but I never expect them to come. Catherine *always* declines. Every year, I receive a letter within three or four days of sending the invitation. Thinking of it now, I do not believe one came this year—but neither did I receive word that they would attend. I certainly would have remembered *that*. Why would she not tell us she was coming to town? Where was she intending to stay?"

"With us, I imagine, never stopping to think of the inconvenience of two unexpected guests—and the multitude of servants she requires—arriving the same night as the ball," the earl said.

"You are not to blame, Aunt," Darcy said, his sentiment repeated by many others. "The only person who should regret their behaviour is Lady Catherine."

"And she is the one who is least likely to," Fitzwilliam added.

Darcy had no intention of forgiving her, even if she saw fit to apologise, not after the way she had spoken to Elizabeth. Besides, knowing his aunt, even if she did eventually express words of contrition, they would be perfunctory, like those he had said to Elizabeth in the churchyard in October, and he did not believe she would ever be capable of understanding why it was not good enough.

Elizabeth. His betrothed. It would take days before he stopped feeling as though he was living in a dream. Already he was making plans to go to Meryton to speak to Mr Bennet; before that, he had to tell Georgiana. She would be overjoyed and possibly beg to go with him to Longbourn, if only so that she did not miss anything more; as it was, she would be bitterly disappointed not to have witnessed his proposal when so many others had. She would probably think he was joking when he described the scene; in truth, he could not believe how he had acted.

*Which is another good reason to go to Hertfordshire as soon as possible.* That way, he could hide from the inevitable gossip about Lady Catherine's appearance, her many demands and insults, and that he had—in front of dozens of people—admitted his love for Elizabeth and asked her to marry him. Was there a way he could avoid London for the next year or two? He must also speak to Mr Bennet before word of the night's events made its way to the countryside, as it surely would. It was a diverting tale—if you were not one of the principal actors, however inadvertently.

The countess said that she appreciated their kind words but still felt terrible about what had transpired.

Elizabeth gave a quiet laugh. "Please do not worry on my part. No harm was done, and I believe we can always learn from occasions such as this."

"What valuable lesson could there be in Lady Catherine's display of…ugliness? Audacity, tactlessness—" Fitzwilliam said, until the earl calmly interjected, saying, "That is enough."

His darling Elizabeth turned to Darcy, her smile widening. "I am not sure yet, but I shall let you know when I sort it out," she said. "Perhaps I shall thank her for encouraging Mr Darcy to propose. That must have been her intention, even if she did not realise it."

Her light-hearted response earned several laughs, with Rebecca adding, "Bramwell too. He might have waited another half a year otherwise."

"I would have ordered him to do it before spring or

leave the house until he came to his senses," Lady Romsley said.

Bramwell turned red and protested he would not have waited much longer, and Frederick Darcy was quick to remind him, "You still have to ask my permission to marry her, young man. I have several very important questions for you." He spoke sternly, even peered at Bramwell through narrowed eyes.

"My father might give you a similar look," Elizabeth whispered to Darcy. She leant close to him, and her warm breath on his skin sent a shiver through him. "He would be no more serious though. He has been strongly hinting that he expected this outcome."

"I plan to speak to him as soon as possible. In two or three days, I hope. I cannot wait to make arrangements for our wedding and removal to Derbyshire."

She lay her hand over his. "I cannot wait to see Pemberley, about which you have told me so much, settle into *our* home, and be yours."

The notion of *that* being his future, of it being just a few months away, made Darcy's heart skip a beat. How different his life would be! He knew many married couples who lived largely separate lives, hardly even seeing each other at meals. He had often assumed that was how his marriage would be, and it might have been, had he chosen a bride based on her connexions and dowry.

"What a vile woman my sister is." Lord Romsley made an angry noise and shook his head. "But, as Miss Elizabeth said, we should consider the good that came from her display of madness. I shall soon gain a daughter-in-law in recompense."

"A niece-in-law too," Fitzwilliam said.

"Do you know, I cannot recollect whether I have offered my congratulations to the four of you yet. Have I?" Lord Romsley asked.

Bingley gave an awkward laugh and half-raised his hand. "If people are going to start offering congratulations, perhaps you can do it for six rather than four?"

Darcy was not alone in gaping at him. Elizabeth was the first to speak, crying, "Jane, did he? Are you?"

Miss Bennet blushed and nodded.

"In all the confusion after Darcy and Lord Bramwell proposed to their ladies, I took Miss Bennet aside, and, well…" Bingley shrugged and scratched the back of his neck.

After this revelation, they all agreed that they needed to have one more final drink of the night so that they could properly toast the three engaged couples.

With a heavy sigh, Lady Romsley said, "I am glad we shall always have some happy memories to look back on when we think of the ball, but what a disaster! It will be the talk of the Season, likely for years to come. I do not know how I shall hold my head up. I believe that in the future we shall spend Twelfth Night in the country. I shall not risk doing anything other than staying at home on the fifth of January ever again."

This year's ball had been on the sixth since Twelfth Night was on a Sunday, but Darcy was not about to mention it.

He looked at Elizabeth, who smiled at him in return and said, "I think it was the most spectacular ball I have ever been fortunate enough to attend."

"As do I," Bramwell agreed, soon followed by Bingley and then their loved ones.

## CHAPTER THIRTY-FIVE

Two days later, Bingley and Darcy escorted the Miss Bennets home to Longbourn. As Darcy had anticipated, Georgiana asked to accompany them; thus, she and Mrs Annesley completed their party.

Mr Bennet regarded both Bingley and him as soon as they joined the family in the drawing room and said, "Mr Bingley first, I think," before leaving the room, Bingley quietly following him and giving Darcy an alarmed look over his shoulder.

Darcy took a seat next to Elizabeth and listened as she and Miss Bennet told their mother and sisters about their sojourn in London. No one asked why Mr Bennet and Bingley were speaking privately or mentioned that Darcy and Elizabeth's hands were clasped together in the space between them on the sofa.

Bingley returned less than ten minutes later, and Darcy stood to go to the book-room, assuming he would find Mr Bennet there. Elizabeth offered him a supportive smile and mouthed the words, "I love you". She had told him that her father would not be surprised when he requested permission to marry her, and he agreed. It seemed obvious to him that Mr Bennet had long ago guessed his feelings for Elizabeth, and if he had disapproved, he would have said something to warn him off. Nevertheless, his hands trembled as he knocked at the door and entered once Mr Bennet called out that he should.

Mr Bennet was seated behind his desk. He gestured for Darcy to take the chair across from him, and said, "So, you wish to marry Lizzy?"

Darcy was aware he was staring at the man, his mouth hanging open. It was the suddenness of the question. He softly cleared his throat and nodded. "I do."

"Let us suppose I have asked you the usual things and you have answered in the usual manner. We are both satisfied that your feelings are what they should be, as are hers, and we both know you can support a wife, even one who does not bring her own fortune to the marriage. I could wish that you did not live so far from Hertfordshire."

"Your family will always be welcome to visit whenever you like, either in Derbyshire or in town, sir," Darcy said. "I have already told Mr and Mrs Gardiner that I hope they and their children will come to Pemberley in the summer."

Mr Bennet gave him a look that appeared to combine a little sadness and, if he was not mistaken, the beginnings of fondness. "That is very kind of you, and I know that you mean it sincerely. You are a good man—far better than I thought when I first heard of you."

Darcy shook his head, intending to dismiss the sentiment. "I must thank you for reminding me to be the gentleman my parents raised me to be. My father would have been gravely disappointed in me, and if you had not demanded I apologise to Elizabeth, if I had not had to labour to earn her forgiveness, I would have lost—"

"A prize beyond measure," Mr Bennet interjected, his tone warm.

"One I shall always treasure," he vowed.

Mr Bennet accepted this with a solemn nod. "Although your father might have been disappointed in his son the night of the assembly last October, his pride in seeing what you did afterwards would have been immense. He is not here to appreciate it, but I am. In another decade or so, I might even believe you are worthy of my darling girl. Sooner if your library at Pemberley is as magnificent as you say it is."

He laughed heartily, and, seeing no other reasonable response, Darcy did likewise.

Elizabeth sat and waited—and waited—for her father and Mr Darcy to rejoin them in the drawing room. Mr Bingley had taken less than a quarter of an hour to ask her father's permission to marry Jane. Twice that time had already passed. What could they be talking about? Surely, her father would not object; he liked Mr Darcy and had spent enough time with him to understand that he would make her a good husband. She did her best to smile and take part in the conversation about London and what the Bennets had done during her and Jane's absence, but inside, she was quivering. It was unlike her to be this anxious. She had known since the Netherfield ball that this day would arrive, had thought that her father knew it too, and did not understand the delay.

*Once they are here, Papa can announce that Jane and I are both engaged, then we can celebrate and begin to discuss the wedding.* She and Jane had spent many hours speaking of it already. Their poor mother might find there was little left for her to suggest or decide, from what the day would be like to their gowns and the type of flowers they would have.

Even thinking of Mr Darcy brought warmth and happiness to Elizabeth's heart. She wondered whether he was informing her father of Lady Catherine's appearance at the ball. During the carriage ride to Hertfordshire, they had all agreed that they must tell the Bennets what had happened. They were sure to hear of it, and it was better to be honest about it at once than try to explain why they had kept it secret. If Elizabeth had not seen signs that her father liked Mr Darcy, she would wonder whether he had doubts about her marrying into a family with such a woman in it, especially when Mr Darcy had initially seemed to have a similar arrogant and cutting character.

For her part, Elizabeth truly was not bothered by Lady Catherine's manner. Her arriving as she had and beginning to scold and make demands in the middle of the crowded room *had* been shocking, and Elizabeth *had* been insulted—far more than she had been by Mr Darcy —but the woman was nothing short of ridiculous, and she preferred to laugh at such people. How could anyone take them seriously? It said a great deal that Lord Romsley had called his sister vile. And Elizabeth had received a rather unique proposal in consequence.

Quietly, she chuckled to herself. What a tale it would be for her and Mr Darcy's children! It had been quite the story already, but this addition to it surely made it unequalled. *Yet, it is enough now. Oh, I hope nothing else so… noteworthy occurs at the wedding or for an extended period afterwards. Several years would do. I wish only to relish being Mrs Darcy and making my husband as happy as possible!*

At last, the gentlemen appeared. Mrs Hill and a footman were behind them, holding a tray of glasses and two bottles, which Elizabeth guessed had come from her father's not-so-secret store of fine wines reserved for special occasions. Mr Darcy returned to her side directly; she stood and held out a hand to him, which he took and kissed. He did not sit but stood beside her, while her father went to her mother, and, as wine was poured and glasses distributed amongst them, made the announcement.

"I would have been very disappointed had Jane and Elizabeth returned from London without ensnaring husbands," he said.

Her father waved off Mrs Bennet's protest of his little joke. "Our girls know I am teasing them, and if their gentlemen cannot bear it, they ought not to have proposed. But propose they did, and I am delighted to inform you all that I have given my permission to Mr Bingley and Mr Darcy to marry Jane and Elizabeth. May you all live long, contented, prosperous lives together."

Elizabeth was smiling too much to make it possible to even sip her wine. She smiled her thanks and approval to her father, smiled at Jane to tell her yet again how pleased she was for her, and smiled at her mother, three younger sisters, and Georgiana as they came to congratulate and embrace her.

Most of all, Elizabeth smiled at her Mr Darcy. Their eyes on each other, he kissed her hand once again, and she then kissed his. It was a compromise since she could not do what she longed to, which was rest her head against his strong chest and listen to his heart beating, wrap her arms about him and hold him close, just as she intended to do for the rest of her life.

# CHAPTER THIRTY-SIX

*Eight weeks later*

The next morning, Elizabeth would be united in matrimony with the only man she could ever imagine marrying. Each day, her heart filled with more love for him, and her certainty that he was what she had always needed, the other half to the person she was meant to be, grew. They had spent the long, dark weeks of winter together in Hertfordshire and London, where she and Jane had stayed at Gracechurch Street for almost a month. It had been an opportunity to shop for their weddings and lives as married ladies, but what Elizabeth especially valued about it was the chance to know Darcy's family further. She liked them all, loved Georgiana as a sister already, and had become good friends with Rebecca. No one had heard from Lady Catherine since the Twelfth Night ball apart from Lord Romsley, who had received a letter that he refused to discuss. Jane had often been in company with Bingley's sisters, and, much to Elizabeth's surprise, the ladies had decided to embrace their brother's marriage and new sister-in-law. She supposed it was either set aside their objections or risk a breach with Bingley, and she was proud of them that they had chosen so wisely.

Netherfield Park and Longbourn were both full of guests for the wedding. Lord and Lady Romsley, their sons, the new Viscountess Bramwell—the couple had married a fortnight earlier—Mr and Mrs Frederick Darcy, Georgiana, and the Gardiners had all travelled to Hertfordshire to take part in the celebrations, as had the Hursts and Miss Bingley. Presently, Elizabeth and Darcy were taking advantage of a day that could be called no better than 'not bad' and had gone into the open air for solitude and exercise. They were confined to the roads, the paths in the gardens and those they had met on in the autumn being too muddy.

"I cannot believe I let you talk me into taking a walk," Darcy said.

"You do not find the damp, overcast weather appealing? I thought that it would hold your interest at least. I knew the company would not." She sighed loudly. "How my power over you has faded. So quickly too! I had hoped it might last until the autumn. Christmas, if I was fortunate."

One of the many things she had learnt about Darcy during the weeks of their engagement was that he was a simple man, in some ways. He did exactly as she expected upon hearing her speak disparagingly about herself—he stopped walking, took her face between his hands, and kissed her until she was nearly breathless. To be sure, he knew she was teasing, but that did not matter; he could not bear any suggestion that he did not love her ardently and would continue to do so for the rest of their lives and beyond. He would not call her perfect. They had discussed the topic in late January. She no longer recalled how it had begun, but they had soon agreed that no person was without flaw; thus, there was no such thing as a perfect woman or man. However, someone might be perfect *for you*, and that they were to each other.

"Minx," he muttered before giving her a quick kiss, tucking her arm about his elbow, and continuing on their way. It was necessary to keep walking since the day was rather cool in addition to being damp and overcast. Only a strong desire to be alone for a short while had driven them from the warmth of Netherfield's drawing room where their families were gathered to spend the afternoon and take dinner together.

"In just a few hours, we shall be separated until we see each other at the church tomorrow morning," she said. "I am finding it almost impossible to believe this day is finally upon us." He made a noise of agreement. "Then off to town we go, and in just a few weeks, I shall see Pemberley at last—as long as there is no more snow, or not very much."

He chuckled. "That is what you are truly anticipating? Not being my wife or there finally being an end to the fuss of planning the wedding and packing what you want to bring with you, which you led me to believe was tiresome work. You just want to see my estate."

She laughed gleefully, unable to hide how happy she

was. "Exactly so, sir. You did not expect anything different. Or did you?" He shook his head, and she would not have been surprised if he had also rolled his eyes at her silliness. Speaking more seriously, she said, "You know very well how I long to be your wife and have you for my husband. I *am* looking forward to seeing Derbyshire, and Pemberley especially, because it will be our home and I have heard so many delightful stories and descriptions of it, but what I most want is for us to be together and embark on our new life."

"My sentiments are exactly the same," he said. "Eight weeks did not seem especially long to wait when we decided on a wedding date, but it feels as if it has been eight months."

Establishing the day on which they—along with Jane and Bingley—would marry had taken a fair amount of negotiation and a number of letters. Mrs Bennet had wanted to ensure she had enough time to, 'do the thing properly! It is not often a family sees two of their daughters married at once, and to such fine gentlemen!' Jane and Bingley's opinions had to be considered, and much to Elizabeth's surprise, they had actually *had* opinions. She generally considered them both to be so good-natured and unwilling to disappoint anyone that they would agree to whatever was suggested to them. In addition, because Darcy's family wanted to be part of the festivities, they needed to be sure the date did not conflict with Lord and Lady Bramwell's wedding or any of Lord Romsley's many responsibilities.

"But it *is* here at last. In less than four-and-twenty

hours, we shall be Mr and Mrs Fitzwilliam Darcy, and we shall set about fulfilling our destiny."

His steps slowed as he turned his head to look at her. "Our destiny?"

Arranging her features into the most serious expression she could manage, she gave a single firm nod and said, "Our destiny. Were you not aware that we had one?"

He scratched a spot between his eyebrows. "No. Perhaps you ought to tell me about it, my love. I would like to know what to expect."

"Since you asked so prettily. I should preface my explanation by saying that this is how our destiny *should* unfold. It is up to us to make it a reality."

"Do I detect some hesitation, Miss Bennet? You said you knew our destiny, and I would like to hear it, if you please."

"Patience, Mr Darcy, patience!" she mock-reprimanded, which earned her another head shake. He also smiled, though, because he loved it when she teased him; he had told her so many times. "We shall have three children, two boys and a girl. Our eldest son should be named for your family, but I have not quite determined what. You will not want to use George, despite it being your father's name." Mr Wickham had spoilt that for him.

"Hugh," Darcy said decidedly. "It was his second name and that of my grandfather."

"I like that very well. Hugh for our first son, and since we are to have two, the second will be named for my family. Rupert, perhaps, after my father. I prefer that to Bennet, and I believe Jane has already decided to use it for their first son. Naturally, I shall love my nephew, whatever my feelings about his name."

"Our daughter too." When she asked what he meant, he explained, "You said we would have a daughter, and she should be called after your mother or one of your sisters. Or you. I *am* particularly fond of the name Elizabeth."

"That is most kind of you, and if my mother knew you considered her name worthy of your daughter, she would be flattered. But I was thinking it should be Anne after your mother. We could add my mother's name, if Jane has not already used it for her daughter, or, as you said, that of one of my sisters. But enough about names. Do you not want to know what else the future has in store for us?"

"Pray continue. I am finding this highly entertaining."

"Georgiana has a brilliant first Season, and eventually she is claimed by a worthy gentleman who loves her dearly and whom she loves in return. I promise you, this man is one to whom even you cannot object."

"I doubt it," he muttered.

Elizabeth pretended not to hear him. "Do not worry, my darling, she will not marry until she is my present age, so we shall have her with us for a while yet, which pleases me exceedingly." Darcy was a little too protective of his sister, in her opinion, and she happened to know that Georgiana was beginning to find it rather oppressive. Elizabeth had promised that she would do what she could to help him accept that his sister was a young woman and could not always remain the child she had been when their father had died and she had clung to him for comfort and stability.

"Jane and Bingley will not always want to remain at Netherfield, and the current owners are unlikely to sell it, in any case," Elizabeth went on. "Since they will need a new estate, you will just happen to know of one less than twenty miles from Pemberley. Their children and ours will grow up being the best of friends, and their son will marry our daughter."

"Your knowledge of our future extends to the next generation?" he asked, his tone disbelieving.

She hushed him. "I am almost finished, and I am approaching the most crucial part. Our children will grow into fine adults, and we shall be enormously proud of them. Hugh will be a diligent eldest son, and Rupert will be a widely respected member of the clergy. He will consider becoming an officer, but he will understand that I would worry excessively. And"—she stopped walking and stood facing him, gazing into his eyes, his hands in hers—"you and I shall be known far and wide as the most fortunate, most perfectly matched, happiest couple the world has ever seen. Forevermore."

## ALSO BY LUCY MARIN

A Matter of Prudence

A Pinch of Salt

Being Mrs Darcy

Christmas at Blackthorn Manor

Her Sisterly Love

His Family Objects

The Marriage Bargain

Mr Darcy: A Man with a Plan

Mr Darcy's Second Chance

Mrs Bennet Makes a Match

The Recovery of Fitzwilliam Darcy

The Truth About Family

Paperbacks Available in Large Print Format

A Matter of Prudence

Being Mrs Darcy

The Marriage Bargain

Collaborations and Anthologies

'Tis the Season

Affections & Wishes: An Anthology of Pride & Prejudice Variations

Happily Ever After with Mr Darcy

Mr Darcy's Second Chance

# ABOUT THE AUTHOR

Lucy Marin developed a love for reading at a young age and whiled away many hours imagining how stories might continue or what would happen if there was a change in the circumstances faced by the protagonists. After reading her first Austen novel, a lifelong ardent admiration was born. Lucy was introduced to the world of Austen variations after stumbling across one at a used bookstore while on holiday in London. This led to the discovery of the online world of Jane Austen Fan Fiction and, soon after, she picked up her pen and began to transfer the stories in her head to paper.

Lucy lives in Toronto, Canada, surrounded by hundreds of books and a loving family. She teaches environmental studies, loves animals and trees and exploring the world around her.

ACKNOWLEDGMENTS

Many thanks to the wonderfully supportive Quills & Quartos crew.

The character of Budge was created in honour of my doggy nephew, Buddy, who crossed the rainbow bridge in April 2024. I am grateful that my sister-in-law agreed to let me include him.

Printed in Great Britain
by Amazon